Frankley Library
Balaam Wood School, New Street. B45 0EU
Tel: 0121 464 7676

Loans are up to 28 days. Fines are charged if items are
not returned by the due date. Items can be renewed at
the Library, via the internet or by telephone up to 3 times.

Items in demand will not be renewed.

Date for return		

J15

Check out our online catalogue to see what's in stock,
renew or reserve books.

http://birmingham.spydus.co.uk

Like us on Facebook!

Please use a bookmark.

Birmingham
City Council

Hot Pies on the Tramcar

Sheila Newberry

ROBERT HALE · LONDON

© Sheila Newberry 2006
First published in Great Britain 2006

ISBN-10: 0-7090-8143-X
ISBN-13: 978-0-7090-8143-2

Robert Hale Limited
Clerkenwell House
Clerkenwell Green
London EC1R 0HT

2 4 6 8 10 9 7 5 3 1

Typeset in 11/13pt Palatino
by Derek Doyle & Associates, Shaw Heath
Printed in Great Britain by St Edmundsbury Press
Bury St Edmunds, Suffolk
Bound by Woolnough Bookbinding Ltd

*Dedicated to the fond memory
of my constant writing companion
a little dog called Lizzie.
1994-2005*

PART ONE

London, 1925

One

THE first tramcar of the day came to a grinding halt at Paradise corner. The huddle of folk under the flaring street-lamp parted ranks and climbed thankfully aboard. A young woman in a tightly belted mackintosh arrived at the last moment just as the bell clanged, shaking the rain drops from her umbrella, crying, 'Wait for me!' The conductor clipped another tuppenny ticket. It would be dark again when she journeyed home after long hours treadling a sewing machine. It was March, but not yet spring in Suburbia.

A light was showing upstairs in No.1 Paradise Buildings, a solid, red-brick Victorian terrace of small businesses with accommodation above. The pie shop at street level still had the blinds down, and the grille was bolted across the adjacent basement entrance.

Josefina gave a final rub at the condensation on the sash window, relishing the squeak her fingers made. She let the curtain fall back into place. 'Rose Marie's gone,' she reported to Florence, returning to her chair by the stove.

'Got wet even in that brief dash across the pavement, I suppose,' Florence observed, moving the big saucepan off the heat, before adding flour to water bubbling with melted lard. She beat the mixture into a glossy ball, then scooped it out on to the floured preparation table. The kitchen was spotless; Florence too was well scrubbed, shrouded in a white apron, her brown hair strained back off her flushed face and concealed under a mob cap. Now, she flattened nuggets of the pastry between her palms and pressed them round the bottle-shaped beech-wood moulds. These would be filled with the chopped cooked pork

9

then topped with circles of pastry, which she crimped with finger and thumb, before the batches went in the oven. The mutton tartlets would be made next, to be baked in the shop oven as required, and sold piping hot.

Josefina wore a pinafore over her school clothes, despite the early hour. On her first morning at Florence's, two years ago, she'd ventured into the big kitchen full of cooking aromas; seen the pestle and mortar bowl where herbs, grown in pots on the windowsill, were ground, and the bowl of hard-boiled eggs which later she'd learn to tap and peel, only to be despatched back to her bedroom with the stern words: 'No sitting around in your night attire! It's unhygienic!'

She'd wept then, because she'd been used to creeping into her mother's side of the bed in the mornings, snuggling up when Stella whispered, 'Go back to sleep, darling, there's a good girl.' Sometimes they'd stayed in a small hotel, with sweet-smelling linen on the beds. More often, they put up in a back street board-ing-house with other theatricals, where there were grease-spotted tablecloths and chipped plates in the dining-room and an overwhelming smell of boiled fish. But the old-style music halls were in decline since the advent of the cinema, and bookings scarce.

Josefina's mother was partnered in her act by her husband, referred to grimly by Florence, her mother's step-sister, as 'that dago'. Jose's smouldering good looks, his expertise with the Spanish guitar, confirmed his ancestry, but he'd been born in the East End of London. Josefina's thick mop of straight black hair, those lustrous dark eyes couldn't be denied: despite her reserva-tions, Florence had insisted he marry Stella six years ago.

I should never have indulged that girl, paying for those singing lessons, Florence often sighed to herself. Stella wouldn't have run off with that wastrel if she'd been apprenticed to a trade like young Rose Marie. Still, Stella does have a lovely voice, a real talent. She might have sung in opera. Her eyes misted over. All she'd wanted was for her to be happy.

But Jose wasn't cut out to be a father. He wanted to take off for Europe with Stella, but not Josefina, then four years old. It was almost time for her to start school, Stella told her sister defen-sively when they turned up at Florence's unexpectedly; she

10

needed a proper home. Florence could look after her; they promised to keep in close touch and send money for her keep. Affectionate letters from Stella arrived spasmodically but not a penny came Florence's way. Not that she worried about that, for Josefina had taken her mother's place as one of Florence's girls.

Now she checked the eggs were cool enough for shelling, advising Josefina, 'Put a couple to one side, then you can mash them with butter and make sandwiches for our breakfast. I'll slice the bread for you when I've lined the tins with pastry. The new tenant upstairs is bringing her little girl down to us at a quarter to eight: I said we'd look after her until it's time to go to school. Her mother has to work, she's a widow—'

'What's that, Aunty Florence?' Josefina rolled an egg in her palms.

'Someone whose husband has died.'

'Like you, Aunty?'

'I've never been married, but nevertheless, I've brought a family up, eh?'

'What about Manny, in the shop?' Josefina asked, a trifle too innocently.

'What about him? I'm his boss: that wouldn't do.'

'He must be lonely, living in the basement by himself.'

'He's lucky to have a roof over his head, and a job, on account of him having a gammy leg. He was invalided out of the army during the war. Anyway he's too young for me - he's not yet thirty,' Florence paused, anticipating what the child would say next.

'How old are you?' She dug a knife in the softened butter to spread on the bread.

'Never you mind, get on with your task.' But she smiled at her niece.

'Why are you Mummy's *sort-of* sister?'

'Well, my father was well over forty when he met my mother, and she was no spring chicken either - you work that one out for yourself! So I was an only child, until my father was widowed and by that time he'd got used to having a woman around, so he married Stella's mother, whose husband had also died. I was fourteen and Stella was only five, but I was really pleased to have a sister. Then, later, Rose Marie came along. I had to care for both girls, after Stella's mother died of pneumonia. Satisfied?'

'Did your father die of - what was it you said? - too?'

'He died of old age - that's as it should be - some time after that. Then I had to run the shop as well as make all the pies. That's when I took on Manny.' Florence put out three plates, cut the sandwiches into quarters. 'The upstairs child may be hungry. . . .'

'Why does it say, W. Flinders & Son, under Paradise Pies on the shop, Aunty? We're all daughters.'

Florence poured the tea, passed a cup to her niece. 'The son was my father, silly. His father set him up here. Before my time. Eat up. I've got pies to fill.'

She was brushing the fluted tops of the pies with beaten egg, when there was a tentative knock on the outer door. Josefina ran to open it. A young woman with shingled fair hair, wearing a shabby coat, stood there, gently pushing her child forward.

'This is Yvette, and you are Josefina, I know. We are a little early—'

'Come in,' Florence called, rinsing her hands at the sink. 'Have you time for a drop of tea? It's not long brewed.'

'Thank you, no. My first day at work - I don't want to rush.' She had a slight accent.

French? Florence wondered, though her surname was Bower. This was a cosmopolitan area. 'See you about two then,' she said. 'Would Yvette like something to eat?'

The child shook her head, compressed her lips mutinously.

'Thank you, no. She had her breakfast,' Yvette's mother said.

'Then take this for your lunch, my dear. I don't suppose you had time to prepare anything, did you?' Florence wrapped the sandwich in a square of greaseproof.

'I - I was too nervous . . . couldn't eat a thing then, but thank you, Miss Flinders.' She put the package in her bag. 'Goodbye, Yvette. Be good.' She clattered down the uncarpeted stone steps to the front door.

'Take Yvette to your bedroom, while I clear up here,' Florence told Josefina.

Yvette followed her reluctantly, through to the room she shared with Rose Marie. 'Your whole apartment smells of cooking,' she said disagreeably. 'Of *pies*!'

12

Josefina looked at her. Yvette was small, pale and skinny, with fuzzy blonde hair which had obviously been curled overnight in rags. She wore skimpy clothes and unsuitable shoes for the time of year, cracked patent leather with thin soles.

'You need a pie or two to fill you out,' Josefina returned smartly, 'or you might get washed down a drain in the rain.'

'I'll tell my *maman* you said that!'

'And I'll tell my aunty I don't want you for a friend. I shan't walk with you to school. Anyway, I don't s'pose you think the Board school is good enough for you!'

Unexpectedly, Yvette began to cry. 'You must take me; Miss Flinders promised!'

Josefina's resentment evaporated instantly. 'Oh, come on, sit down and I'll show you my dolls. This one is Carmen, see, she's dressed for flamenco dancing, because she came from Spain. I'm half-Spanish myself. She's more an ornament really. This is my baby doll, she belonged to Rose Marie—'

'Your sister? She's very pretty. We've seen her from our window.'

'Rose Marie is my aunty too, only she's too young to call that.'

'I've got a doll that was my *maman's*, when she was a little girl in France, that makes *me* half-French! She brought it with her when she got married. The doll is called Clarice, and she has a wax face and real hair. You can comb it and curl it. But you have to be careful with her, like your Carmen. Maman says she is very precious.'

'She cost a lot of money, d'you mean?'

'Oh hundreds of pounds!' Yvette could see Josefina was impressed. 'Maman has a real French perfume bottle too - you can spray it on you, puff, puff.' She squeezed an imaginary soft rubber ball. 'But it doesn't smell so good any more.'

'Like the pies!' Josefina performed a somersault on the unmade bed, and ended up giggling, on the pillow. A feather floated down on to her hair.

'How did you do that? Show me!' Yvette commanded.

'Girls, time to leave for school, and for me to open the shop,' Florence called.

Rose Marie had been entrusted with a special repair today, a tear

13

in the layered skirt of a dance dress. She enjoyed hand-sewing, which gave her legs a rest; it made a nice change to leave the busy hum of the machines behind in the main workroom for the quiet room where two middle-aged seamstresses worked.

'All this modern dancing,' one of her companions said after a while, approving her almost invisible stitching. 'Madam must have caught her heel in that. She always brings her little disasters to us. Are you almost finished? She wishes to wear the dress on stage tonight.'

'Miss Short's having a fitting downstairs for a new gown,' the other seamstress looked up over her wire-framed spectacles. 'She'll collect this, in about an hour.'

'Have we some rhinestones to match these on the bodice?' Rose Marie asked. She'd had an idea. 'I could sew two or three on each of these panels, including one to conceal the repair. What d'you think?' she asked diffidently. She could just picture the effect when the skirt swirled in the dance, and the lights caught the sparkling gems.

'I think you're right. If you go on as you are, my dear, I can see you progressing on to design in the years to come.' She passed the little box of semi-precious stones.

'Thank you,' Rose Marie accepted the compliment gracefully. *How* many years to come? she thought. I want to see more of the world outside this dress shop, like Stella. I want to wear dresses like this, only I'd take care of them, and go dancing in the evenings, not back to the pie shop. 'My sister's on the stage, too,' she added, 'she sings.'

The woman who wore the spectacles removed them, rubbed at a red mark low on her nose. 'I'm glad you haven't had your head turned by that, my dear,' she said.

Lilli Bower had been working industriously all morning, mostly on her knees, sweeping between the tip up seats, dusting down the red plush, picking up the litter from the floor. She thought ruefully that at least she'd learned something from her mother-in-law, how to clean a house. She'd never picked up so much as a duster in her old home, though when the servants left during the war, she'd helped her mother with the cooking.

Every now and then she looked up at the stage, where the big screen was hidden behind the velvet curtains, imagining them swept aside and the dazzling beam from the projection room in the lofty regions above, wavering, then steadying, as the picture appeared, to the delight of the audience.

The Golden Domes cinema in Camberwell certainly lived up to its name, with wonderful gilding and plaster ornamentation. When the music started, the lights dimmed, you'd be in another world, Lilli thought. She'd love to see the new Lilian Gish picture.

She still had the ladies' room to tidy: the powder bowl to replenish, the mirrors to clean. Another cleaner saw to the foyer, and the manager's office at the front.

Lilli straightened up at last, satisfied that she had done all that was expected of her. The splendour of the Golden Domes reminded her of the château in France where she had spent her youth, before she met her soldier husband at the end of the war, and such was the euphoria after the Armistice, she'd married him, despite her mother's disapproval, and come to England, where their daughter was born. It had been a real culture shock. They shared a back-to-back house in the Midlands with her husband's family, all mill workers. After a big row with his mother one day, Lilli had pleaded with her husband to take her away, for them to set up on their own. When he refused, she walked out on him, taking little Yvette. Eventually, she'd ended up in London, having sold her jewellery to help them survive. She was too proud to go home to her own family. This job, menial as it was, meant she could carry on. She was very fortunate to have a kind landlady who'd help with Yvette, and another new friend in the pie shop. It was Manny who'd told her about the vacant flat and the job going at the cinema. She'd have to walk there until she got paid, but life was looking up at last.

Rose Marie was followed by others from the tramcar into the pie shop that evening. Manny served her first, wrapping a hot meat and potato pie in a cloth, then she dashed outside to the waiting tramcar to give it to the conductor, to keep him going until the end of his shift. Her travelling companions emerged from the shop, dispersing in various directions as the tram departed. Even those lucky enough to be in regular employment appreciated a ready meal, and not having to feed precious pennies to the gas meter.

Manny waited by the shop door as usual to exchange another word or two with Rose Marie. He was a cheerful chap, not very tall but of a stocky build. A wide smile transformed his plain features, despite displaying his uneven teeth.

'Had a good day, Rose Marie?'

'Yes. Did you, Manny? Lots of customers?'

He nodded. 'Hot pies always go down a treat in weather like this.'

'Well, I'm hoping for something different for my supper! 'Night, Manny.'

He watched as she opened the door next to the shop, then closed it behind her. He listened to the echo of her footsteps as she climbed the stairs.

Manny limped back to welcome in a new customer.

'Heard your pies are the best,' the man said.

'Made In Paradise,' Manny replied, with a wink.

Rose Marie was not best pleased to discover a newcomer in her bedroom, when she went to get changed. There were two little girls, not one, lolling on the bed, looking at some picture books.

'Out you go,' she told Josefina and Yvette. 'I don't want to be a peep show!'

'Come on, Yvette,' Josefina said. 'She's always grumpy when she gets in from work. We'd better lay the table for supper, as you and your mother are eating with us.'

Florence overheard this exchange. She sympathized with Rose Marie, for she could remember the lack of privacy when she was growing up and had to share a room with Stella. She didn't comment though. She was tired, and still busy cooking.

When Lilli arrived, she sniffed appreciatively. 'That smells good, Miss Flinders.'

'Broth and dumplings; rice pudding: Josefina's favourite.'

'I'm afraid my Yvette picks at her food.'

'Well, she'll have to learn to be grateful for what she's given, won't she? 'Specially when times are hard.' Florence had a feeling that she could have two more lame ducks to care for. Still, it was good to be needed.

Manny shut the shop at eight o'clock. There was a solitary ham and egg pie left under the glass dome on the marble-topped counter. He speared a pickled onion the size of a billiard ball from the jar and placed it beside the pie. Oh well, a cold supper he thought, but first he must clean up. He fetched the mop and bucket from the back room and began his task. Someone tried the door. He called out, 'Sorry, sold out - we're closed!' He doused the light.

He went down the basement steps and opened his front door. The gas fire would soon warm the living-room. He'd eat the pie, then go along to the pub on the far end of the Paradise row for his usual glass of stout.

The barber's, the butcher's and the tobacconist's shops were all closed. The doctor's rooms above the latter were in darkness There was a light still showing in the baker's front window, and he observed the bent back of the cleaner, as she moved around the shop. Poor old girl, he thought, no evening off for her. She'll be working again by six tomorrow. Like Florence. I don't suppose *she's* ever seen the inside of the Paradise Pub, had a good laugh and a singsong. She'd be surprised to hear me render 'The Rose of Tralee', seated at the piano. Some say I bring tears to their eyes. One drink, that's all, and I come over all sentimental for the place where I was born and left as a child. Maybe I sing it for another Rose now - Rose Marie, but I know she's not for me. I could never tell *her* what I've been through; lost my best mate in the war - mustn't think of that. I wouldn't want her to know I sometimes wake in the night, crying out and sweating, the echo of gunfire ringing in my ears.

Florence hung the damp tea-cloths on the airer. Their supper guests had returned upstairs; Josefina was already in bed and hopefully asleep. Florence went into the sitting-room through the folded back double-doors. They only used this room, full of good, but old furniture, in the evenings. The kitchen was the hub of their home.

Rose Marie was curled up on the sofa absorbed in her *Woman's Weekly* magazine. Florence said silently to herself, was

I ever that young and full of dreams? Did my hair gleam golden under the overhead light; was my skin that smooth? She's seventeen and I'm thirty-four . . . romance has passed me by.

She yawned. Soon be time to make the cocoa. But first she'd write a letter to Stella in Barcelona to tell her that Josefina had a new friend. . . .

Two

A Sunday morning in April; Florence turned sizzling bacon rashers in the pan and drank her second cup of tea of the day. She'd enjoyed her sabbath soak, as she referred to it, before the girls were awake. She'd risen at six to light the copper alongside the deep bath, with mahogany surround. She had to siphon the water out but it was a great improvement on the jug filling of years gone by. She used a knob of soda to soften the water rather than bathsalts, but she did indulge herself with a tablet of Pears soap.

Now, she looked younger and more relaxed than all week, in a button-through print frock and hand-knitted cable-stitch cardigan, with her hair still damp and curling at the ends, loose round her face. She'd recently given in to Rose Marie's cajoling and had her hair bobbed, even if she'd insisted that the local barber would do.

A polite tapping on the door, then Manny came in. She'd told him bluntly when he was first working for her she knew he existed on left-over pies all week, and that on Sundays he must eat with the family. The table was ready laid, so he sat down, so as not to get under her feet, watching as she cracked the eggs into the bacon fat and spooned a little over the yolks, the way they both preferred them. After a while, he judged she would be receptive to a little conversation.

'Saw Burton, the butcher, last night.'

'Oh, yes?'

'He said to tell you, if I remembered, mutton is good at the moment.'

'Well, you remembered, and so will I. I hope it's cheaper than the last lot.'

'He has to make a living too, Florence. Folk aren't buying so much meat.'

'So I keep him going, do I? Me and my pies. We all help each other, eh?'

Manny nodded, as she put his full plate before him. 'Thanks, Florence.'

'I might as well have mine with you, cook the girls' breakfast later.' She sat down opposite, poured two more cups of tea. We must look like an old married couple, she thought. Yet I know very little of his life before he came here. Maybe he left a family behind him. He knows me for what I am; the one who holds us all together.

Rose Marie was awake, but loth to rise. She could hear muted voices from the kitchen and guessed that Florence and Manny were tucking into their fried breakfast. The heroine in the serial story she was following in her magazine was accustomed to a continental breakfast of croissants and frothy coffee. She picked fuzzy-skinned apricots, warmed by the sun, for dessert, and every day seemed like Sunday.

Josefina had returned from her ablutions and was dressed apart from her socks. She'd had her bath as usual yesterday evening, so it was a perfunctory wash, but all clean clothes for her today. She'd quickly learned to be independent after she came to live here. Now, she located a neatly rolled pair of cotton socks in her underwear drawer, put them on, then slid her feet back into her slippers.

'Brushed your hair?' Rose Marie asked, without looking up from her story.

'Mmm.' Josefina gave it a guilty smooth-over with her hands.

'Leave me in peace then, eh?'

'Don't worry, I will! And I'll be out this afternoon, too. Aunty Florence said to Yvette's mum, "Why not take Yvette to Battersea Park on Sunday? Good walks and lots to see on the river." So I asked, of course, "Can I go, please, as well?" '

'Didn't she mention the gas-works? Bet you don't know Lilli invited me, as well!'

'Aunty Florence said I had to call her Mrs Bower! Are you coming?'

'I might. If I don't get any better offers . . . Oh, tell Florence I don't want my breakfast yet, please. I'd rather wait until Manny's gone, only don't say *that*, will you?'

'What's wrong with Manny? He's very nice, he makes me laugh.'

'I like him too, but . . . off you go, Josefina!'

Lilli and her daughter had few possessions, having left home with one small suitcase, but Lilli had spotted a discreet second-hand clothes shop on her route to the cinema and determined to buy a few items there after she was paid on Saturday morning.

The clothes were not exactly chic, she thought, but clean and of good quality. Lilli bought a job lot for a florin. The shop owner was shrewd but soft-hearted. As Lilli was about to leave with her neat brown paper parcel, she selected something on impulse from a shelf crowded with dreary felt hats.

'Here, dearie, this would suit you; have it on me. It's unlikely to sell round here.'

The white piqué hat with a flamboyant red flower fixed to the front had probably been worn just once, to a wedding, Lilli decided. She expressed her thanks.

Now, walking along the river path on a nice afternoon, she wore the hat, and heads turned. The little girls were ahead of Lilli and Rose Marie, darting to look at things which caught their eye, but keeping in view as their elders requested. When they stopped for a while to watch the pleasure boats on the lake, Lilli suggested that she and Rose Marie take advantage of a vacant seat nearby.

'I shouldn't have worn these heels,' she added ruefully. 'Not for walking.'

Rose Marie looked down at her own unsuitable footwear, with pointed toes and T-strap fastening. 'You have to suffer to look smart! Florence, of course, doesn't agree. She says I'll have painful bunions when I'm old, but I say, live for the moment!'

'She's very kind, your Florence, isn't she? And she works so hard.'

'I love her dearly, but you won't catch me joining her in the hot pie business.'

'You are a seamstress, is that right?'

Rose Marie nodded. 'Yes, and I must admit that can be tedious

21

too, but it's a skill which could lead to more interesting things. Also, we have a varied clientele.'

'Ah, such as?'

'Actresses and dancers. Noel Coward recommends us. He has *three* plays on, in London! One's called Fallen Angels: Florence thinks that sounds,' she hesitated.

'*Risqué?*' Lilli supplied.

'Well, she didn't put it like that, but I guess that's what she meant.'

'She is the guardian of your morals, is that it? Like a mother.'

'Yes, but she's my *sister*! Stella, though, my other sister, is not stern at all. You're about her age, that's why I'm glad you've come to live in Paradise, so I have you to talk to.'

'Stella must miss her daughter, I know I could not leave my Yvette behind.'

'It's not Stella's fault,' Rose Marie rose instantly to her defence. 'Her husband is the selfish one. He always wants his own way.'

Lilli dare not say she had personal experience of that. She took a little mirror from her bag, examined her makeup, then carefully applied more lipstick. There was a mere stub left in the gilt case. She was well aware that Rose Marie was not the only one watching. Two young men in smart blazers and straw boaters were giving them smiling sideways glances. She pretended to be oblivious to them.

'You don't paint your face yet?' She accentuated her cupid's bow lips.

'Florence said I should wait until I am eighteen.'

'Actually, my mother said the same. Yet she taught me the art when the time came! Anyway, you are pretty enough without it. Did Stella get round this rule?'

'Of course, because she married young and then she could do what she liked in that respect!'

'She was a rebel, your sister,' Lilli observed.

'Yes.' She thought, I couldn't hurt Florence like she did. 'Shall we walk back now? There aren't so many buses on a Sunday, and we're expected back for high tea.'

Florence had seized the opportunity, while she had the place to herself, to relax on top of her bed with an Ethel M Dell novel. She had taken off her frock, so as not to crease it, and unhooked her corset; slipped into a comfortable cotton kimono, Japanese in style, heavily embroidered, an impulse buy by Stella from Berwick Street market some years ago. She'd discarded it when she left, so Florence had taken to wearing it. She was sentimental like that.

As Florence dozed, with the open book resting on her stomach, Manny, in the basement flat, yawned, and tidied the newspaper he'd spread across the table.

'Might have a kip,' he said aloud, disturbing the little white cat curled in his chair. It mewed plaintively. It was a stray. He'd got round Florence, who considered that pets and pies did not go together, by promising he'd keep it out of the shop but saying that it would be useful prowling the cellar at nights. Not that he intended to shut the cat down there. It had endured enough hardship, in his opinion, and was good company.

The hammering on his front door startled him. He wondered who it could be. He didn't invite people into his private quarters, he met enough of the public all week. The pub was a different matter, he could come and go as he pleased there. He was popular because of his music, but he had no close friends or confidantes.

'You're the last one I expected to see!' he exclaimed. 'I thought you were a goner.'

'Likewise,' the big man told him. 'Still, ain't you going to ask me in?'

As Manny stood there, irresolute, the visitor pushed past him in the narrow hall and went through to the living-room, uninvited. Manny closed the door and hurried after him.

'What are *you* doing here?' he demanded incredulously.

The man removed the cat unceremoniously, then sat down heavily in Manny's chair. 'I'm famished. Exhausted. Got any grub?'

'Bread and cheese, I don't do much cooking for myself. Will that do?'

'It'll have to. I've been on the road for weeks. I ain't ate some days, Manny. Is that the moniker you still go by?'

'It's my name, isn't it?' Manny said sharply, passing him a

thick crust and a heel of hard cheddar. 'What's yours?' The tea was stewed, but it would have to do, he thought.

'Well, I was known as Buck in my youth, on account of my teeth, and even though I got 'em knocked out later, that does me all right nowadays. See you're still limping.'

'Almost lost my leg, but luckier than some.'

'Old Pa Flinders still around?'

'He died before my time. I came here just after the war. His daughter employs me.'

'Ah, Florence . . .' Buck took a gulp of tea. 'Best you tell her I'm here.'

'It's her day off; I didn't ought to disturb her. . . .'

'We're old friends. You may find this hard to believe, but I worked for her father when I was a lad. I delivered pies to order, then. Still got the old black boneshaker?'

'No. We can sell enough pies in the shop. I'm not sure—'

'You're not sure she'll want to see me? Well, I reckon she will.' He brushed the crumbs from his moustache, then belched painfully. 'Suffer terrible with me stummick. . . .'

Florence came to, with a start. Had she been dreaming? Then the rapping on the door was repeated, and she heard Manny call, 'Florence, are you there?'

She pulled the kimono round her, tied it in place. Her hair was tousled, but, after all, it was only Manny, she thought. She padded to the door. 'Yes?'

'Can I come in?' he asked urgently.

'I'm hardly decent,' she answered doubtfully. 'Why?'

'I can't tell you here; he might hear—'

'*Who*, Manny? All right, close the door after you.' She saw his pale face. 'What's wrong? You've had a shock, I can tell.'

'He says he worked here years ago. He's obviously been living rough. He says *you'll* want to see him—' he gabbled.

'What's his name?' she interrupted.

'Buck.'

Now the colour drained from her cheeks. 'Buck' she repeated. Then, 'Yes, he worked here, but it was years before the war. He was a young man then; I don't suppose I'd recognize him now. My father, well, he gave him the sack. At the time, I thought that was unfair, but . . . do I gather you know him, too?'

'We were in the army together, in France, 1916. He went missing, presumed killed. I was in hospital, injured, at the time. It was like seeing a *ghost*, Florence.'

'Look.' She'd regained her composure. 'Give me ten minutes to tidy myself, and then bring him up here. I'll sort this out, don't worry.'

'He might ask you for money.'

'If I consider he's in need, I'll help him. I owe him that. Off you go, then.'

'You'll have to give me an 'and with me boots,' Buck told Manny. 'I had to struggle to get the bleeders off.' He twitched his toes in the felted, holey socks. 'I need a bath. Reckon Florence'll let me use her tub?'

'How do I know?' Manny wrestled with the first muddy boot.

'I lived down here in the basement, that time. Just you, is it? No lodger in the spare room? You can put me up tonight, can't you?'

'Well, you can't stay upstairs, the rest of the house is all women. I told Florence I knew you in the army, but believed you'd been lost in action. I'll keep quiet about the rest of it, and I expect the same of you, regarding myself.'

Florence appeared quite composed. She held out her hand to Buck. 'It's been a long time, Buck. I'm sorry to see you've obviously hit hard times.'

'You ain't changed much, I'm glad to see, Florence. No hard feelings, eh?'

'I don't bear grudges. Well, you'll have to get cleaned up before the girls come back and then you and Manny can have your supper with us.'

'Girls? Young Stella still with you?'

'Stella's grown up, married and gone away. I look after her little daughter as well as a younger sister; we lost my stepmother not long after she was born.'

'You never married?' Buck queried.

'No, did you?'

'Not exactly,' he answered evasively.

'Well, I'll get the copper going again. Some of Dad's clothes are still in the hall cupboard. Help yourself; you're welcome to keep them. Have a cup of tea while you're waiting on your bath. Has Manny offered you a bed for the night?'

'Yes,' Manny affirmed reluctantly. 'I'll go, if you don't *mind*,' he emphasized, 'to make the room ready. I'll be back shortly.'

'I don't mind,' she asserted.

Rose Marie and Josefina parted company with Lilli and Yvette at their door. They were surprised to discover that Florence had a visitor, a burly fellow looking ill-at-ease in an old-fashioned suit, with a whiff of camphor balls. He and Manny were seated either side of the kitchen stove. Florence was putting the finishing touches to the supper table. She turned to introduce them. 'My sister and niece, Rose Marie and Josefina; this is Buck, who once worked here. He and Manny are old comrades, too, they were in the army together.'

'Pleased to meet you,' Buck said. With his moustache and shaggy eyebrows trimmed and his hair oiled back he looked better, despite the deep lines which seamed his face.

'And you,' Rose Marie responded, smiling. 'We must go and tidy up, Josefina.'

'Bombay toast,' Florence said, a little later. 'My grandfather was out in India, in the army during the troubles, and he brought the recipe back. I thought it would make a change for high tea. It's really just scrambled eggs with capers and anchovies, and a good shake of cayenne pepper. So watch out, it's rather hot.' She put a generous spoonful on each round of well-buttered toast, two for the men, one each for the girls and herself.

When the table was cleared, it was time for the adults to move into the sitting-room for a while and for Josefina to go to bed.

Florence hesitated, then indicated it was time for the men to retire downstairs. 'Early to bed for us too. Busy day tomorrow. Goodnight.'

'Like old times,' Buck told her. 'Goodnight, Florence.'

'I'll see you before you leave,' she said. She hoped he would take the hint. She was wary of any disruption to her ordered life.

Three

AFTER she'd waved Josefina and Yvette off to school, a few minutes walk past a further row of shops round Paradise corner, Florence went into the shop, while Manny fetched the first batch of pies. She inspected the floor, the tiled surrounds, counter, oven and deep sink.

He came in with the loaded, covered basket as she placed the clean cotton squares in a neat pile under the counter. She looked up. 'Buck awake yet?'

'Yes. He's dressed and ready to go. Waiting to say goodbye to you.'

She tapped her apron pocket. 'He didn't ask, but I'm giving him something anyway. I packed a bag with some necessities; spare clothes, food and a bottle of tea He never had much in the old days, he came to us from the foundling hospital, you see, but it's obvious he called here after all this time, because he's on his uppers.'

'Well, you helped me out when I needed it most, so who am I to say you ought to be wary, though he might come back for more.'

'That's a chance I'm prepared to take, Manny, all right?'

Florence advised Buck, 'Put this in your inside pocket.' She handed him an old purse, heavy with coins. 'Copper mainly, but I hope it tides you over until you get a job.'

'More chance of that now I'm tidied up. Thanks,' he said gruffly.

'Good luck.'

'I've already had that, seeing you,' he said, as she saw him out.

Florence went upstairs to her flat. Should I have said something more, she wondered. But what was the point, raking up old hurts? She dabbed her eyes fiercely. There was still the past week's laundry to parcel up to await collection, but Buck's castoffs could be consigned to the dustbin.

'Miss Short's new gown is ready; she telephoned earlier to request it be delivered to her at the theatre. I wondered if you might enjoy a jaunt on such a pleasant afternoon?' Mrs Belling, the proprietress of the dress shop, asked Rose Marie. 'You should take your folder of pins, needles and thread, in case a minor alteration is needed . . . do I take that smile as a yes?'

'Yes please!'

'Then collect the dress box from the office, in about fifteen minutes. The taxi will be here by then. Good-afternoon, everyone.' Mrs Belling swept out of the workroom.

The other girls were excited for her. 'Lucky you! You might even get home early.'

'I intend to make the most of being out and about up west!' It was fortunate, Rose Marie thought, that Florence had recently decided to have the telephone installed, because she could ring her sister and tell her not to worry if she was late.

'Making a delivery?' the taxi driver asked, as he saw her settled in the back seat of the square black cab. 'Don't worry, I've been told where to go.'

Rose Marie nodded. She clutched the box on her lap. MISS SADIE SHORT, CRITERION. BY HAND. The label read.

She looked down at her own capable small hands, thinking she should have worn her gloves, not the rather dented silver thimble which she'd forgotten to remove. She slipped it into her pocket. It might yet come in useful.

This was one of the modern variety theatres, with twice nightly performances. Here you could be entertained by the top names of the legitimate stage, appearing in melodramatic sketches or classic excerpts; sometimes by a foreign *corps de ballet*; an opera singer or two, as well as popular comedians, magic acts, dancers and speciality turns.

'Take a seat in the stalls, miss,' the commissionaire advised. 'Miss Short is about to rehearse a new number for tonight. I'll tell her you're here when she comes off.'

It was an eerie experience for Rose Marie, sitting in the front row, with all the empty seats around her; the silence from the circle above and the curtained boxes. The house lights were dimmed, the curtains opened, but the orchestra pit was deserted. At the side of the stage, an elderly man removed his jacket, slung it on the back of his chair, rolled up his shirt-sleeves and puffed on a bent cheroot. After shuffling some sheet music, he began to play. A spotlight began to dance about the stage, ready to focus on the dancers. There were two of them: Miss Short, not clad in one of her shimmering gowns but in a crumpled tunic over footless white tights, rather incongruous with silver dancing shoes; her partner, a lithe young man with a disdainful expression, casually attired in jumper and slacks.

The music was staccato and lively, the dancing nothing like Rose Marie had imagined. The dancers did not swirl romantically around the stage, but performed their steps side by side; now and again Miss Short's partner circled her, seized her round the waist, lifted then launched her into space. She landed on her feet, still dancing. Her high kicks were audacious, amazing; Rose Marie gasped, thinking, no wonder she rips her skirts!

'Makes you tap your feet, don't it, all that jazz,' a male voice observed.

Startled, Rose Marie turned to discover that the seat behind was now occupied.

'Mind if I join you? We might as well enjoy this together.' Without waiting for an answer the man vaulted over the top into the seat beside her. He glanced at her face, her flustered expression, and grinned. 'I see I'd better introduce myself! I'm Sadie's brother Russell. I had an appointment in London this morning, so thought I'd make a day of it, pay my sister an unexpected visit. Her landlady said she'd be here. Now, may I ask who you are?'

'I'm . . . Rose Marie Flinders. I have a parcel for Miss Short.'

'You are also a dancer?' he asked. He had what she thought of as a posh voice.

'Oh, no,' she said quickly. 'I'm a dressmaker.'

'You make frocks for Sadie, is that it?'

'Well . . .' She hesitated, then: 'I'm still an apprentice, but when I get a chance. . . .'

'Oh, you'll get that, I'm sure.'

The music stopped abruptly, and the male dancer came to the front of the stage. 'Who's out there?' he called. 'You're putting us off, with your chatter.'

'Russ, and a young lady with the delightful name of Rose Marie, with a parcel for Sadie. We ought to applaud, you were awfully good. Finished your rehearsing, Stan?'

'Well, we can take a break for half an hour. More practice definitely required.'

'Come up on stage both of you,' Sadie beckoned. 'We'll have a cup of tea in my dressing room. I have a new dress to try on, Stan, which may need a stitch or two.'

It was a small room, with a long shelf the length of a mirrored wall, illuminated by a naked electric light bulb. On the shelf was a huge pot of cold cream, a bottle of witch hazel, sticks of greasepaint, a box of powder with a swansdown puff, bottles of scent, and wodges of cleansing cotton. There was a screen in one corner, which Sadie retreated behind with the dress box, after offering the single armchair to Rose Marie. Stan had not accompanied them.

'You can boil the kettle and make the tea, Russ. There's milk or lemon in the cold box. You'll have to take it unsugared, I never indulge, I watch my figure.'

She was a quick-change artiste, emerging from behind the screen with a triumphant 'Ta-ra!' and twirling round for effect. 'There! What d'you think?'

'You forgot to remove the tights - otherwise, fabulous, dear Sis,' Russ said.

Fabulous. Rose Marie hadn't heard that description before. Regarding the vibrant young woman in the misty blue organza dress with the dipping handkerchief hem, low waist, shoestring shoulder straps with *diamanté* clips, she thought, that's *just* the word.

'Coming to the show tonight?' Sadie asked Russ, while twisting her supple body this way and that, so that Rose Marie could make sure the dress was a perfect fit.

'Free tickets?' Russ placed the tea-tray on the shelf. 'Should there be a couple, I'll invite Rose Marie here to join me.'

'Oh, please, you don't need to do that.' Rose Marie straightened up. 'No tucks needed,' she assured Sadie.

'Thank you so much. I'd be delighted for you to accompany my unruly young brother. He's inclined to leap to his feet and cheer on occasion, especially at the bright young things in the chorus; I have to remind him that the variety theatre is not as vulgar as the music hall!'

Rose Marie blushed. This wasn't the moment to tell them about Stella.

'That's settled then. Shall I call for you at home?' Russ asked. 'The first performance is at seven.'

'Where's home?' Sadie enquired, re-emerging from behind the screen in her practice clothes.

'South London . . .' What would they think if they knew she lived over a pie shop?

'Look, I'll be finished here by five, I hope; why don't you both come back with me to my rooms and wait with me until it's time to come back here, eh? Though I'm afraid I always eat out late after the show, so have nothing to offer in the grub stakes.'

'I'm expected home for supper, and I also need to get changed.'

'Can you telephone your folks? I have use of the landlady's instrument.'

'Well, yes—'

'You can borrow something from my wardrobe, too. I must go,' Sadie drained her cup. 'Come back to the stalls, when you're ready.'

'Lucky you were here,' Russ told Rose Marie, when his sister had gone. 'I didn't have to tell her I wasn't offered the job I went for today. They said I needed a haircut.'

She couldn't help smiling at his comical expression. He was probably a couple of years her senior, she thought; fresh complexioned with floppy, sandy coloured hair and clear blue eyes. 'Don't get the wrong impression,' he advised. 'I *need* to work, like Sadie. She's fortunate enough to have found a career which suits her. I haven't yet discovered my forte. Our esteemed father gambled away a small fortune. He shot himself.'

'How awful!' Rose Marie exclaimed, shocked.

'It was years ago. We're over it, as far as one can be. Sadie supports our mother and me. I want to do my bit. Don't be fooled by my accent,' he added. 'I went to a private school, so private that no one's heard of it; my mother lives in a little rented house in Norwood.'

'You didn't need to tell me that.' She rinsed the cups in the hand basin.

'I believe in being honest from the start. How about you?'

'I told you: I work in a dress shop. I live with my sister. Over the family pie shop,' she stated baldly.

'Well, I'll be all right for supper I imagine, when I take you home! You see, I can't afford to treat you. All I possess is my return train-ticket home.'

I'm not sure Florence will approve of him, she thought, but I do.

'I'll be back around ten o'clock,' Rose Marie told Florence over the telephone. 'Miss Short's brother will see me safely home. Can you keep my supper in the warming oven please? Oh, and can you save a pie for Mr Short? He says he'd appreciate that on the way back to Norwood tonight. Thanks!'

Florence swallowed hard. She wanted to say, 'Be careful! Don't give this young man any ideas.' Instead she managed a mere, 'Be good! Enjoy the show.'

She knew she would spend a tense evening until Rose Marie returned.

'Isn't it exciting?' Josefina was, of course, eavesdropping on their conversation. 'I used to watch Mummy and Daddy from the wings when they were on stage. They thought I was asleep in their dressing room, but I didn't like being shut away from them, so I crept out and people went "shush!" and they'd find me a stool and tell me to sit very still.'

'You'll see your parents soon, I hope. Sit on my lap and tell me some more,' Florence invited. She was fortunate to have little Josefina to love and care for, she thought.

Rose Marie was starry-eyed by the final curtain. Then she and

Russ hurried to Sadie's dressing room. She changed quickly back into her ordinary clothes, and hung up the borrowed stylish velvet jacket and skirt behind the door. She'd attracted admiring glances in the circle.

Sadie met them in the corridor outside. She would be on stage again in an hour.

'Thank you, I had a lovely time.' Rose Marie beamed.

'I'm glad. Well, I'll see you again soon, at Belling's. Give Mother my love, Russ.'

'I will. Thanks, Sadie. We'd better dash, I think.'

'Here, take a cab.' Sadie loosened the strings of her dolly bag, passed him some coins. 'I expect your sister will be anxiously awaiting your return, Rose Marie, eh?'

Rose Marie nodded. They're both so nice, she thought, not toffee-nosed at all.

The taxi drew up outside Paradise buildings just as Manny arrived at the basement steps after his visit to the pub. He paused, wondering who would alight, then saw Rose Marie. She waved at Manny, then turned to her escort. 'This way. I live at number one.'

As they closed the front door behind them, Manny glanced up. He saw Florence's face at the window, then she pulled the curtains together.

Oh well, he thought ruefully, it had to happen sometime soon, and now it has. Rose Marie has been out on the town this evening, with a toff no doubt, coming home by cab. I guess Florence will find that hard to accept; I have no right, of course, but *I* certainly do.

Florence found the young man charming and disarming. He apologized for having to rush off, but the cab was waiting to take him to the station. He accepted the hot pie, wrapped in its cloth, gratefully. 'I'm starving! Had nothing since the sandwich my mother made me for my lunch. Thank you, Miss Flinders. I hope to see you both again. Well, goodbye.'

When the cab drew away from the kerb, Rose Marie came away from the window.

'Your supper's on the table,' Florence said. Wisely, she did not comment on the fact that Rose Marie's escort had not provided

her with any refreshment before or after the show. It was obvious, she thought, that Mr Short was short of a bob or two. Was
Rose Marie, in her turn, attracting lame ducks? She gave a little
sigh. 'Eat up, dearie.'

Four

'Do stand still, Josefina,' Florence admonished her niece, yanking back her shoulder-length hair into a tight, stubby plait. She secured the end with a rubber band from her odds and ends drawer under the sink. 'That'll hold it in place.'

Yvette kept a safe distance away. She was aware that Miss Flinders disapproved of her own artificial curls, but her mother had made a special effort with the rags last night, because this was the day appointed for the school photographer. Poor Josefina, she thought: she looks awful with her hair like that.

'Time you were going.' Florence glanced at the kitchen clock. 'Here you are,' she handed the girls a halfpenny each, and a scribbled list to Josefina. 'For the greengrocer. This afternoon will do, tell Mrs Snelgrove. Come on, then. Manny will be wondering where I am.'

The children walked sedately round the corner, then, when they were out of Florence's view, the usual morning fun commenced. They performed a sort of nimble hopscotch along the paving stones, avoiding the cracks. Sweets were not allowed in school, but they paused to look at the tempting array of colourful jars in the little sweet shop, just before the ironmonger's and the greengrocer's. These establishments had wares overflowing on the pavement, which was inconvenient for mothers hurrying along with a pram and toddlers in tow.

The ironmonger was lugging out a basket of cheap china, packed in straw. As if delving into a bran tub, he came up with a single cup and saucer and displayed them on top. There were zinc buckets, broom handles and soft brushes tied together by string; stacks of paint and putty tins; a pair of steps leaning against and keeping the door open. He eyed the children suspiciously. 'Watch where yer treadin'.' They skirted the muddle obediently.

Snelgrove & Sons was misnamed, like the pie shop. Mother and daughters was more like it. They were an awesome trio, over six feet in height and of Amazon build. Mrs Snelgrove had rammed an ancient trilby on her head; she wore a long brown drill overall; a money-bag strapped around her waist, leaving her hands free to weigh vegetables and fruit in the scales, placed on an orange box. Her daughters wore sacking aprons and had cropped hair, as if masquerading as the long-gone sons.

'Lorst your tongues?' Mrs Snelgrove enquired cheerfully. 'A nice rosy apple each?' Her hands, already grubby from the root vegetables, hovered over the tray of polished apples.

'Yes please,' Josefina said. They handed over their halfpennies, and the list. Mrs Snelgrove patted their heads and wished them a good day at their lessons.

The school bell was ringing. Now they had to hurry.

'I pinched a couple of cherries,' Yvette confessed. The stones were in her pocket.

'You didn't! You'd better take 'em back!' Her friend was shocked.

'I can't. I ate them while Mrs Snelgrove looked at the list, but I think she knew . . . You won't tell my *maman*, will you?'

'You needn't worry, I never tell tales.'

They entered the school gates. The pupils were already lined up so they sidled to the end of the queue.

'All neat and tidy for the photographer, children?' the head teacher, Miss Darch, enquired with a smile. Her nickname, Miss Starch, was not deserved, but accepted with good humour.

'I'll undo your hair at break-time, and comb it out,' Yvette whispered.

'Oh, aunty won't like that!'

'You can say Miss Starch did it!'

Josefina was shocked, but silent. She was discovering a new side to Yvette today.

'Here you are, my love.' Mrs Snelgrove put down the heavy box on the table with a sigh; glanced expectantly at the teapot on the hob. 'Make it strong; I need it this afternoon.'

There was a tap on the door. It was Lilli, home from the cinema.

'Care to join us?' Florence didn't wait for an answer, but took down another cup and saucer from the dresser. 'Sit down, Lilli, do.'

'Thanks! My back's aching. Extra cleaning today. Good-afternoon, Mrs Snelgrove.'

'Same to you,' the greengrocer returned.

'Lovely onions,' Florence said appreciatively. 'Spanish, I presume?'

'Yes. I sliced one for us to eat with our bread and cheese at elevenses. Cut up a Bramley, too. They're getting past their best, but I can't abide waste.' She paused, looked at Lilli. 'Seeing you gives me a chance to say, well, your daughter's been at my cherries. Now, if she'd asked politely, I'd've given her and Josefina a couple to dangle from their lugs; I 'member my gals used to like that.'

'Lugs?' Lilli was puzzled.

'Ears. What I mean is, she likes to help herself, Mrs Bower. She ain't the only one, of course, but I'll trust you to see to it. I wouldn't like her to do it elsewhere; some'd come down hard on her, and you.'

'Are you sure?' Poor Lilli looked near to tears.

Mrs Snelgrove patted her hand. 'Sorry, love, but she's done it before. Your gal didn't see,' she added to Florence. 'Don't worry, *she's* not light-fingered.'

When Mrs Snelgrove had departed, Lilli repeated, 'Light-fingered - I can't believe it.'

'Talk to her, but don't be too cross,' said wise Florence. 'She's had a lot of upset in her young life lately. It shows up in different ways. Losing her father - how long ago was that? And you deciding to try your luck in London. . . .'

Lilli was instantly on her guard. She hadn't wanted to lie to Florence, but when she'd told her initially that she and Yvette were on their own, Florence had assumed she was a widow. She'd had to tell her daughter it was best not to talk of their past life. Was this encouraging Yvette to be devious, in more ways than one?

'What about Josefina?' she countered. '*She* doesn't even have her mother with her.'

Florence winced. She took the empty cups to the sink. 'Well, we've both got things to get on with, I'm sure. We must each do what we think is best, with our young 'uns.'

He was an elderly photographer, with old-fashioned equipment, which entailed him ducking his head under a cloth while he activated the flash and recorded each class of children with their teacher, in turn. The result would be amazingly clear in detail; the solemn faces of the children in their Sunday best; the girls in cotton frocks with hair ribbons; the boys wearing collared shirts, knee-length trousers and highly polished boots. Josefina and Yvette sat together in the front row. Their youthful teacher stood behind them, resting a hand on either shoulder. The caption on the photographs would read: Paradise Board School, 1925.

'Your hair!' Florence exclaimed, looking at the photograph in due course.

'Miss Darch gave it a comb through,' Josefina said defensively. This was true.

'Whatever for?'

'She said, "Who did your hair like that?" This was also true. Now came the fib. 'I said, "me, Miss, I just tried to tidy it up...."'

'Well, it's recorded for posterity, that's for sure.'

'Let's all go down the Strand,' Russ sang out rather than suggested. He tucked Rose Marie's arm in his and they marched, giggling into Trafalgar Square.

She'd been hoping he would contact her again after their evening at the theatre, but, in fact, it was another three weeks before his note arrived in the post.

Dear Rose Marie,

Much to my mother and sister's relief, I have at last secured a place in the working world! A dusty little second-hand bookshop, one of many along the Charing Cross Road, but to me an Aladdin's cave. Being less impecunious, I would like to take you out - how about this Saturday afternoon? (I shall be working in the morning.)

We could enjoy the sights of London town, and then I would be delighted to treat you to tea.

What do you say?

If it's 'yes', I will call for you at 2.30.

Yours, Russell Short.

As they stood by Nelson's Column, Rose Marie observed, 'You didn't get your haircut!'

'You should see my new employer! With a name like Elmo Turbot-Watts, you'd expect him to be eccentric, and he is.'

'He's got long hair, you mean?'

'Well, hardly any on top, but a magnificent beard, which he combs through with his fingers when he's cogitating. He wears a velvet waistcoat, with – shush! – a gravy stain or two on the front. He seems very vague, but he can locate any book a customer might ask for, even if it's been tucked away at the back of a shelf for years. There's one other assistant, who's been there for the past twenty-odd years. "Jacob is a law unto himself," Mr Turbot-Watts says, so he hopes I will actually sell some of the books, and make myself generally useful. There's only one rule, as far as I can gather: I'm allowed to read in any slack moments, so long as I don't eat sticky buns at the same time, or make rings on books with my teacup.'

'Are you being trained? Is it a sort of apprenticeship?' Rose Marie wondered.

'I'm learning as I go along. If Mr Turbot-Watts approves of my progress, in time I'll be taken on buying expeditions all over the country. Mr Turbot-Watts has a van; two seats in the front and boxes of books in the back.'

'He needs someone young and energetic to crank up the engine I suppose?'

'I believe I got the job because I can drive, Rose Marie! My grandfather taught me, I used to drive around his estate. My salary is modest, but I believe the prospects to be good.'

'I'm glad,' she said, smiling up at him. 'Now, let's visit the National Gallery, shall we?'

'Why not? Art was one of my favourite subjects at school. However, while you regard the pictures, I'll enjoy looking at your pretty, expressive face!'

She laughed out loud. 'Florence told me to be careful, not to get carried away.'

'I gather she doesn't believe in love at first sight?'

'Certainly not, and nor do I!'

'But you like me, don't you?' He challenged her.

'Oh, I do, Mr Short, I really do!'

The statue of George Washington, outside the gallery, regarded them in a lofty fashion. He'd seen it all before. When they re-emerged into the bright sunshine, the girl in the cream tussore costume and round-brimmed natural straw hat was unselfconsciously holding hands with the young man in the striped blazer and rather crumpled baggy trousers.

Unbeknown to her sister, Rose Marie was paying a small weekly amount for her summer outfit, an offer from her kindly employer she could not resist. She loved to wear smart clothes. Rose Marie surmised that Russ's mother was no expert with the smoothing iron, and that nor was he.

They'd looked at pictures both great and small, impressive and formal. Rose Marie had lingered by the impressionists, where apparently simple brush strokes conveyed the story behind the picture.

'It's all to do with *light*, they were originally called open-air painters,' she informed Ross solemnly. 'Bright colours, shadows.' She was still bemused by what she'd seen.

'But nothing clearly defined,' he observed.

'You really liked the Turner pictures, you said you could almost smell the steam from the locomotive; well, I love the dreamy feel of Monet ... see, my booklet says that in 1874 he painted a series called Cathedrals, including the one in Rouen several times, in changing light. Oh, and his views of London recall how it was here at the turn of the century.'

Now, Ross observed, 'Here we are at St Martin's church in the Fields. The doors are never closed, they say, no one is ever turned away. The crypt is full of homeless folk at night.'

Rose Marie gave a little shiver. 'All those poor down-and-outs ... I don't want to feel sad on such a lovely day.' She glanced up at the wide black steps to the entrance.

'Come on then. Let's go on to St James's park for a while, and then we'll have our tea!'

'We mustn't eat too many cakes; Florence will have supper ready for us at eight!'

Florence thought, as if I haven't made enough pastry this week. She rolled the rough puff pastry to fit the pie plate. Still, she had an eager assistant in Josefina, mixing breadcrumbs into warmed golden syrup, then adding a squeeze of lemon. Then she carefully scraped the mixture into the pastry case. Florence smiled to herself as Josefina sucked the spoon clean.

'One less thing to wash up, Aunty,' Josefina said hopefully.

Florence prodded the jacket potatoes on the bottom shelf, and turned them over before she put the treacle tart in the oven.

'Now, wipe the table over and we'll prepare the salad. I thought it best to keep the meal simple - I didn't want to be all hot and bothered and dabbing my brow when our guest arrives.'

'He's not a guest Aunty Florence; he's Rose Marie's beau.'

'Wherever did you hear that old-fashioned expression? He's just a friend, Josefina.'

'Like Manny? He's invited to supper, too. Why couldn't I ask Yvette? She's *my* friend.'

'She practically lives with us as it is! She ought to spend more time with her mother.'

As soon as she said that, Florence regretted it. It was over a year since Josefina had seen Stella, after all. She added quickly, 'Remember you promised to get yourself off to bed after supper, my girl!'

The three of them met at the front door.

'This is Manny, who looks after the pie shop - Manny, meet Russell Short,' said Rose Marie.

'Russ for short, if you'll forgive the pun,' Russ said, shaking Manny's hand.

'Have you had a pleasant afternoon?' Manny asked awkwardly.

'Very nice,' Rose Marie told him, as she opened the door. 'We walked down the Strand, we went to the National Gallery, we looked at the church next door, St Martin's in the Fields – d'you know it? Then we walked a while in Green Park 'til I started hobbling in these silly shoes - well, Florence did warn me, I would! - but we had to walk some more before we found a tea-shop and I could sit down thankfully and enjoy a muffin dripping with butter while a sad-faced man played a violin in the street outside.'

They'd arrived at the door of the flat. From the stairwell above, Yvette, piqued at not being invited, peeped through the bannisters at them, and then went to report to her mother.

Florence had seen Rose Marie and her escort arrive in the taxi. She'd sighed ruefully as she turned away from the window. The tram was due along shortly. Getting his first wage packet had obviously gone to young Mr Short's head.

Manny brought up the rear. Rose Marie plumped down in a chair, removed her shoes, and wriggled her toes. 'You were right as usual, Florence, no blisters, but very tired feet.'

'Ready for your supper?' Florence asked. 'I hope you like crab - may I call you Russ?'

'Of course you may. And I do. You dressed the crab yourself?' He was impressed.

Florence nodded. It had been a slow process, if not a too arduous one, because she could sit at the table to prepare it. She'd scraped the meat carefully from the small claws into a bowl, mixed it with the left over breadcrumbs and lemon juice; a nut of butter; salt and pepper, and the inside of the crab. Then she'd cleaned the shell, put it in the centre of a large serving plate, and spooned in the mixture. The white meat was flaked from the large claws; this was piled on either side of the shell. Josefina decorated it with chopped parsley.

'You must try our grape punch,' Josefina said, squeezing in between Rose Marie and Russ. 'It's ginger beer and grape juice. I'm allowed it, 'cause it won't make me tiddly.'

Florence motioned Manny to sit next to her. She could tell he felt out of it. 'Help yourselves,' she said. 'Pass the bread and butter, Josefina, please, and remember what I said about bedtime, earlier.'

While Manny helped Florence with the washing up, Rose Marie and Russ took their cups of coffee into the sitting-room.

'I must keep my eye on the time,' he said, looking at his wristwatch. 'How often do I say that? My sister bought me the time piece for my birthday because of it.'

'Florence will make sure you don't miss the last tram,' Rose Marie told him. She winced. 'I'll have to soak my feet in salt and water, before I go to bed.'

He reached down and gently rubbed one stockinged foot and then the other. 'Easier?'

'Yes, thank you. But - I don't think Florence would approve,' she told him.

He straightened up. 'I'm sorry, I didn't mean—'

'I know you didn't. But can't you think of anything better to do?' She leaned towards him expectantly. 'You may kiss me, if you want to.'

'I want to,' he admitted. 'It's just that I'm not too experienced at that lark. . . .'

'Well, nor am I, but I'd like to be!'

'How can I resist such an invitation?'

'Quickly then - before Florence bursts in!'

He made his mind up; he slipped his arms around her, pulled her close. Their first kiss was rather a hit and miss affair, but both of them hoped it was the start of something very special.

'He's got good manners, been nicely brought up.' Florence handed Manny another plate to dry, then to slot in the wooden plate-rack on the wall.

'They told me they'd enjoyed their London jaunt,' he said. He cleared his throat. 'It brought back memories, Florence, of you-know-when, Rose Marie mentioning St Martin's in the Fields.'

'Where that kind bobby found you that night? The one who sent you here?'

'That's right. I don't suppose I told you all of it.'

'I don't reckon you did, my dear.' She rinsed her hands, dried them on the towel hanging under the sink. 'We'll have our coffee in the kitchen, eh?'

'I was on my beam end, I felt I couldn't go home in that state.' Manny took a gulp of his coffee. Florence had given him a decent-sized cup, not one of those small cups she kept for visitors. It was things like that which made him feel almost like one of the family.

'Yes?' she encouraged him. She passed him the plate with the last slice of treacle tart.

'It was bitterly cold; I'd been sleeping rough for a month or so. The bobby took me back to the police station. The sergeant gave me some grub, a mug of tea, then allowed me to sleep in an empty cell, but they didn't lock the door. He said he'd have a word with a colleague who might be able to help me find a job. It seems he'd heard you were looking for an assistant in the pie shop. He said he knew what war did to a man's mind as well as his body.

'In the morning, I was fitted with a decent pair of boots, a jacket and trousers. I was given a bowl of warm water, soap and a towel, the loan of a razor to shave and scissors to cut my nails. I began to feel like a human being again.'

'Like Buck,' she said quietly.

'And like you, they gave me a shilling or two to carry me through. But I paid them back, as I promised I would.' He sounded almost fierce.

Florence rose, took their empty cups to the draining board. 'I knew, of course, who sent you to me. I'm glad they did. One day, maybe you'll tell me what happened before that.'

He remained seated at the table. Sensing there was more to come, Florence sat down again too.

However, he talked of more recent times. 'We've all heard Dick Sheppard on the wireless, the parson at St Martin's, eh? The one who preaches and prays for peace in the world? I went back there one Saturday night, I don't know why. There was that very same bobby. He introduced me to the Reverend, who showed me how the down-and-outs were welcome now in the crypt of the church.

'It was packed full. Folk lying on benches, covered with old coats. Some asleep. Some just sitting, leaning one against another, for warmth and support. The newcomers were given a bowl of hot soup and a thick slice of bread. The helpers didn't ask why the folk were there. They'd seen it all before, but I must say it did me good to see what was being done. . . .'

After a long moment Florence said, 'Well, we'd better join the others, and remind young Russell that he'll need to leave in less than half an hour.'

She was completely taken by surprise when Manny put his hands on her shoulders and kissed her cheek. 'Thank you, Florence,' he said.

Florence gave herself a little mental shake. She thought, I mustn't read anything into that. I'm a good listener and he appreciated that.

Five

LEAVING the cinema each afternoon after work, Lilli had become increasingly nervous all week. She glanced over her shoulder involuntarily as she hurried home; she knew it was irrational, but she suspected that she was being followed.

There were others walking the same way, of course, but none she could class as furtive. Once she'd swung around fearfully when there was a glancing blow to her back, but it was only the bulging shopping bag of an elderly woman, as she shifted it to her other arm.

'Sorry dear,' the woman apologized, with a wry smile.

It was Friday before she convinced herself that she must be imagining things. On a sudden impulse, she stopped by the flower seller on the corner and bought two bunches of mimosa, one for herself, because it reminded her of France, and the other for Florence, who now had two small girls to look after in the school holidays.

Yvette, she thought, I must buy her a little treat. There was a baker's shop across the road. The proprietors were Polish; the cakes were more fancy than in the Paradise shop.

Lilli stepped out into the road, wondering if there would be any Madeleines left. Yvette declared they were delicious, those little dome-shaped cakes brushed with jam and rolled in desiccated coconut, with a shiny glacé cherry on top.

There was a screech of brakes. Lilli was jerked backwards by strong hands and propelled to the pavement. Dazed, she saw that the motor car had flattened her flowers on the road. The driver wound down his window and shouted at her, before he drove on.

'You've had a shock,' a man's voice observed. She took in a

sallow-skinned face, sleek dark hair, deep-set eyes. She was reassured by his look of concern.

'I ... suppose I should say thank you ...' She was shaking now; near to tears because of the ruined flowers.

'There's a tea-shop just along here. Allow me to buy you a cup of tea, and then, if you permit it, I will be pleased to escort you home,' the man said.

Lilli allowed him to take her arm, as they walked a hundred yards or so to the shop.

As she gratefully quaffed the hot tea, her companion said suddenly, 'If you will excuse me for a few moments - I assure you I will be back.'

When he returned, he presented her with more flowers, to replace the crushed ones.

'Oh, I didn't expect ... this is so kind of you. Thank you.' She reached for her purse.

'No, my pleasure, I insist. The flower seller advised me. Now, you were about to purchase bread from the bakery across the road, I believe?'

'Just some cakes, Madeleines, my daughter's favourite.' Why had she added that?

'Then you are in luck, *madame*, under the glass on the counter here, see: two Madeleines! Is that sufficient, I wonder?'

Even as she wondered at his use of *madame* and his pronunciation of Madeleine, he called to the waitress as she came past with another order, to put the cakes in a bag and to add to the bill.

'We haven't introduced ourselves,' Lilli said. She was beginning to feel rather uncomfortable about all this attention. 'I am *Mrs* Bower.'

'And I am Philippe Solon. I am French by birth, as I believe you to be.'

She chose not to comment on his assumption. 'I must thank you again for your kindness, but I must be going. My daughter will wonder where I am. There is really no need for you to accompany me, Mr Solon, I feel quite restored.'

'Allow me to see you out,' he said gallantly. He opened the door and gave her a little salute. 'Goodbye Mrs Bower, I'm glad I was able to help.'

As Lilli walked away, he went back inside the tea-shop to pay the bill.

Lilli was relieved that Mr Solon had not insisted on seeing her home. However, the disquiet resurfaced. She quickened her pace. Was her imagination playing tricks?

Florence was pleased with the mimosa. Yvette and Josefina ate their cakes there and then.

'I'm sorry I was late,' Lilli told Florence.

'That's all right dearie, but I was a bit worried about you; you're usually so punctual.'

When Lilli arranged her spray of mimosa in a jug, upstairs, she saw that her hands were dusted yellow, from handling it. She wondered if the man who had saved her from being knocked down by the motor car was even now washing the powder from his hands, too. . . .

'It's my Saturday on, at work,' Rose Marie said to Florence late that evening.

'I hadn't forgotten. Are you going shopping afterwards I wonder?'

'Well, perhaps. Russ suggested that I call for him at the book-shop. He finishes an hour later than me, at one o'clock.'

'You'll be back for supper?' Florence asked.

'Well,' Rose Marie repeated, 'I can't say. We might go to the theatre, to see his sister. She's going off on tour next week.'

'I think Lilli will be disappointed not to have your company again,' Florence said gently. 'She must get lonely, with just Yvette for company. Couldn't you invite her to join you?'

Rose Marie flushed. 'We were looking forward to—'

'Like that, is it? Two's company.'

'You don't understand, Florence!'

'My dear, I do. Another saying comes to mind: there's safety in numbers, eh? You're very young, Rose Marie. . . .'

'And what does that mean?' Rose Marie asked rebelliously.

'It means: don't get too serious too soon about this young man.'

'You like him, don't you?'

'Of course I do. But do think about what I say.'

'What do *you* know about it?' Rose Marie realized this was

48

cruel, even as she said it.

Florence flinched. 'I'm not going to argue with you, Rose Marie. Don't be too impulsive, that's all I ask.' She wanted to add, 'Remember Stella,' but she didn't. She thought, if only I hadn't been so anxious about Stella and Jose, questioned her as I did, Stella might not have rebelled and run off with him. I mustn't make the same mistake with Rose Marie.

There was that nagging pain in her side again. She sighed. She always felt emotional at this time of the month, but the cramps were becoming much worse. She ought to see the doctor, she knew that, but how could she take time off? She was much too busy.

The pie shop closed after the lunch-time rush on Saturdays. Manny turned the sign to CLOSED. While Florence bagged up the takings, he began to clear up.

'Not a very busy morning,' he observed. 'Apart from jellied eels. In this weather, folk are not wanting hot pies.'

'That's why I made more ham-and-egg,' Florence said. 'Well, I'd better go and see to the girls. It's not good for them to be indoors in the summer, but I have to keep an eye on them. Lilli will be home shortly. I'll suggest she takes them out this afternoon.'

'You look tired, Florence,' Manny told her, concerned.

She forced a smile. 'Didn't get much sleep last night, it was too warm.'

The knock on the shop door startled them.

'Can't they read the sign?' Manny grumbled. He shot back the bolt and opened up.

The man standing there politely removed his hat. 'Good-afternoon. I believe Mrs Bower lives here?'

'She's not at home.' Manny stepped aside to let Florence deal with the stranger.

'I am sorry to have troubled you,' he said. 'Would you be so kind as to tell her that her friend called?'

'I wasn't aware she had any friends in this area, apart from us,' Florence was wary. 'You'd best give me your name.'

'Philippe Solon. I, too, am French.'

'Oh, are you a friend of her family?'

'I know of them, yes,' he smiled. 'Well, I will try again.' He replaced his hat, and walked off, round Paradise corner.

Quite suddenly, Florence felt giddy; she clutched at Manny's arm. The next thing she knew she was slumped in a chair, and Manny was holding a glass of water to her lips. His face was drained of colour, like her own.

'Can you manage the stairs yet? You gave me such a fright! Thank goodness Lilli just arrived, I haven't had a chance to tell her about the visitor yet - I said the doctor was probably still in his rooms, and to fetch him here.'

'Thank you . . .' she managed. 'What would I do without you, Manny?'

'What would we all do without you?' he said huskily.

The children had already eaten their sandwich lunch, so Manny offered to take them to the newsagents to buy comic papers and a bag of lemon drops to share in the park nearby.

While the girls were out, Lilli acted as chaperone, while the Doctor examined Florence in her room. On his instructions, she mixed a powder in a medicine glass of warm water.

'You must remain in bed,' the doctor said. 'You should attend a clinic at the hospital as soon as possible. You are obviously very anaemic. How long have you had this problem?'

Florence felt drowsy; the pain had subsided. 'I can't remember. . . .'

'That means a considerable time,' he observed. 'I have held a surgery in Paradise for almost fifteen years and you have never called on my services for yourself during that time. Of course, I recall you bringing young Rose Marie to see me, from time to time, and latterly, your niece, Josefina, but—'

'I didn't want to bother you,' Florence said defensively.

'Does that really mean you don't wish to know the cause of all this?'

'Perhaps. I don't have time to be ill.' Her eyes closed. The sedative was working.

The doctor motioned to Lilli. They went out, closed the door behind them.

'Are you available to help out here, Mrs Bower? She must rest up for a week or so.'

Lilli made up her mind instantly. 'I can look after her.' She thought, I may lose my job, but it can't be helped - I owe so much to Florence.

She had to know. 'Doctor,' she asked anxiously, 'Is Florence seriously ill?'

'Try not to worry. It appears to be a common problem. Minor surgery would hopefully alleviate the symptoms. There is ah, a permanent solution, but one she may not consider, being still of child-bearing age.'

'Florence isn't married; she has no children of her own.'

'You haven't known her long?'

'No. . . .'

'Then you and I should respect her privacy, eh? I will call again, if you think it wise.'

Rose Marie was amazed at the number of bookshops along Charing Cross Road. Many of these came under the banner of second-hand books, a few were serious vendors of rare old tomes. Dust inevitably added to the hazy interiors of all the bookshops; shelves were crowded, books piled haphazardly on chairs, awaiting their turn on display. The front shop windows were packed solidly with rows of books as well, which accounted for the twilight effect within, but during the summer months, to counter this, the shop doors were propped open. There were stands of cheaper novels in racks on the pavement to attract and halt the progress of the casual reader; boxes of dog-eared postcards and other ephemera.

She recognized Mr Turbot-Watts from Russ's graphic description. He appeared out of the gloom to welcome her in.

'Miss Flinders, I presume? Mr Short is attending to a customer just now. Please look around while you have the opportunity. Mr Short tells me you have catholic tastes in reading.'

Rose Marie was not quite sure what that meant. 'I go to the library,' she said lamely.

'You should be building up your own library, my dear. A few pence will buy you a new paperback edition of a classic book, or you may find an earlier, bound copy on my shelves. . . .'

'I mainly read romantic novels,' Rose Marie admitted. Better to be honest.

Mr Turbot-Watts beamed. He ran his fingers through his luxuriant beard, while he reflected on that category of his stock.

'Romance . . . not penny dreadfuls I presume, they appear to have had their time and place. There are the passionate writers of the past, like the Brontë sisters, who write of romance, yes, and unrequited love, of joy and of loss—'

'I have a copy of *Jane Eyre*. My sister gave me that for my fourteenth birthday. I read it again recently; this time I understood it. After all Jane Eyre and Mr Rochester went through, well, I was so thankful it had a satisfactory ending! Oh, and I haven't read Jane Austen since I was at school, but I loved *Pride and Prejudice*.'

'I know where I have a copy, and if you will excuse me, because your young man is trying to catch my eye to remind me it is he you have come to see, I will deal with the customer and then I will reunite you with Elizabeth Bennet, before you leave.'

'Thank you,' Rose Marie said shyly.

Russ came over and his happy grin told her just how pleased he was to see her. He took both her hands in his and squeezed them gently.

'Come into the back room. I must spruce myself up, and put on my jacket. How d'you manage to look so cool and smart after your morning's toil?'

'I changed in the cloakroom at work,' she admitted. She wore the cream two-piece again because he'd said how much it suited her, last weekend.

'I've a present for you,' he said. 'A novel by Netta Muskett. It looks your sort of book.'

'Yes, it does, thank you.' She slipped the gift into her raffia shopping bag. She whispered in his ear, 'Your boss is finding me a copy of *Pride and Prejudice*. . . .'

'He approves of you, I can tell!'

They enjoyed a light lunch in a small restaurant. A perfect poached egg on toast and a frosted glass of lemonade. Then they took a bus to the West End and did some window-shopping, before they took tea with Sadie in her dressing room at the theatre.

'You're not going up in the Gods,' she insisted. 'I have tickets for the stalls. It's my last night here. I shan't see you for a while, we are touring until December.'

When the lights dimmed, Rose Marie anticipated the moment

Russ would slip his arm around her. She didn't have to wait long. She was vibrantly aware of his hand on her back.

Sadie dazzled the audience in the dress Rose Marie had delivered, was it really only a month ago? It was thrilling to watch the sensuous tango; the smouldering looks the dancers exchanged; the fluidity of their movements. Surely they must be in love, Rose Marie thought.

She said naïvely when the lights went up. 'D'you think they'll get married one day?'

'We-ell,' Russ said slowly, 'I don't imagine so. You see, Stan is otherwise inclined.'

'What do you mean?' She looked puzzled.

He smiled at her. 'Oh, Rose Marie, how sweet you are; how innocent!'

'Tell me!' she demanded.

'Not my place to do so. Ask Florence.'

'Don't worry, I will!'

They caught the last tram to Paradise corner. Russ stayed on it, bound for the station. Rose Marie waved him goodbye. As she stood outside her door, she became aware that a taxi was drawing up at the kerb. The driver helped a young woman alight. She paid him, and he carried her bags across the pavement.

'Thank you, ma'am. Goodnight.'

By the light of the street lamp, Rose Marie recognized a familiar face.

'*Stella*!' she exclaimed. 'Whatever are *you* doing here?'

'And what are you doing, little sister, out so late in the evening?'

Then they were hugging, and Rose Marie cried happily, 'Oh won't Florence, and Josefina, be surprised to see you. Come on, let's go inside!'

Six

'HERE she is, thank goodness,' Lilli exclaimed in relief. She'd promised Florence that she would wait for Rose Marie to come home, and to explain what had occurred. The little girls were upstairs in Lilli's flat, tucked up in Yvette's bed.

Manny had decided to keep her company, instead of going as usual to the pub. He'd told her about the man who'd called earlier that day. Lilli did not say much, but he recognized the flicker of fear in her eyes.

The door opened and there were two young women, instead of one.

'Lilli, Manny - didn't expect to see you! Where's Florence? Lilli, this is Josefina's mother, my sister, Stella!' Rose Marie spoke loudly in her excitement.

'Shush!' Lilli warned them anxiously. 'Florence is asleep, she had a bad turn, earlier; we had to call the doctor.'

Rose Marie was alarmed. 'Florence - she's *never* ill! Oh, I should've been here!'

'What's wrong?' Stella asked. This was hardly the welcome she'd anticipated.

Lilli glanced at Manny. He took in her embarrassment. Time to be tactful, he thought.

'I should go,' he said. 'Call me, if you need me. Goodnight.' He left immediately.

'Cocoa? There's a jug keeping hot on the stove,' Lilli offered. 'You shouldn't disturb Florence tonight; leave the explanations until the morning. I'll get back to my own place, and the girls now.'

'I was hoping to see Josefina!' Stella exclaimed. She was rummaging in her bag, and she added, 'I could do with a cigarette. Can either of you help out?'

Rose Marie was shocked. 'You always said smoking would ruin your voice! No, I don't smoke, you know Florence doesn't approve, and nor do you Lilli, eh?'

Lilli shook her head. 'I really must go. I'll bring Josefina down after breakfast.'

After she'd gone, Stella decided: 'I'll have a wash, and then get to bed. You can bring my cocoa in, can't you, Rose Marie? At least there'll be more room in the bed, with Josefina not in it!' She yawned widely. 'As your friend suggested, we'll leave the talking 'til morning.'

She'd had such a happy day, Rose Marie thought ruefully, but now, she guessed there would be plenty to worry about ahead. Who would make the pies, for one thing?

Later, she hung her best outfit in the wardrobe, undressed swiftly by Josefina's little night-light, then extinguished it. She slid into bed and said softly, 'Goodnight, Stella,' in case her sister was still awake.

There was a stifled sob from the other side of the bed.

'Stella? What's up?' she asked.

'I didn't know how to tell you. I was expecting a big hug from Florence and a cuddle from my Josefina, you see . . . I've left him, Rose Marie; my marriage is over!'

'You've left Jose? But why?'

'He found another woman, that's why. He's been unfaithful to me for months. Don't you go falling in love, Rose Marie - I wouldn't like you to get hurt.' Stella turned over, her back towards her sister.

No more was said. Rose Marie lay awake for a long time. It's too late, she told herself. I'm already in love with Russ, and I believe he feels the same way about me.

Florence awoke just before seven o'clock. Oh dear, she thought, I've overslept. Then she realized it was Sunday. Why did she feel so groggy? She sat on the edge of her bed, recalling hazily the events of yesterday.

Sunlight streamed through a gap in the curtains; Lilli had been too busy last night to ensure they were properly closed. The linoleum was chilly to her feet; someone had rolled up the bedside rug. Florence became aware that she was trembling. She wanted nothing more than to subside beneath the covers again, but first she must make her way to the bathroom.

Rose Marie, alerted by her footsteps passing her bedroom door, leapt out of bed herself. She glanced down at Stella, still slumbering. Then she followed Florence to make sure she was all right, before she locked the bathroom door.

'I was intending to have a bath,' Florence told her. 'But. . . .'

'Not this morning, eh? Look, I'll go and tidy your bed while you freshen up. Could you do with a nice cup of tea?'

'Could I! Off you go then, I don't appreciate an audience!'

Florence insisted on sitting at the table to drink her tea. 'Josefina not awake yet?'

'Not as far as I know. She's with Lilli and Yvette. Oh, and there's something I'd better tell you right away: Stella's come home!'

'What d'you mean she's come home?'

'She'll tell you all about it, I'm sure. It's not my place to do so.'

'What about breakfast?' Florence worried. She put her hand to her head. She still felt weak and dizzy. She attributed that to the doctor's potion.

'Finished your tea? I think it's time I learned to cook, don't you?'

'Manny. . . .'

'He won't expect to join us this morning, I'm sure. And Lilli can feed the girls. Back to bed for you, Florence dear.'

'I'm feeling much better . . .' Florence said unconvincingly.

'Doctor's orders!' Rose Marie managed a bright smile.

'What else did he say?'

'Not much to worry about, I'm sure, but Lilli will tell you. I wasn't here after all.'

'Oh, how did your afternoon and evening go?'

'I'll enlighten you later! But we had a lovely time. Take my arm, Florence, that's it.'

The bacon was over-cooked, she'd broken the yolks of two of the eggs, so Rose Marie decided to scramble these rather than drop them in the spitting fat. Breakfast was rather a disaster, she thought ruefully. She spooned some of the rubbery-textured egg on to buttered toast, arranged a tray and took it in to Florence.

'Just what I could do with,' Florence told her kindly. 'Is Stella up yet?'

'No. I'll tell her you're waiting to see her, when she is.'

Rose Marie ate a solitary breakfast, the first meal she had ever cooked, she realized. She was opening the kitchen window to put her bacon rinds out on the sill for the birds, when she heard excited voices, and Josefina burst into the room.

'Where's Mummy?'

'Still in bed—'

Josefina didn't hesitate, she was out of the kitchen in an instant without waiting for Rose Marie to add, 'She's still asleep!'

'Sorry,' Lilli apologized, holding her own daughter in check. 'How is Florence today?'

'Not too bad it appears. Are we making a fuss about not much?' Rose Marie asked hopefully.

Lilli shook her head. 'I should leave Florence to tell you, I think. Yvette and I will go upstairs now, and come back later. Can you manage?'

'Of course I can! Thank you for all your help yesterday, Lilli.'

'I'm so fond of Florence. She has helped us very much, also.'

'Darling, it's wonderful to see you,' Stella cried, as Josefina kicked off her shoes, and jumped on the bed, making the springs groan, as Stella sat up.

'Oh, Mummy, I missed you so much! How long can you stay?' She smothered her mother's face with damp kisses.

'As long as you want me to. . . .'

'That's for ever!' her daughter assured her fervently. 'Is Daddy coming back soon?'

'I'm not sure,' Stella hesitated, but felt unable to impart the bald facts. 'He sends his love, anyway.' That much was true. 'Now, go and see Rose Marie, because I must get up, and then find out how Florence is.'

Some time later, Stella joined Rose Marie and Josefina in the kitchen.

'What d'you fancy for breakfast?' Rose Marie asked.

The smell of burnt bacon lingered, despite the open window.

Stella said quickly, 'Oh toast will do, Rose Marie, thank you. I can get that myself. But is it all right if I look in on Florence, first?'

'Yes, of course. Don't *say*, well, too much, will you?'

'I won't.' Stella stifled her minor irritation. Rose Marie was patently the sister-in-charge this morning. She realized belatedly that she couldn't just arrive back and expect things to be as they were before she left home seven years ago. Rose Marie was a young woman now.

Stella tapped on Florence's door and then entered her room.

'Florence dear, this isn't like you, in bed on such a nice morning! I arrived just at the right moment, eh?' She leaned over and kissed her sister. 'What's up?'

Florence motioned to Stella to sit on the side of the bed. 'Just one of those tiresome female complaints, the doctor says. He wants me to have a proper examination at the hospital clinic. I may need a minor operation - you really mustn't worry about me! How about you? Why didn't you let us know you were coming?'

Stella began to sob, she couldn't help it. She mopped her face with her handkerchief.

'You're very thin, and pale; you don't look well yourself,' Florence said, concerned. 'Come on, tell me, you'll feel better if you get it off your chest.'

'It's the old story.' Stella sniffed. 'Jose is a *rat*, like you said he was.'

'Oh my dear, did I say that? I know I called him a dago, but—'

'Well, he was. He is! He's got a new partner, in both senses of the word. He wants to be free of me - of us, oh, my poor Josefina! How can I tell her that?'

'You don't have to yet. She can think you are here on holiday. Personally, I think you have arrived just at the right time! I imagine Rose Marie and Lilli have been wondering how on earth they can cope with their work, as well as looking after me for a week or two. . . .'

'Well, I'll put their minds at rest. *I'll* look after you, of course.'

'I feel better already! But I suppose the pie shop will have to close until I can get back to the baking - unless Manny can help out there.'

58

'I'll ask him, and remember, I enjoyed my role as pie-maker's assistant when I was not much older than Josefina! The main thing is, you mustn't worry. It will all work out.'

'I hope it will for you too, my dear,' Florence said. 'And I don't just mean the pies. . . .'

'Mummy,' Josefina called. 'Can I come in and see Aunty Florence?'

Florence answered immediately, 'You know you can!'

Florence found it very frustrating resting in bed on Monday morning, while Stella and Manny made their first batch of pies in the kitchen. She couldn't help feeling grateful that Rose Marie was not involved, after the unpalatable scrambled eggs she had served up for Sunday breakfast. Stella's offering had been edible, if not inspiring. Two slices of toast and honey, to give Florence energy, she said.

Rose Marie had caught the tram as usual, and Lilli had brought the children downstairs when she went to the Golden Domes. She'd warned them to be good and not to worry Florence until she returned in the afternoon, when she promised to take them out. They were settled in the sitting-room with draughts and dominoes, and a pack of patience cards.

'No ham-and-egg pies today, so you've got the morning off,' Josefina was told.

Manny was more dextrous than Stella. He followed the recipes in the tattered exercise book which Florence kept in the table drawer. The pastry pie cases were duly filled and seasoned, then went in the oven. They relied on an alarm clock to time the baking.

They didn't talk much, concentrating anxiously on the task in hand. Now and again Manny glanced thoughtfully at his companion. She was taller than her sisters, of a height with himself. Her long dark hair was braided round her head and hidden by the cotton cap. He didn't know her well, having come to Paradise Street after Stella had left home, but at their previous brief encounters he had observed her vivaciousness, overheard snatches of her lyrical singing as she entertained her daughter. He thought, she doesn't look too well herself, but maybe it's because she isn't wearing lipstick this early in the day.

'A bit lopsided,' Stella sighed, over the final batch of meat patties. 'D'you think the customers will mind?'

Manny shook his head. 'A couple of hungry bites, and they're gone!'

'I'm hungry, too, how about you?'

'I could do with a cup of tea . . . but first I must take the pork pies down to the shop and put a note on the door saying we'll be opening an hour late—'

'Due to circumstances beyond our control? Isn't that what they usually say?'

This time he nodded.

'The girls are suspiciously quiet. I'd better check on them. Thanks Manny for all your hard work.'

'It's what I'm employed for,' he said a trifle shortly, as if remembering his place.

'So am I now, I suppose; I must earn my keep.'

'You'll be here a while then?'

'Yes. Just as well, isn't it?'

Just as well, he thought. Florence and Josefina would be glad to have her home. But how about Rose Marie? She hadn't looked too pleased this morning, when Stella told her she could manage without her. . . .

Florence made her mind up. She insisted that she would visit the hospital this afternoon. Get it over with it, she said, emerging from her bedroom fully dressed.

Stella, slumped wearily in Florence's chair, after all the early morning chores, suppressed a groan. There was still the washing to sort and bag up for the laundry, with most of the contents of her luggage to add to that: she had certainly left Spain in a hurry. She literally had a few coppers in her purse, but she didn't need to worry Florence further by telling her that.

'Are you sure you're up to it?'

'Yes. The doctor said "as soon as possible". I've no pain, thanks to his horrible medicine. We can leave when Lilli comes home. I'll be extravagant: call a taxi for once!'

The outpatients clinic was at the rear of the hospital. They walked down echoing corridors with polished floors, where trolleys squeaked on rubber tyres, and nurses coiffed like nuns, hurried past to where duty called. The smell of carbolic was overwhelming, not reassuring; in fact this made them afraid, wondering what was to come.

They glanced through the glass partitions beyond which the ward stretched; rows of beds with plain white covers, with patients lying propped on pillows; chairs in which slippered men in checked dressing-gowns sat reading newspapers. They heard a rattling cough and saw a pale young woman reaching for a glass of water.

'Here we are, I believe,' Florence said, as they approached a waiting area, where women of all ages sat patiently on long benches or wooden chairs. They handed in the doctor's letter at the desk.

'This is a free clinic,' the receptionist informed them, placing the letter on the pile. She sized them up. 'Although if you can afford to pay something for your treatment, the hospital will be grateful. There is no means test, we leave it to your discretion.'

'I understand,' Florence said.

'Take a seat. There may be a long wait, but everyone will be seen and we have three doctors here this afternoon.'

'It's quieter than being in church,' Florence murmured to Stella. The faces around wore impassive expressions: one or two even had their eyes closed. Only their fingers, gripping their baskets or handbags betrayed the fact that they were not asleep.

Two long hours went by before at last Florence's name was called, and the two of them were ushered into a small consulting room.

Florence was concerned when she saw how youthful the doctor was. He was drying his hands on a towel, but he smiled and tried to put them at their ease. 'Now, which of you is my patient?' he asked.

After he had perused her own doctor's letter, he asked Florence to undress behind a screen, to don a robe and to climb on to the examination couch. He pressed a bell. 'There will, of course, be a nurse in attendance. Call me when you are ready, please.' He saw Stella's uncertainty. 'Oh, don't go. Your sister will be glad to have you with her when I tell her what I have discovered about her condition. . . .'

Florence submitted to the examination without a word of

complaint. She knew it would be over quicker if she kept calm. There were reassuring murmurs from the doctor and the kindly nurse patted her hand and approved of her stoicism. Then it was over, and she was suddenly shaking and unable to manage putting on her clothes without help. The nurse buttoned her up, and even tied her shoelaces. 'Well done, my dear. Ready to see the doctor now and hear his verdict?'

I've got to get a grip on myself, Florence told herself sternly. I mustn't alarm Stella. She pulled the curtains aside and walked out, managing a smile for her sister.

The doctor looked cheerful. 'You've allowed this to go on longer than you should, but I think this problem can be alleviated. I am going to tell you now that there is no indication of any malignancy. . . .'

A huge wave of relief washed over Florence, and she said faintly, 'Oh, thank God.'

He continued. 'In a week or two, when there is a bed available, I recommend that you come into the hospital for things to be put right. You should rest as much as you can, in the meantime.' He now addressed Stella, 'Can you help with that?'

'Of course I can!' she agreed.

'Sometimes,' the doctor said kindly, 'a possible recurrence can be resolved by the patient deciding to add to her family. You might consider that, Mrs Flinders, at your age.'

Florence flushed. 'It's *Miss* Flinders, doctor.'

'I do apologize! I just assumed—' He paused. 'Well, go home and don't worry. All will be well. Just await a letter from the hospital.'

'I will. Thank you so much, doctor,' Florence rose. Stella offered her arm.

As they walked back down the corridor, Stella said, 'It's such a relief, Florence, isn't it, to know things can be put right. I'm sure the doctor didn't intend to embarrass you.'

'Don't mention it to Rose Marie, or Lilli, will you? Or I'll be embarrassed all over again!'

Seven

Rose Marie was feeling decidedly fed-up. Florence appeared to have handed over the running of the household to Stella and encouraged her to manage the pie shop with Manny.

'It'll help to take Stella's mind off her own affairs if she's kept busy,' Florence told Rose Marie. 'You shouldn't have the burden of all this at your age.'

It was Lilli who thought of a temporary solution.

'You've only the two bedrooms and it must seem very crowded in your room, with the extra bed moved in there for Josefina; naturally she wants to be with her *maman*, but. . . .'

'It's *me* who has the truckle bed!' Rose Marie confided.

They were in Lilli's flat, where it was quiet, while Yvette played downstairs with Josefina.

'Yvette can come in with me, and you can have her room. What do you think?'

'The thing is, would Florence mind? But honestly, I haven't had a sound night's sleep since Stella arrived. That small bed is awfully hard.'

'I'll suggest the idea to Florence, I'd be glad of the company. We get on well, don't we?'

'I used to get on with Stella,' Rose Marie said ruefully. 'But I was younger then.'

Florence had observed the little flare-ups between Stella and Rose Marie, and thought privately that the arrangement would be a relief.

'Rose Marie can eat with us, that should help Stella I think, not having to prepare her meals,' Lilli said.

'In that case,' Florence told her, 'Rose Marie must pay you for her keep, not me.'

There were two letters in the post mid-week. One was for Florence from the hospital informing her there would be a bed available in the hospital on Sunday, that her operation would be the following day and she should be home again on the Wednesday of next week.

The other letter was for Rose Marie from Russ. She opened it in the privacy of her new bedroom. His writing was, she mused, cheerful and confident, like the man.

My dear Rose Marie,

My mother has expressed a wish to meet this wonderful girl I am forever talking about!

This being my Saturday morning off, and, fortunately, yours, too, I would like to call for you at about ten o'clock and then escort you back to our house for the rest of the day.

What do you say? Yes, I hope!

Please advise by return of post.

Salutations,

Russ.

She showed the letter to Lilli. 'I'll have to see what Florence thinks.'

'How can she mind? He asks so charmingly.'

Florence was too preoccupied with her own news to say then what she later thought, that it was rather early in their friendship for Rose Marie to meet the young man's mother.

Her friends were excited for Rose Marie. Mrs Belling appeared in the workroom unnoticed.

'More chatter than clatter!' she reproved them mildly, seeing the sewing machines idle. 'Anyone care to tell me what all the fuss is about?'

Rose Marie owned up. 'I've been invited to visit my young man's mother!'

'Oh, have you? Tell me, is the young man by any chance Miss Short's brother?'

'How—?' Rose Marie wondered how Mrs Belling knew that.

'The workroom grapevine, my dear. I imagine you are undecided what to wear?'

'Well, I have my tussore costume, of course, but he's seen me in that several times.'

'I'll send one of the sales ladies up here at lunch-time with a box of clothes we have sorted out for the summer sale. Look through and see if there is anything which will suit, eh?'

'I'm not sure if I can afford. . . .'

'Don't worry about that now.' Mrs Belling looked round at the other girls. 'The offer goes for the rest of you, too! Now, some treadling would not come amiss! I really came to say we need more of the voile blouses to display downstairs, they are selling very well. Thank you.'

When the box duly arrived, a work table was cleared, and the garments displayed. Some were too big, or too matronly for Rose Marie's slight figure, but there was a white cotton frock with a fine silvery stripe, short sleeves, dropped waist and buttoned bodice. The collar, slightly soiled due to a careless trying-on by a customer who had applied too much pink face powder, had a detachable poppy-red bow.

'I'll rub the stain with a damp, soapy sponge, then with a clean damp cloth. It'll soon dry, then I can press the collar. First, I must make sure it fits!' said Rose Marie. She mused, I've white cotton gloves, and maybe Lilli will lend me her little white hat.

On Saturday morning, Rose Marie popped downstairs to say cheerio to Florence. She discovered Florence pottering around in her kimono, making a fresh pot of tea.

'Stella and Manny are already busy in the shop. Josefina is having a lie-in - my suggestion! She will stay awake at night until her mother gets to bed. You're all ready for your big day, I see.' She smiled at Rose Marie. 'I expect I'll be tucked up by the time you arrive home. You'll come and wish me luck, won't you, before I go to the hospital tomorrow?'

'I'm going with you! You're not worrying too much about it, are you?'

'No, but I'll be glad to get it over with. Off you go, and have a good time.'

'Thanks, Florence, I will!'

Rose Marie waited outside the shop. Stella spotted her through the window and waved. 'Enjoy yourself!' she called.

Manny was serving an early customer, but gave her a little nod.

She didn't have to wait long. A small box-bodied green van with gold lettering on the side, E. T-W RARE BOOKS, drew up at the kerb. To her astonishment, it was Russ who opened the driver's door and jumped out.

'Don't look so surprised! I struck a bargain with the boss! The van is mine until tomorrow, when I've to collect Mr Turbot-Watts because we have a sale to attend after lunch.'

Once they were driving along, they exchanged the news since they'd last met.

'I've become more independent,' Rose Marie said. 'I'm sharing the flat upstairs with Lilli and her daughter. It's too crowded in our place since Stella arrived home .'

'Is that a permanent arrangement?'

'That depends on Stella. She'll have to live where she can find work, I suppose.'

'Well, Florence must be glad to have her help at present.'

'I suppose so . . . It's noisy this engine, isn't it?'

'It's a very reliable motor, a Trojan; ten horse power, if that means anything to you?'

'I'm afraid it doesn't.'

He continued, 'The engine is under the floor, a two-stroke, hence the vibration. But the chassis, as they call it, is well sprung, and I'm sure you noticed the solid tyres? The Trojan is well named, it can get up any hill with ease.'

'I only saw *you!*'

'That's nice. Dare I ask if you are looking forward to seeing my mother?'

'I . . . I'm not sure,' Rose Marie admitted. The bucket seat was uncomfortable and she felt a little sick. She hadn't travelled so far in a motor before, and Lilli's idea of a good breakfast, on her own working morning, left-over cream cake and hot chocolate, probably didn't help. . . .

'Don't allow her to intimidate you, that's my advice.'

Rose Marie gulped. 'You'll have to stop - oh *hurry!*'

Russ's large pocket handkerchief saved the day, and her dress, but Rose Marie arrived in Norwood with a wan face and woeful expression.

'Wait a moment, Russ,' she put out a restraining hand, as he switched off the engine.

Rose Marie opened her bag and took out a small bottle of eau de Cologne. She dabbed some behind her ears, and in the hollow of her throat.

'There! I hope I smell sweeter now.' She glanced out of her window. It was a quiet suburban street with neat rows of identical terraced houses. Not a shop or public house in sight, and no children playing outside. Not at all as she had imagined, despite Russ describing his home as 'a small house in Norwood'. Did anyone actually live in this place?

'I have a key, but I'll knock, as Mother may be busy in the kitchen, or out in the garden,' Russ said, as they walked up the little path, flanked by leggy rose bushes, to the door.

However, Mrs Short had obviously been watching out for their arrival, and the door opened immediately.

She was a tall, elegant woman in her mid-forties, wearing a linen skirt with a pretty, ruffled blouse which Rose Marie recognized instantly as one of those which had been selling like hot cakes in Belling's dress shop. She could have machined it herself, but, of course, it would be impolite to say so, she thought. Was Mrs Short aware that was where she worked?

Mrs Short's blue eyes had a definite frosty glare. She shook hands before Rose Marie could remove her gloves, looked her up and down, then opened a door off the minute hall.

'You can entertain Miss Flinders for ten minutes while I make some coffee, Russell.'

They sat together on a hard-stuffed sofa. The windows were closed; it was an airless room. Rose Marie removed her hat and put it on the occasional table with her gloves.

'Quick,' Russ murmured in her ear, 'how about a kiss before Mother returns?'

She demurred. 'D'you think we should?'

'Shush. . . .'

They sprang apart guiltily when Mrs Short came in carrying a silver tray with two steaming bone-china cups. She looked askance at the hat and gloves. Before Russ could remove these items, she pushed the tray on the table, the hat fell to the floor. Mrs Short managed to tread on the brim, as she bent swiftly to retrieve it.

67

'I'll put this on the hallstand,' she said firmly, not deigning to apologize.

'Aren't you joining us, Mother?' Russ asked.

'I have lunch to prepare,' his mother reminded him.

'May I help?' Rose Marie offered, even as she wondered if Lilli's hat was damaged.

'That's not necessary. My son seems to have his own ideas on how to spend the time before we sit down to eat. By the way, Miss Flinders, the bow at your neck appears to have come unfastened . . . Now, if you will excuse me.' She swept out.

'Oh dear,' Russ said with feeling. 'I think you can say that's put a stop to *that*, eh?'

'Russ, are you sure your mother was anxious to meet me?'

'I suppose,' he admitted, 'it was more wishful thinking on my part.'

'She probably thinks we're too young to be serious; I know Florence does.'

'Florence is nice to me, nevertheless, she makes me welcome when I see her; Mother is, there's no other word for it, an out and out snob!'

'Well, she knows how to make good coffee,' Rose Marie said, as she took the first sip.

Lunch, too, was an agreeable surprise. Slices of cold chicken and ham; tiny waxy new potatoes with melted butter and parsley, served on Royal Doulton plates; a colourful bowl of salad stuff; fresh-made mayonnaise in a cut-glass jug and mango chutney in a matching dish.

Over dessert, apricots and cream, the probing began.

'I understand your sister runs a long-established business - may I call you Rose Marie?'

Rose Marie almost choked on a mouthful of food. She managed a nod, while Russ poured more water in her glass. She swallowed. 'Yes, of course you may use my first name.'

'Miss Flinders seems too formal for one so youthful,' Mrs Short told her. 'My daughter tells me you are an accomplished dressmaker.'

'Rose Marie wants to go on to clothes design, don't you?' Russ put in.

Rose Marie realized that Mrs Short was deliberately patronizing her. 'I intend to be successful in whatever I choose to do, in the future.'

'You appear single-minded, but I imagine that in your case, an early marriage is on the cards.' There was no mistaking the malice in Mrs Short's voice.

'Why should you imagine that? What are you implying?' Rose Marie demanded. She put down her spoon with a clatter. She looked at Russ. 'Your mother obviously doesn't like me, Russ. Maybe you should take me home.'

'Don't go!' Mrs Short surprised them. 'You're wrong, Rose Marie, I do like you. I don't want my son to commit himself to . . . a liaison, before he's carved out a career for himself.'

'My sister married too young, I won't make the same mistake.'

'Mother, can't you understand? There's a strong attraction between Rose Marie and me. We enjoy being together. That doesn't mean we want to rush things.'

'I know you, Russell. You're too impulsive, like your father.'

'Please,' Rose Marie put in, sensing that the argument would become heated. 'Can we forget this conversation? We've both told you how we feel, Mrs Short. There's nothing for you to worry about, is there?'

'You're very charitable,' Mrs Short observed. 'Well, shall we adjourn to the garden?'

The garden came as a surprise to Rose Marie. It was more or less private because of the high hedges which separated the neighbouring plots on either side. There was the ubiquitous square of lawn; a crazy-paving path and neat flower beds, but at the end there was a gazebo where they could sit in the shade and think themselves somewhere much grander.

'Take the comfortable seat,' Mrs Short told Rose Marie, indicating an armchair with embroidered cushions. All the simple furniture, including a small table, was made of cane.

Hanging from a stout hook to one side of the entrance was a gilded bird cage containing a trailing fern. There were jardinières containing miniature shrubs sited around the gazebo, and comings and goings on a bird table to watch. Rose Marie was also intrigued by a stone statue alongside a tiny pond, green with moss and obviously very old, of a lissom young woman holding her skirts up as if she was about to ford a stream.

'Russell moved that to a safe place for me, before the auction of our old home. The antiques had to be sold, too, to cover my husband's debts. All we had left was the furniture we needed for this little house, dutifully provided by my brother-in-law. An aunt gave me the gazebo to make me feel at home. That, I must say is something I have yet to experience. But Aunt Bea was right, this does help.'

'I'll make a pot of tea and bring it out, shall I?' Russ looked from one to the other.

'You think you can trust me not to bite her head off, is that it?'

'Mother! That wasn't necessary.'

'Off you go, then,' his mother said.

When they were alone, Mrs Short asked Rose Marie, 'Would you like me to put you in the picture regarding our past life?'

'I think you already have.' Rose Marie felt apprehensive, wondering if Mrs Short realized that she knew the facts about her late husband's demise.

'Well, I have certainly hinted that Russ is not in line for any inheritance. Nor is my daughter. My own background may have helped them to come to terms with that. You look puzzled, so I'll enlighten you. Sadie is actually following in my footsteps, as it were. I was a dancer, too. Russell's father saw me in a London show and pursued me thereafter. It was an exciting time but it was unexpected when he proposed marriage. My own mother urged me to accept him. I think she feared the alternative was certain seduction and disgrace! Unfortunately, the latter was destined to come. Mine was a respectable lower middle-class family, we were in trade like your people; they didn't approve of my being on the stage. I take the opposite view, I am very proud of Sadie.'

'I'm sure Russ will make you feel the same way about him.'

'I'm afraid he has too relaxed a view on life.'

'That's what I like about him,' Rose Marie said defensively.

'Talking about me?' Russ asked, as he arrived with the tea.

'Not exactly - more about seduction,' Rose Marie said, with some justification.

'It never entered my mind,' he averred, with a cheeky grin. 'Now, after the tea, how about a walk to the Crystal Palace?'

'Too hot for me,' his mother said. 'But you two go. I don't mind.'

Eight

'I should leave soon, I think,' Rose Marie said. 'Have you everything you need?' She looked anxiously at Florence, sifting beside her hospital bed, awaiting the attentions of a nurse.

'You know I have. You're off to meet Russ, are you? Or does this place make you feel uneasy, like it does me?'

'We-ell . . . Russ is working today; driving Mr Turbot-Watts to Surrey to collect the contents of what he calls a modest library.'

'You didn't say much about your visit to his mother's house yesterday. How did it go?'

'Mrs Short wasn't very welcoming at first; she seemed to think I was pursuing her son for his money, and of course I'm aware he hasn't any! But we sorted out our differences and Russ wisely kept quiet; she actually kissed me when we left, saying she hoped to see me again.'

'I suppose she's just over-protective, as mothers are. What did you do at Crystal Palace?'

Rose Marie felt the colour rise in her cheeks. 'Phew! It's too warm in here,' she said, in case Florence noticed. 'We didn't go over the palace this time, but walked in the grounds, plenty going on outside. There was a crowd watching a hot air balloon taking off.' She didn't add, we found a quiet spot away from there, and enjoyed a cuddle in the long grass. Russ spread his jacket for me to lay on, but my new dress still got rather creased. Lucky his mother didn't know about that.

'I was young once myself, but it wasn't much fun,' Florence observed. 'Off you go then. Tell Stella to telephone the hospital tomorrow afternoon.'

'I love you Florence.' Rose Marie felt suddenly choked.

'I know you do. Look, here comes the nurse! Don't worry, will you? I'll be all right.'

'Someone delivered this lovely bunch of cream rose-buds for you in reception,' the nurse smiled. 'Here's the card. I'll put them in water.'

'Thank you, nurse. Now who on earth. . . ?' Florence opened the tiny envelope.

Rose Marie wasn't going until her curiosity was satisfied.

'All the best,' Florence read aloud, then, 'The card's signed "Manny".'

'Her bed's at the end of the ward, near a window,' Rose Marie told Stella.

'Well, she'll soon be home again, thank goodness, and fortunately, the children go back to school on Tuesday. Lilli and l can relax a little, then.'

'Stella, I didn't like to ask before, but does Jose know you're here?'

'Where else would I be? I suppose I ought to contact his family, and see if they know what's happened.'

'They haven't shown any interest in Josefina since she's lived with us.'

'We didn't tell them about that arrangement, they wouldn't have approved. When are you returning to our flat? The last thing I wanted was to put you out.'

'It didn't seem like that to me,' Rose Marie admitted.

'Look, when things are back to normal, and Florence is in charge again, I'll have to seek work, in earnest. I don't want her to think I've given up singing for pie-making! I may have to leave Josefina here, I wouldn't want to unsettle her again.'

A tap on the door, and Manny came in. He said, 'I hope you don't mind, I just wanted to know if Florence has settled in, in hospital.'

'You didn't ask at the desk then, when you brought the flowers?' Rose Marie asked.

Manny looked sheepish. 'They wouldn't tell me, not being family. How did you know?'

'I was just about to leave myself, when a nurse gave Florence the roses. She said they were from you. She was obviously pleased at the kind thought.'

'What kind thought?' Lilli and the girls had just returned from their walk.

'It was nothing much.' Manny cleared his throat. 'I'll see you first thing tomorrow, Stella.'

'Business as usual,' Stella observed. 'We appreciate all your extra efforts, Manny.'

The fragrant roses, now unfurling, were the first thing Florence focused on when she came round after her operation later on Monday morning. She was back in the ward, with the screens around her bed, becoming aware of the daytime routine going on; the squeaking medicine trolley, the cheerful voice of the nurse: 'Thermometer under the tongue, please.'

Then the screen was removed and it was her turn. 'Good – awake, I see! Let me put another pillow under your head. How do you feel, my dear?'

'Still rather sleepy,' she yawned.

'You weren't out long, dear. The operation went well. The doctor will see you this afternoon. You'll be sitting up by then. Just relax now. Ready for a cup of tea?'

'Yes, please! And a couple of biscuits – I wasn't allowed any breakfast, as you know.'

'Well, that's a good sign. Right. Thermometer under the tongue. . . .'

After the tea and biscuits, Florence pulled the covers up and slept until lunch-time.

The doctor was smiling and reassuring. 'I hope we won't need to see you again.'

'When can I resume work?' she asked.

'Well, you need to get over the effects of the anaesthetic as well as the operation. Say, a fortnight. You will be sent home with a large bottle of iron tonic. It tastes vile, but make sure you take it to the bitter end, eh? In a month or two you will feel rejuvenated.'

'Thank you doctor, for everything.' All that secret worry, she thought, over the past few months, and now, thank goodness, she was free of that. She could make plans for the future.

Later, the nurse told her, 'Your sister, Mrs Lopez, telephoned.

She and your other sister are visiting you this evening.'

'But I'll be home in a couple of days—'

'They want to see for themselves how well you are!'

The ward doors were opened on the stroke of seven and relatives filed in.

Rose Marie and Stella brought Florence black grapes and a bottle of lemon barley water.

'Oh,' Stella delved in her bag. 'Wine gums from Josefina and a magazine from Lilli.' She passed these to Florence, adding, 'And a letter from Manny.'

'Not his resignation at being worked so hard, I hope,' Florence said. She tucked the letter under her pillow. The girls were obviously curious, but she wasn't opening it yet!

Florence actually forgot about the letter until it was almost time for lights out. As the nurse tidied her bed and plumped her pillows, she asked, 'What's this?'

Feeling rather like Josefina, Florence read the letter under the covers.

Dear Florence,

I was pleased to hear all is well.

I have not found the extra work too tiring and if possible I would like to continue, after you are able to get back to the pie-making. That is if you can afford to pay me a bit more. Will you be so kind as to think about it and let yours truly, Manny, know.

Florence smiled to herself. She refolded the letter and replaced it in the envelope. A sudden preposterous idea struck her. Was it the effects of the gas, she wondered. 'Think about it', he said. Well, she certainly would, and he might well be surprised at her thoughts! But first, there was Stella to sort out, and that might not be an easy task.

Josefina and Yvette went off to school on Tuesday morning. They were glad to be back to normal - gazing in the shop windows and skirting the cracks in the pavement. The only thing was, Stella hadn't thought to give them their apple money. Josefina clutched the greengrocery list. She entered the shop while Yvette waited outside. She knew Mrs Snelgrove watched her.

There was the usual haphazard display of fruit on a trestle table. Oranges, Yvette noted. She glanced furtively around, then through the greengrocer's window. Mrs Snelgrove and her daughters were asking after Florence.

Yvette put out a stealthy hand. Her fingers curled round a large orange. She hesitated. Where could she put it? Her pockets weren't capacious enough to conceal it.

There was a touch on her shoulder. She let the orange go, spun around. A tall man stood there, a stranger. Maman had warned her about talking to people she didn't know.

'I don't think your mother would like you to do that,' he said reprovingly. 'You are Mrs Bower's daughter, I believe, Yvette?'

She nodded mutely. The man raised his hat politely, as if she was a grown woman.

'Please tell your mother I have been away, but that I will see her soon. Now, you should hurry on to school, I think. The bell is ringing.'

'But, who are you?' Yvette faltered.

'Philippe Solon. She will know when you say the name. Goodbye for now, Yvette.'

Mrs Snelgrove had spotted them in conversation, through the window. She came hurrying out, followed by Josefina.

'Who was that?' she asked, arms akimbo, as she stared after the retreating figure.

'A friend of Maman's, I think,' Yvette faltered. She daren't look at the oranges.

'Here,' Mrs Snelgrove took a small vegetable knife from her pocket and sliced a juicy fruit in two. She wrapped the sticky orange pieces in paper. 'Half each, instead of an apple. Off you go, then. Be good, girls!'

Miss Darch was waiting at the school gate for the stragglers. 'Hurry up!' she called to Josefina and Yvette. 'I'm sure you were sent off in good time - you've been dawdling!'

'Oh dear,' Lilli exclaimed, when Yvette passed on the message from Philippe Solon. She'd called in at Florence's flat after work to see Stella and they'd enjoyed a chat while they waited for the girls to return from school.

'What's up?' Stella asked, intrigued.

Lilli hesitated. Then she said, 'You two should get changed before tea. Off you go.' When she and Stella were alone, she continued. 'This man, I can't be sure, but I think he's been following me. Oh, he doesn't seem to be - oh, how can I put it - *sinister*, but he obviously has a purpose. I don't think it's a coincidence that he is French, either.'

'Maybe he was asked to find you, eh?'

The girls emerged from Josefina's room. 'Just going up to Yvette's now, back in five minutes!' Then they went off upstairs.

'I don't think five minutes is long enough to tell you my story,' Lilli told Stella. 'Even Florence doesn't know all of it, and Rose Marie, well, she's too young to confide in. But I think *you* will understand because you also have abandoned your husband.'

'I certainly didn't abandon him – it was the other way around!' Stella sounded affronted.

'I'm sorry, of course, you are right. But you couldn't live with him any more, eh?'

'That's true. But you were widowed, that's different.'

'Stella, my husband, as far as I know, is alive, and probably he is very angry because I left him and did not say where I was going. In fact, then I did not know myself.'

'So it looks as if I may be right about this mystery man!'

'What do you advise me to do?'

'We'll talk about it later, here come the children! But I think you are in more trouble than I am, Lilli. Let's keep it to ourselves.'

Florence arrived home on Wednesday afternoon, early closing day in the shop. Manny came rushing out from the basement, to assist her from the taxi and to carry her bag.

'Are you sure you should have come home so soon?' he asked anxiously.

'Stop fussing, Manny, you know me better than that.' But Florence smiled.

Stella was ready to receive her, with Florence's chair drawn up to the stove, because an unexpected nip in the air was a reminder that Autumn was in the offing.

'Stay, Manny,' Florence said, when he turned to leave them.

'I'd like to have a little talk with you; no time like the present, eh? We can retire to the sitting-room after we've had that cup of tea. Thank you, Stella, just what I can do with.'

'I'll get on with the supper, shall I?' Stella asked. She had something to tell Florence herself, but that could wait. She hoped that Florence was to ask Manny to continue with the pie-making after the brief span she'd reluctantly decided to allot to her convalescence.

'Yes please. You came home at the right time, Stella - just when I needed you!'

Stella bit her lip. I can't play happy families here, she thought, I *can't*.

A little later, Florence and Manny adjourned to the other room.

Manny fetched the small footstool for her to rest her feet on. 'You must be weary.'

'Actually, I find I am. I want to do so much, but I realize it's not possible just yet.'

He sat in the armchair opposite the sofa. 'You have something to say, Florence? Is it about my note? Perhaps I shouldn't have asked you what I did - not yet, anyway.'

'I had the feeling when I read it, there was more you wanted to say.'

He cleared his throat, but didn't confirm her supposition.

Florence said, after a long pause, 'I realized when I was in hospital that I have been concerned with pie-making since I was not much more than a child, and with the demands of the family, that I'm becoming middle-aged before my time. Before I know it, Rose Marie will leave me, as Stella did; though I pray she won't make a mess of her life as her sister has. Stella, I can tell, is already restless, and will be off again, with or without Josefina—'

'At least you'll still have *her*,' Manny ventured.

'Oh, I love her as if she was my own flesh and blood, but the fact is, she isn't. Stella must face up to her responsibilities. Soon, I could be on my own, and this place could seem far from paradise then. Manny, how would you like to become my partner in the business? I realized you'd had a decent upbringing, an education, when we first met, despite the circumstances. The girls won't want to take it on in the future. We are a good team.

I trust you. What do you say?' It almost sounded as if she was pleading with him.

'I want to say yes, and thank you, Florence. But, are you sure?'

'I'm sure. In fact, that's not all.' She took a deep breath. 'Why don't we put it on a proper footing and get married? I realize you don't love me, I've seen those wistful glances you give my Rose Marie, but you must realize nothing can come of that. You and I get on very well together, and as I said, I don't want to be left on my own.'

'You're a good woman, Florence.'

'I'm a *normal* woman!' she flashed back. 'I'm thirty-four, does that seem too old to you?'

'Of course not, I'm not much younger, but there's things you don't know about me. . . .'

'Unless you already have a wife somewhere, the past should be buried.'

He shook his head vehemently. 'No wife.' Then he realized that her eyes were brimming with tears. He moved quickly to her side. His arms encircled her, comforting and strong. She didn't attempt to break away. He held her close for some time, but nothing more.

'Are you trying to tell me, yes?' she whispered tremulously.

'I suppose I am,' he said wonderingly.

Nine

FLORENCE waited until supper-time to spring the news, when Rose Marie joined them. Florence didn't press Manny to stay, and Josefina was already in bed. They were eating late.

Savoury mince and dumplings; Florence didn't tell Stella she'd had the same for lunch in the hospital. She toyed with the mashed potato.

When the plums and custard were eaten, she spoke up at last.

'I'm not sure what you two will make of this, but Manny and I are to be married.'

Rose Marie was the first to speak. 'Why?'

'It seems the best solution. . . .'

'To what?' Stella demanded.

'To be honest, I want to free you girls from any obligation to me,' Florence responded.

'I don't understand,' Rose Marie told her.

'You've your own lives to lead. You don't have to be tied to the pie shop like me. There's another reason. Father left everything to me, on condition I looked after you both. I was happy to do so. There was a clause in his will, typical of the man he was. Cautious, stern, but on the whole, fair, with one exception . . . I won't go into that. Some of the capital was not to be released until I married, or reached the age of forty, whichever came first. I suppose this was to be my reward for bringing you up.

'This hospital business - it made me think. I feel I had a lucky escape; I want to change my life. *Now!* I don't want to wait another five and a half years. I intend to share the money with you both. Stella, you can be independent of Jose, and Rose Marie, your future is assured. Don't look so shocked! We'll *all* be set up!'

'It's just that, why *Manny*?' Rose Marie asked.

'Who else? This is no place to meet eligible men. We're comfortable, he and I. If you're wondering, he doesn't know yet about the money, and you're not to tell him. I'm realistic. I'm not looking for romance.'

'A companion, you mean?' Stella tried to make sense of it all.

'Not just that, I hope.' Florence smiled. 'Does that shock you? I'd like to know what all the fuss is about!'

Rose Marie rose to the occasion. 'If you're happy, I am, too!'

'So am I!' Stella added quickly. She decided to keep the news that she had a job in the offing, to herself, for now. 'Let's have a glass of sherry to celebrate, rather than tea, eh?'

Florence surprised them again. 'Something stronger for me; I want to sleep tonight!'

Stella spent a restless night, wondering how much money might be involved - she thought it would be indelicate to ask Florence that - and how it would make a difference to their lives. When Manny arrived to help her with the early-morning pie-making, she decided to tell him she knew about him and Florence.

'Congratulations Manny! I had no idea, nor did Rose Marie.'

'You don't mind, then?' He sounded anxious.

'Of course not. So long as its what you *both* want.'

Manny wasn't quite sure what she meant by that.

Rose Marie came through into the kitchen, ready to leave for work.

'Good news, Manny! When's the wedding to be?'

'You'll have to ask Florence about that,' he said shyly. 'She'll decide.'

'I have already,' Florence said, from the doorway. She wore her comfortable kimono. She had a broad beam on her face and looked younger, with her hair all ruffled.

'You promised to stay in bed until the baking was done!' Stella chided.

'Oh, I won't lift a finger to help you, that's another promise! Manny, I'll be fit and ready to marry you in six weeks' time, mid-October. We'll shut the shop for a few days and have a holiday. We both deserve it. Stella, I've a feeling you've something to say - am I right?'

'I've been offered a solo singing engagement, and more to come, if I do well.'

'When is this?'

'I told the agency I have to do my bit here while you're resting up, Florence.' Stella felt guilty, because she had used the telephone to good effect during Florence's absence.

'I must go!' Rose Marie chimed in. 'See you tonight!'

'We'll talk more then,' Florence said. 'Is that all right with you?'

'Yes,' they agreed.

'Good. Now I'll go back to bed, until you've finished the pie-making.'

Belling's was putting on a display of their winter collection. The news in the workroom was that the agency mannequin booked to model the younger styles had failed to turn up.

'Mrs Belling might pick one of us!' the excited girls hoped.

It wasn't too much of a surprise that Rose Marie was the chosen one.

'You will have someone with you to help you change,' Mrs Belling told her. 'Come through the showroom when the signal is given, walk naturally, display your outfit, and smile at the clients. You won't be the first model on, so you will be able to observe how it is done. Now, come with me, Rose Marie. You will be shown how to arrange your hair and to apply make-up correctly. There will be a press photographer present during the show.'

Prior to this, there was a dress rehearsal and the girls from the workroom were invited to view this in the salon downstairs. When Rose Marie made her appearance, there was a concerted gasp. She wore an elegant top coat in pale grey wool with an astrakhan collar and matching cuffs to the wide sleeves. Her hair was set in unfamiliar deep waves but almost obscured by a wide-brimmed felt hat. She'd resisted any drastic plucking of her eyebrows, but her lips were a startling dark red. She looked like a sophisticated woman about town.

Regarding herself in the long mirror before the curtains parted, Rose Marie felt awed.

She was to model four outfits. Her favourite was a two-piece in green crushed velvet with a shoulder cape and silver buttons. There were accessories to change around, too; bags, gloves and shoes, but the jewellery was the same, a single strand of good, imitation pearls.

At two o'clock the show began, with a little light music played on the gramophone. There wasn't a large audience, but all the gilt chairs arranged in a semi-circle were taken. The photographer set up his equipment to one side, and a lady reporter flipped to a new page in her spiral-bound notebook and fiddled with her propelling pencil.

Mrs Belling provided the commentary. There was polite clapping; an anxious girl from the accounts department hovered over the turntable.

It was time for Rose Marie to make an entrance, to smile, to turn around, to display the outfit from all angles. She could hear muted sounds of approval. She saw a familiar face, then another. Sadie was in the front row, with her mother. Then came the applause, and she wasn't nervous any more, but elated.

'You'll be the star of the show in this!' her attendant whispered in the changing room, when she helped her with her final costume, the green velvet. She was right. The camera flashed repeatedly and as Rose Marie blinked, the clapping increased in fervour.

Later, back in the changing room, where the models jostled for space, Rose Marie put on her own clothes. She was about to slip away to return to work, for there was still an hour to go before home-time, when Mrs Belling called her out.

'Rose Marie - friends to see you!'

She emerged, to find Sadie and her mother waiting with Mrs Belling.

'You're a natural!' Sadie enthused. 'I've ordered the green velvet outfit! Well done! I'm having a short break at home before I move on to a new venue next week, so I decided to give Mother a day out, and, yes, to buy her a new outfit, too!'

'We're meeting Russ for dinner - is there any chance you can join us?' Mrs Short asked.

'I - I'm not sure. I'd have to let them know at home, that I'd be late. . . !'

'Use the telephone in my office,' Mrs Belling offered. 'I'm sure you are much too excited to do any more work today, so you're free to go right away, Rose Marie. After all, you have been responsible for the sale of the most expensive outfit of the show!'

Rose Marie thought she wasn't really dressed for eating out, but her new hair-do gave her confidence. She hadn't expected to see Russ until the weekend, so this was a chance not to be missed! Even though they would not be alone together.

When she spoke to Florence, with a request to pass the message on to Lilli, Florence said cheerfully, 'Don't worry; Lilli and Stella are taking the children to the early evening performance at the cinema. It's the new Charlie Chaplin picture, *The Gold Rush*. Being on our own, Manny and I'll have a chance to make a few wedding plans, eh?'

'Oh,' Rose Marie said. Florence had remarked, 'That's nice!' when she explained about her unexpected role that afternoon and how Sadie and her mother were involved. She felt rather cheated of her moment of glory. Florence obviously had other things on her mind! Josefina and Yvette were bubbling over with excitement at the prospect of the film.

'You'll have to keep very quiet and not fidget,' Lilli cautioned them. 'Children are supposed to attend the Saturday matinées, and sit at the front. The manager's given us complimentary tickets for the middle. Think how lucky you are.'

'Don't tell your teacher tomorrow that you were out late, either,' Stella added.

They didn't have to join the lengthening queue at the Golden Domes but were whisked away by a conspiratorial usherette and shown straight to their seats.

'This is like a palace,' Josefina said to her mother, awed by her surroundings.

'Well, they call these places picture palaces! You two sit between us, eh?'

The lights dimmed; the music began, as a late-comer took the seat next to Lilli. She was aware that it was a man, but she didn't look at him, not wishing to get into conversation.

The Little Tramp character and his partner, played by Mack Swain, were portrayed in the Klondike territory of Alaska, as would-be prospectors hoping to find rich deposits of gold in the gravel of the tributaries of the Yukon river. The unworldly tramp harboured a secret passion fur a dance-hall hostess in the rough-and-ready Gold Rush town. There were thrilling scenes of bitter snow blizzards in the wilds, where, sheltering in a ramshackle hut, the starving hero boiled up an old boot and sat down to eat it with exquisite manners.

'Mummy, I think the boot must be made of liquorice!' Josefina whispered.

'Don't spoil the illusion,' Stella murmured back, as the tramp finished off the bootlaces.

There was another culinary high-spot, the dance of the bread rolls, manipulated on a pair of forks. Chaplin was a supreme master of the mummers' art.

The stapstick scenes made them laugh until their sides ached, they gasped over the frenzied fight between the tramp and his partner, who was maddened by hunger, when they feared for their hero; the sad moments had them wiping their eyes.

When the credits rolled, the lights went up, and there was a concerted groan from the audience; they hadn't wanted the story to end.

'I'll get the ices!' Stella suggested, being nearest the aisle. The little girls insisted on following her. There was already a long line of people waiting.

It was then that Lilli realized who had been sitting next to her throughout the film.

'Good evening, Mrs Bower. Do you agree this is Chaplin's best film so far?'

Lilli didn't deign to answer his question. She was angry, and afraid. 'Mr Solon, you must stop following me. If you don't, I will have to inform the police.'

'Believe me, I mean you no harm.'

'Someone is employing you, is that it, to - to—'

'Watch out for you. I have your best interests at heart.'

'Tell me who it is! Oh, I can guess, but I want to know for sure.'

'It is not for me to say. But think of me as your friend.'

'I can't do that!'

'It would be better for you, if you did. You will need my support, if—' He paused. 'The ice-cream bearers are returning. I shall leave now, before the next film. Will you meet me in the tea-shop tomorrow, after you finish work? I will explain more then, if I can.'

Stella passed along the little tub of vanilla ice-cream, with its wooden spoon.

'Who was that Lilli?' she asked curiously.

'Somebody I know slightly. He asked my opinion of the film, that's all.'

Russ's first reaction on seeing Rose Marie with his mother and sister, was disconcerting.

'What have you done to your hair? It doesn't suit you!' he exclaimed. 'And your lips!'

'Oh.' Rose Marie put her hand up to cover her mouth. 'I meant to wipe it all off—'

'Apologize to Rose Marie, Russ,' his mother told him. She turned to Rose Marie. 'Well, I can put his mind at rest: no man, apart from that intrusive, ancient newspaper photographer, was present to see you make your debut as a mannequin at the Belling Winter Collection.'

'Your picture is going to be in the papers?' Russ sounded even more agitated.

'Probably,' Rose Marie flashed back, disappointed at his reaction, especially in front of his family. They had met him outside the bookshop, in Charing Cross Road, and walked through a maze of streets where eating establishments abounded.

'I'm sorry,' Russ said belatedly. 'I was rude. I had no reason to be. Look, let's go in the restaurant now, I booked the table earlier. Mr Turbot-Watts recommended this place.'

'It looks rather bohemian.' Mrs Short didn't sound as if she really minded that.

'Well, we are in Soho, Mother. My boss likes French cuisine, but we could have had Greek, Italian or Spanish, I suppose. Very cosmopolitan round here, as you can see.'

There were low ceilings, pitted beams downstairs and a sweep of stairs to a gallery, with tables for two, four or six, where their places were reserved.

'Shall we go to the cloakroom, Sadie, to tidy up?' Mrs Short suggested. 'I imagine that Rose Marie and Russ would appreciate ten minutes to themselves, eh? We'll order on our return.'

Rose Marie studied the menu. She was still feeling rather ruffled at Russ's reaction to her appearance earlier.

He reached out for her hand. 'Come on, you're not cross with me, are you? I wasn't expecting to see you, but, of course, I'm glad to be with you, and now I can tell you my plan for the coming weekend: on Saturday, I'm driving to Norfolk for another lot of books, and Mr Turbot-Watts suggests I take you with me, and that we put up in a bed and breakfast somewhere, and enjoy the morning in the country on Sunday, before we come back. Do you think Florence would agree?'

'Well, Florence is more interested in her own affairs at the moment, it seems,' Rose Marie said. That still smarted with her. 'Yes, I'd love to come.'

'The boss is paying for our accommodation, too! Look, here they come? I haven't told mother yet, so—'

'Don't worry, I won't say a thing!'

'My treat,' Sadie said, taking her seat. 'Not necessary to hold back! I'm starting with French onion soup, a favourite of mine.'

'Lilli - my French friend - made that for me once. She served it with little toast cubes and grated Parmesan on top. I'll have it too,' Rose Marie decided.

Russ smiled at her. 'And me. See, we're in accord again!'

Florence and Manny carried their coffee cups into the sitting-room. This time, Manny was bold enough to sit close to her on the settee.

'I shan't expect you to do this every evening after we're married,' Florence told him. 'You must still see your friends at the pub.'

'I only started that because I was lonely,' he admitted.

'Ah, but I don't want the rumour going round that poor Manny is being henpecked.'

'To be honest, Florence, it'll take me some time, I reckon, not to think of you as the boss.'

'I told you I don't want all that responsibility any more: equal partners, that's it. But can I make a suggestion?'

He nodded. 'You know you can. We're not married yet!'

'That's what I want to discuss with you. Where to get married.'

'Go on.'

'How about St Martin's?'

'I . . . I'm not sure if that's possible. I'm a lapsed Catholic you see.'

'Look, I'm not going to be a blushing bride in a wedding gown – a nice costume for me, and a smart suit for you, all right? The pie shop can pay!'

'It takes time to fix up, doesn't it?'

'Quicker at the Register Office. It's daft, but I don't even know your first name, or where you were born – just that you answer to Manny because your surname is Manning.'

'Patrick Joseph; I was born in what's now the Republic of Ireland. My mother was English; my father died young, then she brought me over here.'

'She's gone too, is that right?' Florence asked gently.

'Before the war. From asthma. She suffered terrible with that. I don't have any other family, Florence.'

'Well, you soon will have. And when they fly the coop, we'll have each other.'

'I like the sound of that. . . .'

'That's good,' Florence said.

Ten

LILLI felt obliged to tell Stella she would be home later than usual, though hopefully before the children returned from school.

'Be careful,' Stella cautioned. 'But I suppose it's something you're meeting in a public place. I'd be really worried if this man had suggested you calling where he lives.'

'So would I! I will tell him he must stop shadowing me.'

At two o'clock precisely, Lilli arrived at the tea room. The entrance was deserted; she peered through the window trying to glimpse the interior, above the gingham half-curtain.

'Good-afternoon.' He approached so quietly, she was startled. 'Shall we go in?'

The late-lunchers were making ready to leave. A waitress asked them to wait a moment while she swept the crumbs from a table and removed the crockery. They sat down.

'Just tea,' Lilli said to the waitress. She was hungry, but she felt too tense to accept her companion's polite offer of something to eat. 'Now,' she addressed him. 'Would you please tell me what all this is about. Does this concern my husband?'

'Your husband,' he repeated. 'I do not receive my instructions from him. However, I was asked to question him regarding your disappearance. Mr Bower was angry; he wants you to return his daughter, but he indicated that he would not take you back.'

'I would not go, and I will not part with Yvette.' Lilli poured tea from the silver pot. She willed her hands not to shake.

'Can you not guess who the, ah, interested party might be?'

'If it isn't my husband, I must presume my mother. Yet we have not communicated since I left France. She made it clear she had disowned me, though there was little to come! My uncle inherited the estate from my father after he died in the fighting. He, his wife and son moved in with my mother after the war.'

'Did she turn against you because you married a man not of her choice?'

'Partly. I don't know why I should tell you this, but I will. She was disappointed in me; I was already pregnant by this man who, as you say, was not of her choice.'

'You have been frank with me; now I shall tell you something. I have not had dealings with your mother. I was approached by a certain other person because I am discreet. I was not told by whom this agent was commissioned. If I enquire too closely, I can expect to be discharged from my duties. I have learned enough about you to ask myself if this surveillance is justified - I believe not. I think you should consider another move.'

'But we have settled here - we have good friends. I have my job. . . .'

'My dear Mrs Bower, I have your safety very much in mind.' He drained his cup. 'Well, I have given you my warning. You must be vigilant at all times. I shall continue to be concerned for your welfare, I assure you. If you need me, here is my card.' Mr Solon rose. 'Are you ready to leave? Then I will settle the bill.'

It was a business card. It read, *Philippe Solon. Private Investigator*. The address was in Piccadilly. Lilli tucked it into the back of her purse.

Rose Marie and Russ made an early start, before anyone else in No. 1 Paradise Buildings was stirring. Just after five on Saturday morning, she crept downstairs and opened the front door to see the Trojan Horse as she had nicknamed the book van, already parked outside.

'Oh, it's beginning to rain,' she exclaimed, as she handed her overnight bag to Russ to put in the back of the motor. She was glad she had donned her mackintosh because the morning was chilly. The weather didn't appear too promising for a weekend in the country, but then it was nearing the end of September, she thought, stifling a yawn.

'We couldn't get away without someone seeing us,' Russ said cheerfully, as the milk cart came clanking along. 'The horse won't tell tales, but maybe it looks as if we are eloping!'

'Do you wish we were?' Rose Marie asked jokingly, as they drove off.

'What do you think? I bet you haven't had any breakfast.'

'Can you hear my tummy grumbling?'

'Well, my mother wouldn't allow me out of the house without sustenance. She also packed us some sandwiches and a Thermos flask for along the way.'

'That was kind of her. Normally, I'm sure Florence would have done the same.'

'She didn't raise any objection to our weekend away, did she?'

'Not really. She said she trusted you.'

'Oh dear,' he grinned. 'Still, even my sister came up with some advice!'

'They both mean well!'

Later, in the broad light of day, they stopped in a leafy lane in Essex and wound the windows down to breathe in the fresh country air after the rain. They ate their egg sandwiches and drank weak tea from beakers.

'Where exactly are we going?' Rose Marie asked.

'To a windswept village near the coast; see, I've marked it on the map. Not that grease spot from my sandwich - the pencil circle. Mr Turbot-Watts's uncle collects and sells books too, it must run in the family. Chapel House Books, that's the place we have to find. His lease has run out, and he has to dispose of his stock. T-W warns we'll find him eccentric, but he's a nice old boy.'

'More eccentric than your boss, I wonder?'

'Well, it'll be some hours yet before we find out. Ready to move off?'

She nodded. 'I think I'll catch up on my beauty sleep.' She leaned back in her seat.

He kissed her cheek. 'Sweet dreams, Rose Marie. Make sure they include me. . . .'

It was raining again and windy too, when they finally parked the motor by a deserted village green, overlooked by several dwellings; the local hostelry, where they were to stay overnight; a general store, with the sign indicating it was shut; and a dilapidated building with double doors and arched windows,

91

obviously the former primitive chapel. Above the entrance, in flaking white paint, was the legend BOOKS. Over the road was the chapel's red-brick replacement, with inscribed foundation stones, laid by local worthies some fifty years ago.

Rose Marie imagined that this solid building was looking in dismay at its predecessor.

'The bookshop appears to be closed,' she remarked to Russ.

'We're expected, though. Oh, look, the doors are opening.'

A man emerged, clutching an armful of books. Behind him loomed a tall figure.

'That must be him! Quick, Rose Marie, before he disappears!'

'I was expecting you earlier than this,' Mr Turbot-Watts senior greeted them.

'We had to make a stop or two; it was a long drive,' Russ told him.

'Well, come in, come in. The reason I hoped you'd get here by lunch-time will now be obvious to you; the electricity has been disconnected. I'll light the paraffin lamp. Sit down, if you can find a space, young lady. I have a spirit stove, so I can at least make you a cup of tea, but I presume you have ordered your evening meal at the White Hart. The books for my nephew are already boxed, but goodness knows what will happen to the rest.'

As the lamp flared and dispelled the gloom immediately around them, Rose Marie saw that the old man was attired in pyjamas, slippers with flapping soles, and an ancient dressing gown. There was a definite resemblance to Mr Elmo Turbot-Watts, particularly the shiny bald pate and whiskers, though in this case his beard was unkempt. Books were all over the place, in leaning piles, and there was a musty smell. A steep staircase led to a gallery.

'I sleep up in the Gods, as it were,' the old man said, shaking a milk bottle hopefully. 'Solid - goes off quickly in thundery weather . . . you must excuse my attire: my clothes are all damp, due to that damn leaking roof.'

'Where will you go?' Rose Marie asked him, worried about his welfare.

'I shall be all right, my dear. I have, um, a lady friend - completely batty of course, must be to fancy me, but good-hearted. I can rest my bones in her attic with the spiders and mice, but she'll feed me in return for, um, what she calls favours.'

Rose Marie blushed. She hoped he meant chopping firewood or other chores.

'I shall go there tonight, don't worry. Close the doors on this lot. I sorted out the best books for Elmo. How is my nephew?'

'He's well.' Russ felt in his pocket and brought out a fat envelope. 'He sent this for you,' he said awkwardly. It was obvious this was a packet of banknotes.

'He didn't need to do that. He's a good boy. Mind, I can do with it, bills to pay and I haven't a bean. Oh, I lie. The chap you saw gave me a shilling for a bundle of books.' He poured water in a teapot. The brown liquid crawled out slowly through a blocked spout into a stained tin mug. 'We'll have to share this, I'm afraid. I have a solitary sugar lump.'

'No, please, you have it. May I begin loading the boxes? Then we'll leave you in peace. Unless we can help you with your moving out?' Russ asked.

'My dear young man, I intend to just abandon the rest, as I said. It's the only way.'

Later, Rose Marie and Russ were glad to sit by the fire in the visitors' room and warm up before they sat down to a satisfying meal cooked by the publican's wife.

'We should have asked the poor old uncle to join us,' Rose Marie worried.

'Mr Turbot-Watts did warn me how things would be.'

'You should have told me!'

'I wanted you to think of it as a romantic weekend.'

'Hardly that,' she said, pouring gravy over her fillet of steak and rings of onion.

'The night is still young,' he said audaciously. 'Anything could happen. . . .'

Their rooms were under the sloping eaves, with a connecting door.

'Where's the key?' Rose Marie asked their hostess.

'Key, dear? First time I've been asked for that! But there is a bolt, see?' She left them to find out that it was too stiff to shift into place.

'Call out if you need me,' Russ said, before he kissed her goodnight. 'Sleep well.'

Rose Marie had the bigger room, with a double bed. She undressed quickly, washed at the marble stand. She was anxious to try out the soft feather mattress. Her bones ached after all that travelling. She turned the bedside lamp low, reluctant to douse it in an unfamiliar room, and snuggled gratefully under the covers, as she was in a thin cambric nightgown.

The light attracted a large moth which frightened her, though she knew it was harmless. It fluttered round and round the lamp, batting itself against the china globe. When it flew, dazed, into her face on the pillow, Rose Marie let out a muffled shriek.

Instantly the door opened and Russ came in. He had a towel slung round his bare shoulders and toothbrush still in his hand.

'Help! Don't just stand there - kill it!' she cried.

'Certainly not. I'll put the poor thing out of the window. You are a ninny!'

She sat up then, indignant. 'Hurry up, then!'

When he had disposed of the moth and closed the window, he came over to the bed and looked down at her. 'Don't I get a reward?' he said softly.

She knew it was dangerous but she couldn't help herself. She stretched out her arms. Invitingly. 'Oh, come on, then!'

Then they were kissing as they never had before, and she didn't resist when he slipped into bed beside her. He reached out and extinguished the light.

'Don't worry, darling, as I said, Sadie gave me some practical advice . . . I'm acting on it. But if you want me to stop right now, well, I will.'

'Isn't it too late for that?' She felt light-headed, breathless. His hands were now caressing her body, after gently unfastening her bodice. She hesitantly touched his bare chest. His skin, too, was smooth, slightly damp due to the excitement of the moment. She thought, this can't be wrong, I love him so much. . . .

At some time during the night he returned to his own room. Rose Marie rolled over into the warm hollow he had left, and pressed her face into the dent in his pillow. She was sobbing, in little gasps; she couldn't understand why, because she was blissfully happy.

94

They didn't converse much over breakfast. Every time Rose Marie caught Russ looking at her she felt the tell-tale tide of hot colour flood her face.

After a while, he whispered, although they were on their own in the dining-room, 'Do you forgive me?'

'What for? I knew it would happen. I wanted it to. As much as you did.'

'Most people would say it was too soon, that we're too young.'

'If by most people you mean your mother and Florence, yes. But I won't tell, will you?'

'You know I won't. The only thing is, it will be difficult to repeat the experience.'

'Perhaps that's just as well,' she said ruefully. 'But I guess we won't be able to stop ourselves . . . we'll find a way.'

They drove the short distance to the coast, the sandy beach was deserted, the sea rolling. They walked along hand-in-hand. Rose Marie tightened the belt on her mackintosh and turned up the collar. The spray from the waves was chilly, yet she still felt aglow inside.

'Time to make tracks home,' Russ said regretfully. They turned around to retrace their steps to the motor.

Rose Marie called in to say goodnight to Florence when she arrived back. Stella had already gone to bed. Florence was sitting in the kitchen with Manny, drinking cocoa.

'We waited up - wanted to be sure you were safe,' she said. 'Like a hot drink?'

'No thanks. It was such a long drive; I just want to get to bed. Work tomorrow!'

'Goodnight, then,' Florence said. 'Tell us all about it tomorrow evening. Haven't seen much of Lilli all weekend, but maybe she was tired too. Oh, Stella's off tomorrow - but again, that'll keep for now - but it means you can come back to me, if you want to.'

'I'd best go, too,' Manny said. 'Monday morning, early start! For you too, remember.'

Rose Marie gave her sister a hug. 'You should be in bed,' she reproved her.

'As I said, I needed to know you were home safely. Goodnight, my dear.'

When she had gone upstairs, Florence turned to Manny. 'I suppose I have to face the fact that she's a woman now. I mustn't fuss over her so much. Give me a nudge if I do.'

'I can do better than that.' Manny surprised himself. He took her hands, pulled her up from her chair, wrapped his arms round her. It wasn't his usual brief peck on the cheek, but a real kiss, full of warmth and promise, part of a long embrace.

'We-ell,' Florence said slowly, as he released her, looking sheepish. 'I think you had better go, otherwise, who knows where that could lead us?' And I hope it does, she thought, smiling to show him she wasn't outraged, but not before we're wed. Only three weeks to go. A great many pies to make before then, but I'm looking forward to it, with my partner.

Rose Marie discarded the crumpled nightdress when she unpacked her bag. No need to look glamorous tonight, she mused ruefully, as she put on winceyette pyjamas. She thought about what Florence had said, about things returning to the way they were. But it wouldn't be for long, didn't her sister realize that? She wasn't a child to be looked after, like Josefina, and, more significantly, Manny would shortly be sharing Florence's bed, a prospect which rather embarrassed Rose Marie. Not that she thought there would be anything much going on, they were far too old, but they would need their privacy.

Eleven

MANNY was concerned that Florence should not overdo it that first morning. She watched with a bemused smile while he made the hot-water pastry and then the pork pies. However, he allowed her to glaze them before they went in the oven.

'I've been thinking,' she said, as she tapped the hard-boiled eggs for the ham-and-egg variety, Josefina not yet having emerged from her bedroom for her usual task. 'We really don't want all this going on in our domestic quarters. Young Yvette's right, the whole flat smells of pies! When we get back from our holiday, we must plan a new kitchen at the back of the shop and get one of those big, commercial ovens put in. It would make life a lot easier.'

'Can you afford it?'

'Soon it will be can *we* afford it, Manny.' She hadn't yet told him about the money coming to her. In any case, that was not certain until after their marriage. 'Have you any bright ideas of your own?'

'Well,' he said diffidently. 'Maybe we could improve business if we had two or three small tables and chairs in the shop, so that folk could eat their hot pies on the premises, if they wanted to. It'd make more work, of course, but with a proper kitchen we could provide the extras, like bread and butter, mushy peas and mugs of tea.'

'More washing-up,' Florence pointed out, 'but it's worth considering.'

'With extra money coming in, you - we could employ some-one to do all the odd jobs.'

'We could indeed.' She was pleased he was responding to her encouragement.

Footsteps outside, then Rose Marie came in. 'Morning! I've got time, I hope, to wish Stella good luck.' She skirted the cooking area and went through, calling out, 'Stella, it's me!'

'Come in, excuse the muddle in your room! I just sent Josefina to wash. She doesn't want me to go, of course, but I'll be back for the wedding, or earlier, if things don't work out . . . Florence'll tell you all about it later.'

'Stella, I'm sorry if I've been a bit moody while you've been here—'

'I can understand that. Bossy older sister - I've got one myself!'

'Oh, Florence! *She's* almost perfect!'

'Not quite, but she's surprised me lately! Well, have a good day, young Rose Marie.'

Rose Marie embraced her, suddenly tearful. 'I'll look after Josefina. . . .'

'I know you will, thank you. I suppose I had her before I was responsible enough to care for her properly. Keep *your* young man in his place, I should!'

Rose Marie wanted to say, 'Too late for that.' But she had no regrets.

'Must catch the tram. All the best, Stella.'

'All the best,' Stella echoed.

'My mother's going to sing in a club in Bradford, she's got top billing,' Josefina told Yvette.

'What's that?' Yvette was curious.

They were on their way to school. Josefina's consolation gift from her mother was tucked in her pocket, a spinning top and whip, actually a stick with string to wind round the top to set it rotating. Playground toys kept the children's circulation going in colder weather.

She said in a patronizing way, 'Don't you know? She's got a lovely voice, that's why.'

'I thought she sang on stage with your father.'

'She did, but she's just as good without him.'

'Don't you miss him?' Yvette asked.

'Not now. I haven't seen him for a long time, you see. How about you?'

'Do I miss my father? Of course I do. But he can't care about me, or my *maman*, else he'd come and fetch us home, wouldn't he?'

Josefina stopped in her tracks, in astonishment. 'But your father's *dead*, your mother said so, to Aunty Florence, when you came to live in our house.'

Yvette realized she had revealed their secret. Her mother would be very cross.

'Mind your own business!' she cried. She gave Josefina a shove. Her friend tripped over an uneven paving stone and fell heavily on her arm. Josefina let out a shriek, but managed to scramble to her feet, resisting Yvette's attempts to help her.

'You can walk by yourself!' Josefina stormed off ahead, clutching her right arm to her.

Yvette stood irresolute for a few moments, ashamed of herself. Then she saw the top lying on the ground. She picked it up and stuffed it in her own pocket.

'I must return you home,' Miss Darch exclaimed, when she saw that Josefina was in pain. She indicated to the other teachers that they should call the classes into line. 'Miss Flinders should take you to the doctor's. The arm could be broken.' She looked at Yvette, lurking miserably behind Josefina. Miss Darch read the guilty expression, but would not waste time probing now. 'Into school with you, Yvette,' she said. 'I will talk to you when I return.'

Florence was in the shop with Manny. She saw them from the window and rushed outside. Miss Darch placed a comforting arm round Josefina's shoulders, as the child dissolved into tears from the delayed shock.

'Miss Flinders, I'm afraid your niece had a nasty fall on her way to school. You ought to take her to the doctor without delay. He will advise you if you need to go on to the hospital. Here.' She unwound the silk scarf from around her neck. 'I should have done this right away.' Together they made a sling for Josefina's arm.

'I'll fetch your jacket and bag,' Manny said from behind Florence 'Wait in the shop.'

99

'I must go,' Miss Darch said. 'Yvette can let me know how she gets on.'

A few minutes later, at the doctor's surgery, Josefina was the first patient of the day.

The improvised sling was removed, then Florence helped Josefina to slip out of her coat, cardigan and blouse. The doctor examined the swollen arm gently but thoroughly.

'It appears to be what we call a greenstick fracture. The bone should knit together within a few weeks. She will need a plaster from elbow to wrist. Well, do you feel up to a visit to the hospital again, Miss Flinders? Josefina should be seen there this morning.'

'I'm very well now, as you can see. I'll call a cab.'

'You'll soon be back at school, plaster and all, and quite a heroine to the other children, eh?' the doctor reassured Josefina.

She was feeling in her coat pocket with her good hand. She dissolved into tears once more. 'My top! I've lost it - Mummy only gave it to me this morning.'

'We'll find it, if not I'll buy you another,' Florence tried to comfort her.

'But that wouldn't be the same, *it wouldn't!*'

Back at the school, Miss Darch spoke to Yvette outside the classroom. She did not raise her voice, that was not her way.

'Would you like to tell me what happened Yvette?'

'We - we had an argument. I got cross because I said something I shouldn't have and I knew Maman would not like it . . . I gave Josefina a push, but I didn't mean to hurt her. I didn't, really, and . . .' Yvette was sobbing now.

'Now, Yvette, I believe you, but you can see what happens when you lose your temper. I'm afraid I shall have to call to see your mother. Will she be home from work, if I accompany you after school?'

Yvette nodded.

'Where is your handkerchief? In your pocket?' Miss Darch pulled the hankie out for her. The hidden top fell to the floor. 'What's this?' she asked.

'It's Josefina's,' Yvette wept. 'I picked it up after she ran off to school. I didn't *steal* it, honestly, Miss Darch.'

'Did I say you had?' the teacher said evenly. 'Leave it with me. I will return it.'

Not only were the two small girls subdued that evening, but Lilli was quiet and withdrawn after talking to Miss Darch. She'd learned a few unpalatable facts about her daughter. Yvette was suspected of taking small items from other children at school, such as marbles or hair-slides.

'I shall do nothing about this, but it must stop, Mrs Bower,' Miss Darch said. She looked at Lilli, taking in her anxiety. The discussion was between the two of them. Yvette was in her room. Miss Darch added, 'Talk to your daughter, find out what is troubling her. She is showing signs of insecurity. It is a lot to contend with, losing one parent.'

'I realize that.' Lilli felt like crying herself. She called Yvette to say goodbye to Miss Darch.

'Now, Yvette,' said Miss Darch. 'We believe it was an accident, but caused through your impulsiveness. You must prove to Josefina you are genuinely sorry. I'll see you tomorrow.'

When she'd gone, Lilli hugged her daughter reassuringly. 'We will talk, but not today, I think. You have had a shock, too. So have I. We'll have an early night after our supper.'

Downstairs, when Stella rang to say she had arrived safely in Bradford, Florence tried not to make a drama of Josefina's fall. She didn't mention the cause of it. She asked Rose Marie when she came in from work, 'Will you stay with Josefina tonight? She needs a bit of comforting.'

'Of course I will,' Rose Marie said instantly. She realized that she would be glad to be back home with Florence, the food was better for one thing, but she was aware that things would change again when Florence was married, and Manny installed in the flat. She added, 'Though Lilli will be expecting me for supper. I'll join you later.'

It was short commons for supper upstairs. Lilli hadn't felt like cooking. Under her instructions, Rose Marie whipped up a quick omelette. Lilli merely said, 'I shall miss your company, Rose Marie, because I imagine it will not be just one night. . . .'

'I'll see you often, like I did before,' Rose Marie said instantly, even as she knew that it would not be the same, because, of course, her weekends now revolved around Russ.

The two girls walked sedately to school now, both on their best behaviour. Miss Darch's wise words had been taken to heart by both of them. Josefina's plaster was no longer a source of interest to other children, who were eager initially to decorate it with indelible pencil, and she and Yvette were inseparable once again.

Last night, their favourite dolls had exchanged places; it was Yvette's idea. 'My Clarice and your Carmen need a holiday, I think. You must be very careful with Clarice, of course, because she is delicate, and I promise to keep Carmen in her dancing pose, on my dressing table, and not to play roughly with her.'

'I promise to put Clarice on top of my chest of drawers; I'll tell Rose Marie to move her pot of Pond's cream and ornaments over to one side!' said Josefina. She was excited to have the beautiful Clarice for a few days because Yvette had not allowed her to even touch the French doll before. She guessed that Yvette was trying to make up for her accident.

There was a black cab cruising slowly along the road beside them, as if the driver was looking out for a particular place. The children glanced over curiously, then Yvette let out a little shriek. 'It's my *father*!'

'Don't be silly,' Josefina cautioned, embarrassed. She saw Mrs Snelgrove looking out curiously from her shop doorway.

The cab stopped and the passenger door opened. A tall man in a dark overcoat came swiftly across the pavement. Yvette shrieked again, then hurtled herself into his arms. Josefina stood there, as if rooted to the spot. She saw the man's face, with tears rolling down his cheeks. In that split second she registered his likeness to Yvette; the sharp features and pale hair. He had a bushy moustache.

'Here!' he called to Josefina, while still holding on to Yvette with one hand. He had a blue envelope in the other. 'Take this to my wife, Mrs Bower!' As she stood, irresolute, he threw the letter in her direction. Then he scooped Yvette up and carried her to the taxi. The door slammed, and it drove away, fast. It had all happened within the space of a few minutes.

Mrs Snelgrove came quickly over to Josefina. 'Who was that?' she demanded.

'Yvette said,' Josefina gabbled, 'that man was her father!'

The blue envelope still lay on the ground. Mrs Snelgrove bent to retrieve it.

She called out to her girls, 'Hold the fort! Need to see Florence right now!'

Florence and Manny were in the shop. Florence hurried out when she saw them.

'Whatever's happened now?' she exclaimed. 'Not another accident, surely!'

'Better go upstairs,' Mrs Snelgrove advised. 'Don't want the whole of Paradise to know.'

Florence could hardly comprehend what she was hearing. She repeated several times, 'But, Lilli lost her husband before she came here. . . .'

'D'you think we should get in touch with the police?' Mrs Snelgrove asked.

Florence had the letter clutched in her hand. She looked at the writing on the front.

'This is addressed to Mrs Lilli Bower. We must show this to her first. Josefina seems convinced that it was Yvette's father who took her away.'

'She'll be at the cinema by now, won't she? Telephone there and ask her to come home immediately,' Mrs Snelgrove suggested. 'Remember, I witnessed what happened, and I'll say what I saw, of course. Look, I have to get back to work now, but I'll tell Manny something's come up, eh?'

'Thank you, you've been very good, Mrs Snelgrove. I'll take your advice. . . .'

While Florence was busy talking first to the cinema manager, and then to a frantic Lilli, Josefina went into her room. Florence hadn't said she must go to school, and she didn't want to, because she would be late for class. On an impulse she took the French doll from its resting place on the chest of drawers, and tucked it up in her bed.

She said aloud, 'Don't worry, Clarice. If Yvette doesn't come back, I'll look after you. . . .'

'It's him, all right.' Lilli's hands shook as she read the few lines on the notepaper. I AM TAKING YVETTE HOME, WHERE SHE

103

BELONGS. YOU MAY WRITE TO HER, IF YOU WISH, BUT YOU MUST BE CAREFUL IN WHAT YOU SAY. SAM.

'Oh, Florence, can you forgive me for deceiving you?' she appealed.

'I'm sure you had good reason,' Florence said evenly. She looked at Josefina. The child still looked dazed from the shock. 'Play in your room, I should, dearie. Don't upset yourself. It seems you were right. It was Yvette's father. She won't come to any harm.'

'He loves her, I know that, Florence. I didn't fit in with his family. It was a shock, I can tell you when I met them. His mother didn't approve of me. Rather like my own *maman*.'

'Lilli, I don't think this is the time for confessions. The important thing is, what can we do about this?'

'If my husband is determined to keep his daughter, then he will. I can't afford to engage a solicitor, and the police would say Yvette was not taken against her will. You see, she loves her father, just as she loves me.'

'Do you think he has done this to force your hand; to get you to return to him?'

Lilli shook her head. 'No! I was told - oh dear, this is another thing I have not confided to you, Florence!'

'My dear, you are entitled to your private life, though I hope you think of me as a friend.'

'Of course I do! The day you were taken ill, do you remember that a person called here, asking for me?'

'A man, wasn't it? Someone you know?'

'I have met him, briefly on several occasions. I would not say I know him.' Lilli rummaged in her bag. 'He gave me this. He tells me, he cares about my welfare. He warned me that my husband wanted Yvette back, but not me - I am not forgiven.'

Florence studied the business card. 'Do you think this Mr Solon told your husband where you are?'

'That is what I must find out. I have the rest of the day off. I will call on him shortly!'

104

Twelve

PICCADILLY Circus, and the famous fountain with the figure of Eros, but Lilli gave it no more than a glance. The only thoughts of love she had today, were for her daughter. She was in Piccadilly, that busy thoroughfare, but she was lost. Belatedly, she realized that she should have telephoned Philippe Solon first, because the address on the card was too vague.

Then she heard his voice from behind her. She spun round.

'Mrs Bower - Lilli – I was on my way to see you when I spotted you standing here. I am very sorry for what has happened.'

'You already know, then? Or did you arrange the abduction?' she accused him.

'Look, we cannot talk here, it is too noisy. Allow me to escort you to Green Park where we can discuss this.'

'There is no need for discussion. I just want my daughter returned to me!'

He took her arm. 'There is a police officer, see, over there? Don't pull away, or he might apprehend me, and how would that help?'

'If you are guilty, it is what you deserve!' However, she allowed him to walk with her. They did not speak again until they reached the park and found an unoccupied bench.

'Now, what do you know?' she demanded. They sat well apart, but she turned to face him, so she could observe if he was telling the truth or not. She hadn't really taken in his image before. Just the olive complexion, dark hair and eyes. Now she realized that he was not as old as she had calculated, perhaps in his late thirties or early forties, and that he was regarding her with obvious sympathy.

He gazed back at her, at her pale face, the haunted look in her red-rimmed eyes; the beret she had pulled on carelessly at an unflattering angle to cover her fine, flyaway hair.

'What do I know?' he repeated. 'In the beginning, I was obliged to reveal your circumstances, the place where you and your daughter were living and where you worked. I regret that my recommendations regarding you were ignored, as was my decision to drop the case. The person whose name I cannot divulge calculated that if your husband was given this information he would act exactly the way he did, and remove your daughter from you. I swear I knew nothing of this, until I received a telephone call a short while ago, advising me to contact you and to elicit certain facts from yourself.'

'I - I don't understand. What does this person want from me?'

'I was told *you* would know.'

'But I don't! You must believe me!'

'My dear Lilli,' he used her first name again, 'I do believe you. It appears to me that the deceit you practiced was against your husband. I can understand that. As I told you before, I want to help you, to protect you, if I can.'

'Who are you?' Lilli asked.

'I am who it says on the card. Philippe Solon, Private Investigator. What I was before, during the war especially, need not concern you. I am your friend, Lilli. I support your cause.'

'You would help me to get Yvette back?'

'It will not be easy. Your husband is angry, he needs time to think things over. I see both sides of this. Yvette will be well cared for by her father, don't you think?' She nodded reluctantly. He added, 'Come, shall I take you home now?'

Lilli rose. She managed a tremulous smile. 'Yes, please.' This time she slipped her arm in his voluntarily, but when he realized she was shaking, he disengaged himself and supported her with his arm firmly around her shoulders, as they walked along.

When they arrived at Florence's door, it opened immediately. Lilli said simply, 'This is Mr Solon, you met him briefly once. Florence, he wants to help me.'

'Thank goodness you are back!' Florence exclaimed. 'Yvette is on the phone!'

Lilli dashed to pick up the instrument. 'Yvette, where are you? Are you all right?'

'Don't worry, Maman. We stopped at the post office to ring you; we are just around the corner from Granny's! I will write to you tomorrow and tell you all about it. I have to go now. I love you, Maman!' Then Lilli heard the receiver replaced on its rest.

'Good news?' the tall man asked.

'Yvette is about to go to her grandmother's house. She – she said I am not to worry.'

'That *is* good. I shall go now, but I will be in touch. Please think about what I said.'

'I will, but, it's a mystery to me. . . .'

After he had gone, Florence said briskly, 'We'll have hot pies and tea. I'll give Manny a call. None of us have had lunch, after all. Now, please be cheerful for poor Josefina, she's still very upset. This Mr Solon comes from the same place as you, doesn't he?'

'I believe he does,' Lilli said softly.

Florence was determined life must get back to normal, as far as possible, for Josefina's sake. She encouraged Lilli to return to work the following morning, and, later, she took her niece to school, knowing that explanations were due.

As she had anticipated, Mrs Snelgrove was waiting for her outside the greengrocer's.

'Any news?' she enquired anxiously.

'Yes, we know that Yvette is safe, thank goodness; as Josefina told us, she went off with her father. Lilli spoke to her on the telephone yesterday afternoon. She asked me to thank you for your concern and help.'

'He shouldn't have gone about it, the way he did,' Mrs Snelgrove said forthrightly.

'No, of course he shouldn't, and Lilli will have to deal with that, but in the meantime please excuse me, I must talk to Miss Darch if I can, before school begins. . . .'

'You don't know when the child will be back then?' Mrs Snelgrove called after them.

Florence answered, 'Not yet. Thank you again,' as they hurried off.

As they approached the school gates, Florence saw the local bobby standing there.

'I was hoping to have a word with you, Miss Flinders,' he greeted her.

'You've heard what happened yesterday, then?

'Yes. Nothing was reported officially.'

'No. I'll explain . . . Josefina, run along now, and tell Miss Darch I'm here, please.' She bit her lip. There were children going past and mothers casting covert glances.

The policeman suggested, 'Shall we talk with the head-mistress in her study?'

Florence agreed that would be more private. She thought, oh dear, I should have told Lilli to do the explaining. I'm not the one responsible for Yvette, after all. . . .

It was some time before she was able to rejoin Manny at the pie shop. He pulled out a chair behind the counter for her to sit on.

'Other people's children,' he said, because he'd been waiting anxiously to hear how she'd got on at the school. 'You shouldn't have all this worry, Florence. It's not fair.'

'It can't be helped.' She managed a smile. 'I care about them as if they were my own, you see. I had to reveal more than I think Lilli would have wanted me to, but I hope I made it clear that Yvette is all right. Oh dear, we don't want any more upsets before the wedding, do we? Look, I must tidy up the flat. See you at lunchtime if you get a spare moment!'

Lilli worked extra hard to catch up on the jobs she had left undone yesterday. When she emerged from the cinema, she was exhausted; she had neglected to comb her hair and apply fresh lipstick as she usually did before leaving, and there were dark shadows under her eyes due to her lack of sleep last night. She was also aware that her hands still reeked of bleach after scrubbing out the cloakrooms.

She wasn't really surprised to see Philippe Solon. 'I came to see how you are,' he said. 'You have time to spare for the tea shop, I hope?'

'I have nothing to hurry back for now.' Her voice betrayed her hurt. 'I need black coffee, not tea, with plenty of sugar, and a toasted tea-cake—'

'You haven't eaten since yesterday?' he asked, obviously concerned.

108

'No. I feel, ah, hollow, inside. I need something hot and buttery.'

They sat at the same table as on the last occasion, Lilli toying with her tea-cake, but drinking the coffee in grateful gulps.

Philippe, as he asked her to address him, signalled to the waitress to bring the coffee-pot.

Lilli removed the beret, ran her fingers through her hair. 'I look terrible.'

'You are an attractive young woman,' he contradicted her.

Their cups refilled, they drank their coffee and contemplated in silence for a while. Then he reached across the table and lifted her left hand.

'Your wedding ring, you have removed it,' he observed.

'I feel betrayed, by a man I once loved . . . It was a symbolic gesture, I suppose.'

'Did you ever consider how he might feel, not knowing why, or where you had gone?'

'He knew why. I was desperate to get away; I had no idea where, at the time.'

'You should settle things, arrange a divorce.'

'It's not so easy. I don't earn much, part-time. I have nothing to spare for legal matters.' She suddenly realized he was still holding her hand, and she withdrew it from his clasp.

'I have an idea. You could work for me, in my office. I would pay you well.'

'I have not trained as a secretary. . . .'

'I deal with my own correspondence, that is not a problem. You could take notes; answer the telephone, I presume; deal with callers when I am out; keep my diary. What do you say?'

She looked ruefully at her hands, reddened from her morning's labours, with more than one broken nail.

She said, with a sigh, 'My hands still smell of bleach; how I hate that! Mr Solon - Philippe - perhaps I am being rash, but I accept your offer! I will have to work the week out at the Golden Domes, though, that's only fair.'

Later, as she continued her walk home, alone, she thought, I can catch the tram with Rose Marie in the mornings, and perhaps meet her after work sometimes, when she is not seeing Russ. I will feel safer with a companion I know.

Rose Marie had been invited to stay in Norwood for the weekend. It was her eighteenth birthday on the Sunday, but Florence had been good about it, and just asked that she bring Russ back for a special tea that day, saying, 'You ought not to disappoint Josefina.'

Rose Marie had omitted to tell her sister that Mrs Short would not be there. She was spending a few days with Sadie and was going to her latest show. Rose Marie wasn't sure whether Russ's mother knew of her son's plans for the period of her absence.

Russ was on duty at the bookshop that Saturday morning, so Rose Marie arranged to meet him when he finished work. They planned to eat a modest lunch out and then to go shopping for her birthday present, before they went on to Russ's house.

He was in an ebullient mood, anticipating what was to come later. Rose Marie, on the other hand, was now experiencing niggling doubts. She wanted so much to repeat the events of the night they'd spent in Norfolk, but she was aware that one lie would lead to another. What about her previous firm resolve not to make the same mistakes as Stella? Yet, she argued with herself, the culmination of their passion had been inevitable.

'You're very quiet,' Russ said, as they waited for their tomato soup and rolls, in Lyons.

'Russ, I'm so sorry, but I can't go through with it!'

'Through with what?'

'You *know*. Letting Florence think your mother invited me to stay overnight! Did she even agree to our arrangement?'

He was honest with her. 'I hoped you wouldn't ask that question, Rose Marie.'

'Well, now you don't need to answer it, eh?'

'Look, I'm disappointed. However, I'll respect your decision. So long as we spend the day together, and go shopping for that special birthday present. . . .'

'Of course we will! But you mustn't be extravagant, Russ.'

'Wait and see. Mr Turbot-Watts kindly gave me a bonus this week in return for all my hard work! I suspect my mention of your birthday, several times, was the real reason.'

'He takes a fatherly interest in you,' Rose Marie told him.

110

'Like his uncle, he's a confirmed bachelor. But he seems to approve of me!'

They spent the afternoon looking in shop windows. They laughed a lot, and sighed a little over things they couldn't afford. Rose Marie was aware that she was being led in a certain direction, but she was taken by surprise when they halted by a small jewellers'.

'Come on,' he urged her, 'let's go inside.'

'But Russ, look at the prices! You can't afford those!'

'You'll see. My sister recommended this place. They also sell second-hand jewellery at sensible prices. That chap, see, the one with the moustache, is expecting us.'

The assistant beckoned them to follow him to a corner cabinet. He withdrew a tray full of sparkling rings and placed it on a small table. 'Take a seat. Allow me to measure the young lady's finger before selecting any rings. Has madam any preference, say a silver ring set with garnets? Something more modern? Or is it your wish for diamonds?'

'I'm not sure. . . .' Rose Marie said.

'Take your time considering these, while I attend to another customer.'

Rose Marie seemed dazzled by the display before her. After a long pause, she asked Russ quietly, 'Are we looking for an *engagement* ring? You haven't even asked me to marry you yet, or spoken to Florence - or your mother, I presume.'

'I just assumed you felt the same way,' he said in an injured tone.

'You know I do! But I'm not walking out of here with a ring on my finger. You must ask Florence's permission tomorrow. Even if she agrees, it will be a long engagement!'

'You continually surprise me, Rose Marie,' Russ told her ruefully.

'*Never* take me for granted,' she said firmly. Then, she turned her attention to the tray. A slender gold band with a blue sapphire and tiny diamonds was the first ring she tried on.

The assistant congratulated them on a good choice. The ring dated back to the late Victorian era, he told them. It fitted as if it had been made for Madam. A little worn, perhaps. . . .

'I don't mind that.' Rose Marie meant it. She'd tell Russ

privately later that she fancied the ring had been much loved, like the woman who once wore it.

Seven guineas didn't break the bank. Russ was relieved at that!

Florence found herself on her own on Saturday evening. She'd encouraged Manny to meet up with his friends at the pub, saying she'd invite Lilli to join her, as she might want to talk. However, Lilli was busy sewing a fresh collar and cuffs to a dress she had bought at the second-hand clothes shop, which she hoped would be suitable for her new job.

After supper, when Josefina was asleep, Florence decided to have a bath and hair-wash that evening, rather than the next morning, to pass time. She was undressed ready for bed, wrapped around with her favourite kimono, drying her hair by the stove, when Manny called out, 'Anyone at home?'

'Come in!' she responded, glancing at the clock on the mantle-piece. It was half-past eight - he had only been out for an hour.

She was about to excuse herself to get dressed again, then she dismissed the idea, because, after all, they would be married in a week's time.

Manny seemed more relaxed with her this evening, more talk-ative, she thought, caused, no doubt, by his visit to the Paradise Arms!

'Let me have the towel,' he offered. 'I'll give your hair a good rub.' He bent over her and she was glad that he couldn't see her face, because she knew that, uncharacteristically, she was blush-ing at the intimacy of the moment.

'There, that's done.' He removed the damp towel, and Florence gave her hair a swift brush-through and smiled her thanks.

'Shall we go in the sitting-room?' she asked. 'We can put a match to the fire.'

They sat together on the settee, watching the flames curling round the coal, in companionable silence for a while.

Then he drew her closer, whispered, 'I always thought you were rather straight up and down, Florence, but without all those whale bones beneath your clothes. . .' He slipped his hands under the folds of the loose robe to explore the contours of her body, tentatively at first, then with increasing confidence.

'I'm an emancipated woman these days. I threw away my corsets after I came back from hospital. I realized the restriction hadn't done my insides any good.'

'I always admired you, you know, but I never thought you and I would get *this* close.'

She surprised herself. 'Not close enough . . .' she murmured. She took a deep breath. 'Do you want to stay here tonight, with me, Manny?'

'What about—'

'Josefina? You can slip away before she wakes up in the morning.'

'Are you sure?' he asked.

'I don't say a thing if I don't mean it.'

Even as they rose to go to the bedroom, they heard Rose Marie in the kitchen.

'Florence, have you gone to bed? I've come home after all!'

Florence adjusted her kimono for propriety's sake. She ushered Manny through into the kitchen. 'Goodnight Manny. See you tomorrow,' she said.

When he had gone, she asked Rose Marie, 'What's up?'

'I could ask you the same question,' Rose Marie was quite shocked to see Florence all flustered, and Manny looking sheepish. Something had obviously been going on, she thought.

'There's nothing for me to confess. How about you?' Florence queried.

Rose Marie sat down abruptly. 'All you need to know is I thought better of something I intended to do. . . .'

'You and Russ, I suppose. My dear girl, I understand. I suppose I had responsibility for you girls thrust on me, too young.'

'Stella said that about herself, marrying and having a child so young,' Rose Marie wept.

'All I have ever tried to do, was to steer you away from, well, making mistakes. Yet I almost made one tonight, myself. I feel ashamed you guessed.'

'Oh, Florence, I'm sorry, but, in your case, getting married next week, how can it really be wrong?'

113

Florence looked at her. In your case, Rose Marie said. Had she and Russ. . . ?

'A cup of tea, a good night's sleep, with a clear conscience, eh? Your birthday tomorrow.'

Thirteen

'OOH, you're here after all, Rose Marie! Happy birthday!'
Josefina squealed in her excitement when she awoke,
bright and early on Sunday morning.

Rose Marie mumbled her thanks, with her eyes still closed.
The next moment, a parcel was thrust under her nose.

'Guess what it is! It smells lovely! So will you, when you use
it.'

Rose Marie gave in. She yawned, sat up in bed. 'Talcum
powder?' she guessed.

'No, pull the paper off and look!'

'Perfume . . . my favourite, lily of the valley.' Rose Marie
uncapped the bottle, sniffed it.

'It's from me, and Yvette, even though she isn't here. She
helped me choose it.'

'Give me a kiss - no, two: one for Yvette eh? You must miss
her, Josefina.'

'I do, but Lilli had a letter yesterday, and there was a note
inside for me. Look.' She withdrew a creased piece of lined
paper from her pyjama pocket. 'Yvette can't write as well as me,
yet, but as Aunty Florence said, I mustn't comment on that. But,
oh dear, I *have*!'

The uneven printing was in green crayon, which made it difficult to decipher.

Dear Josefina and fambly
    I am staying with my daddy and his fambly. They was
    please to see me again.

115

Will you look after Clarice for me? I hope Florrance will look after Maman. I am going back to my old school.

Will you write to me please?

Love from Yvette xxx

'Now you have a pen-friend. That's nice,' Rose Marie observed, with a smile.

'And *you* have all these cards and parcels which I hid from you yesterday,' Florence said, overhearing this remark as she came into their bedroom, bearing gifts.

She sat on the edge of the bed. 'Happy birthday, dear Rose Marie!'

'Wait - Clarice wants to see everything, too!' Josefina propped the doll between them.

'I'm glad I decided to come home last night,' Rose Marie said softly to Florence.

'I'm glad, too. Still, I realize you'll soon spend your birthdays with someone else. . . .'

'Why don't you say with *Russ*,' Josefina cried impatiently. 'Oh, do open up!'

'I hope you don't mind,' Rose Marie said to Florence, 'but I told Russ he could come and spend the day here.'

'He's always welcome,' Florence assured her.

'He's like one of the family! I can't see his present here,' Josefina told Rose Marie.

'He's bringing it with him, later.'

'D'you know what it is?'

Rose Marie smiled. 'I do, but I'm not telling you!'

Later, when Russ arrived, Florence suggested that he and Rose Marie take Josefina out for a stroll in the park, to ensure a good appetite for the Sunday lunch she and Manny were preparing. She added, 'Why not ask Lilli to go with you?'

Lilli, however, was about to go out herself. The bright lipstick she'd applied emphasized the pallor of her face. 'I am meeting Mr Solon. He thought it might cheer me up, to get out of the flat for a bit. Happy birthday, Rose Marie! Have a lovely day.' She looked wistfully at Rose Marie and Russ, standing on her landing, hand in hand.

'When shall I speak to Florence?' Russ asked Rose Marie, as

Josefina clattered down the stairs ahead of them.

'When you can get her to yourself for a moment, I suppose!' she replied.

'That might be difficult. . . .'

'I always find it better to delay mention of important matters until after we've eaten!'

'You make it sound like bad news,' he said in mock reproach.

'What are you two whispering about?' Josefina called impatiently. 'Do hurry up!'

'That's what I want to do, if only Rose Marie will allow it!'

They sat down to Rose Marie's favourite meal - roast chicken, festooned with tiny chipolata sausages and a waistcoat of well-crisped bacon slices round its plump middle. The final decoration was a sprig of watercress, to add colour.

Florence carved as usual, mainly white meat for the ladies, plus a wing or leg for the two men, Russ and Manny, who passed the dishes of vegetables along the table. There were roast and boiled potatoes, mashed, peppered swede, chopped cabbage and diced carrots.

'Oh, good,' Rose Marie exclaimed. 'Mushrooms in the white sauce!'

Russ said, 'With my plate piled so high, where do I pour the gravy? This is splendid, Florence. My mother's a good cook, but not as superb as you are!'

'Don't you dare say that to her,' Florence reproved him, but she couldn't disguise her pleasure at his compliment. 'I would have been more adventurous if I'd known you were coming to lunch! I expect your mother is wondering what to do, with a large joint of meat!'

Rose Marie exchanged a swift guilty glance with Russ.

'I chose the afters,' Josefina said. 'Egg custard.'

'I crossed my fingers it wouldn't curdle,' Florence told them. 'On your special day.'

Rose Marie thought, it will be even more special, when we tell her our news.

Manny said firmly that they were to leave him to do the washing-up.

'I'll make the coffee then,' Florence said. 'Rose Marie, why don't you and Josefina take your presents into the sitting-room, so we can all enjoy looking at them later, eh?'

'May I have a word with you, please, Florence?' Russ put in, with a glance at Manny, already busy at the sink, with his back to them.

'Of course you can. You can help me. Put the cups on the tray on the table. Now, what d'you want to say?'

'I . . . I would like to ask your permission for Rose Marie and I to become engaged. Don't worry,' he added in a rush, before she could answer, 'We're not thinking of marriage yet.'

'I'm relieved to hear that.' However, Florence was smiling. 'You'll tell me next, I suppose, that you already have the ring in your pocket?' He nodded. 'And that she has said "yes"?'

'Yes, she has! But what do *you* say, Florence?'

'Don't look so anxious, my dear. It's what I expected. Of course, I give my consent.'

'Thank you, Florence!' Russ took the coffee-pot from her hand and put it down on the tray. 'Allow me to give you a hug!'

Manny turned his head then, to see Florence receiving a kiss. He grinned happily. She deserves it, he thought. She always comes up trumps. There was something he could do for Florence now. He abandoned the sink full of dishes; dried his hands on his apron.

'Just popping downstairs to fetch something,' he told Florence.

'Don't be long - we must all see Russ present the ring.'

One of Manny's few treasured possessions from his past life was a rather worn leather wallet. It had been his father's. His mother had given it to him when he started work as a clerk in a railway office. He had carried it with him throughout his service in the army. In the field hospital in the last year of the war, a kind nurse had taken his mother's wedding ring, which had been tucked in the wallet, threaded it on a cheap silver chain which she fastened round his neck. The wallet was kept with a few personal items, awaiting his release from hospital. The chain had long since broken; the ring returned to its hiding place.

Now, he took it out and regarded the ring thoughtfully. It was a solid, plain gold band. It gleamed as it must have done on the day his mother received it. He thought, with a pang, I didn't give

118

Florence an engagement ring. It all happened so quickly, and she, of course, proposed to me! But maybe she will want to wear my mother's ring. I can only ask her. . . .

'You have to go down on one knee, doesn't he Rose Marie?' Josefina was thoroughly entering into the spirit of the occasion.

Russ obliged. Rose Marie held out an imperious hand and queried, 'Well?'

'Will you marry me, Rose Marie?'

'Certainly!' she said. She waggled her finger. 'Come on, where is it?'

Then they were crowding round the betrothed couple to admire the ring.

'Congratulations and happy birthday, once again!' Florence said softly.

Manny cleared his throat, said, loud and clear, 'Florence, it's a bit too late for us to get engaged, seeing as we're getting married next Saturday, but I'd like you to try on this wedding ring for size - it was my mother's - she was a wonderful woman and I know she'd have been pleased for you to have it.'

He slipped the ring on Florence's finger. Yes, it fitted well.

'I should have said too, if you want a new ring, or to wear your own mother's ring, if you have it, well, it must be your choice.'

'It's perfect,' Florence told him. 'You must keep it for now, of course, but I'll be proud to wear it at our wedding, Manny.' Then, in front of the others, she kissed him on the lips.

Not wishing to be left out, Russ embraced Rose Marie.

Josefina's voice reproached them. 'Oh how soppy you all are! What about cutting the birthday cake *now*, Aunty Florence, to celebrate?'

Florence regarded herself solemnly in the cheval mirror in her bedroom. The heather-mixture woollen jacket had a smart mauve velvet collar. The skirt was shorter than she was used to, but revealed well-shaped legs in fine silk stockings. Rose Marie had made sure the seams were straight at the back. Her wedding costume and other new clothes, including lingerie, had been purchased at Belling's, with a generous discount allowed because of Rose Marie.

Stella, who'd arrived home mid-week to help with the preparations and to look after her daughter while Florence and Manny were away, placed the purple cloche hat on Florence's head, trying not to ruffle her hair.

'There! I know you had your doubts about the colour, but it's just right, isn't it?'

The bride's attendant, Josefina, advised by her mother to sit still and watch, couldn't resist swinging her legs, and looking down with satisfaction at her new, shiny shoes.

'You should've worn a long white dress, Aunty Florence,' she observed.

'I'm no spring chicken, dear.' Florence thought happily that the mirror reflected otherwise.

'What's that?'

'Shush . . .' her mother told her, while outlining Florence's lips with a touch of colour.

'The flowers have come; where shall I put them?' Russ's voice. He'd arrived early, as Manny's best man, and driver of the wedding carriage, courtesy of Elmo Turbot-Watts.

'On the table. We're just coming out. You'd better take your button-holes and drive Manny to the Register Office. We need you back here at ten minutes before ten, to collect us.'

'I put some camp stools in the back of the van. Sorry there are no other seats.'

'Well, at least I get the front seat,' Florence said, emerging first from the bedroom.

'I've got my ring on today,' Rose Marie showed it off proudly. 'Jewellery isn't permitted in the workroom.' She tweaked Russ's button-hole, a white carnation, into place. 'I bet Manny's not as calm as the bride!'

'I never thought we'd see this day,' Stella said tactlessly. She added, 'It's a pity Lilli decided not to come.'

'She was worried she might spoil a happy occasion by crying,' Florence reminded her.

Stella thought, I shed a few tears myself, thinking of my own wedding, last night.

In his flat, Manny picked up and stroked his little cat, then had to apply the clothes brush to his grey suit to remove the stray hairs. *Blanche*, Josefina and Yvette had named her for him.

Yvette told him imperiously that meant 'white'. He didn't say he knew a little of the language, having spent four terrible years in dug-out trenches in France during the war.

'You'll be all right. Russ is staying down here while I'm away to keep an eye on the girls, and the shop, at nights. He'll feed you. When we come back, you'll have to make your mind up if you want to stay in the basement, or join us upstairs; that's if Florence agrees.'

Russ assured him he looked smart. New suit; white shirt, with stiff collar and cuffs; a grey, silk tie; gold cuff-links with his initials PJM, his wedding gift from the bride. Manny had visited the barber a couple of days ago for a short-back-and-sides; the floppy locks at the front were now restrained by brilliantine. He'd only the small mirror propped above the sink to check his appearance. He took one last look, as he fixed the carnation in place.

'Ready?' Russ asked. 'Lets go!'

It was a short service; simple words, no music. Florence handed her sheaf of hothouse red roses in a froth of delicate fern to Josefina, then took her place beside Manny. His solemn expression was instantly transformed by one of his infectious smiles when he saw her. He wanted to whisper that she looked really nice, but realized that wasn't enough. Instead, he squeezed her hand tight to let her know how he was feeling. Excited, but a little nervous.

Then the wedding ring slid smoothly on to her finger, the vows were made, and it seemed no time at all before her sisters were hugging her proudly and congratulating them.

They all piled into the book-van this time for the short drive to their chosen restaurant for the wedding breakfast; a modest affair because it was still only mid-morning, and the newly-wed pair were leaving after this, on what Florence referred to as their holiday. Toasts were made in delicious fruit-cup, and the rich, dark, iced wedding cake was ceremoniously sliced.

A few pieces of confetti, thrown by Josefina outside the Register Office, floated down from Florence's purple hat on to her plate. She smiled. 'I didn't expect that!' she told her niece.

'I got you something else!' Josefina loosened the strings of her dolly bag.

Florence and Manny regarded the large paper silver horse-shoe. GOOD LUCK ALWAYS!

The wedding party rose again, glass in hand, to echo that.

They sat opposite each other in the train, not talking for a while, each wrapped up in their own thoughts. They weren't going as far from home as the family imagined; Florence had kept their destination a secret, shaking her head at the guessing games. The West Country? Lake District? Ireland to discover Manny's roots? 'Tell you when we get back,' she said.

Now and again Manny's hand strayed to his pocket. He was reassured to find his wallet still in place. It was bulky with notes, four large white fivers.

'I went to the bank and told them of my change of name,' Florence had said yesterday. 'I withdrew forty pounds, and here is your share.'

'But,' he began uncertainly.

'No buts, Manny. We will set up a joint account after our holiday.'

Now, she broke the silence. They were the only occupants of the carriage. It seemed to her to be a good time. 'Manny, there's something I should tell you. I didn't, before today, in case you got the wrong idea about why I proposed to you.'

'I'm glad you did. You made me realize I didn't want to spend the rest of my life on my own.' It was quite a speech from him.

'Manny, I have come into some money now we are married. My father left it in trust for me until that day, or if I remained single, I would have had to wait until I was forty.'

'I don't understand; why should he have made those conditions?'

'He was a hard man, Manny. I . . . I disappointed him when I was younger, you see. There was more to it than that, though. The real condition was that I should bring up my sisters, and keep the business in the family.'

'You've done that, all right.'

'Would you have changed your mind about marrying me if you'd known before?'

'No,' he said positively. 'But, maybe it could have seemed to

122

the family I was marrying you for your money, Florence. I'm not that sort.'

'I know that,' she patted the seat beside her. 'Come over here. . . .'

Later, she said, as she straightened her hat, and then his tie, 'Manny, I hope you don't mind, but I am dividing the money - £2,000 - between Stella, Rose Marie and myself. You and I can manage comfortably on our share, can't we?'

'It still seems a fortune to me. You're very generous, Florence.'

'Well, now I think we can call this our *honeymoon*, can't we?'

It was a start, she thought. One secret revealed, but more to come, in due course. Would it be the same for Manny, too?

They were in Sussex, Hastings, staying in one of the many tall white stucco hotels along the front. Their room was on the top storey, so they could view the beach and the sea from their window. They were not far from the pier, almost deserted now the summer season was over.

'Looks wild out there this afternoon,' Florence observed, seeing the grey skies and rolling sea, with spray dashing on the shingle. She spotted a lone fisherman, hunched against the wind, and a woman and two children walking with a large, lolloping dog.

She removed her hat, laid it on the bed. 'Time to get changed for tea, I think.'

Manny remained tactfully at the window while she unhooked her skirt and stepped out of it, and hung that with her jacket in the wardrobe. This was hardly the bridal suite, she thought ruefully, as pictured in the hotel brochure, but old habits die hard, and she had booked a modest double room 'up top'. The bathroom was on the floor below.

'We'll be glad of that eiderdown tonight, I reckon,' she said. 'It's cold near the sea.'

They were only sixty miles from London, but the hotel was still solidly within the late Victorian era. The dining-room, to which they had descended three flights of turkey-red carpeted stairs, was rather gloomy, with dark oak sideboards, tables and chairs. The royal portrait over the fireplace had not been updated. Edward VII, that genial, stout monarch weighed down, it appeared, with his regalia, stood alongside his Queen consort, the beautiful, seemingly ageless Alexandra, who was now approaching the end of her life.

They were shown to a table for two; a waiter switched on the lights, and the room instantly appeared more cheerful. The fire was lit, and a modest blaze encouraged. Other guests came in, settled at their tables, and muted conversation began.

A pretty young waitress came up to their table, smiling, and took their teatime order.

'Would you like sandwiches? Or scones, jam and cream? A selection of cakes?'

Manny looked at Florence. They suddenly realized they were hungry. They hadn't eaten since the wedding breakfast. Dinner wasn't until half past seven; it was now just after four.

'All of those, if we may!' she told the girl. 'With a large pot of tea, please.'

A little later, they unfurled pristine white damask napkins and enjoyed their feast. They said as much to their waitress, when she came to clear their table.

Encouraged by their friendly conversation, she suggested, 'You ought to have a stroll before dinner, else you won't be able to manage another morsel!'

They climbed the stairs again to their room, intending to collect their coats and hats.

'Phew!' Florence exclaimed. 'I feel more like a snooze, after all that food.'

'So do I,' Manny agreed.

'Let's take our shoes off then, and our top clothes, and plump down on the bed.' Florence, in her petticoat, did just that, and closed her eyes.

Manny took his time about joining her. Eventually, when he thought she was asleep, he gently eased the eiderdown from under her and arranged it carefully over her legs, avoiding touching the seductive silk stockings. Then he laid down beside her. She stirred, turned on her side towards him.

He felt a mixture of emotions; uncertainty because he wasn't sure what she expected, unlike the other night, when she had made the first move. He'd been relieved then when Rose Marie arrived home unexpectedly, he admitted to himself.

'Manny,' she whispered, shifting closer.

He had to tell her. 'Florence, maybe it didn't seem like it, when, you know, we were about to . . .' he floundered.

'What are you trying to say?' He sensed that she had tensed up now, too.

'I haven't had any experience. I suppose you could say I was rather a mother's boy; I wasn't at all wayward in my youth. Then there was the war, but I didn't seek, well, *comforts* in the way some of the other soldiers did, when we had spells away from the front line.'

'It'll be all right, you'll see,' she comforted him. 'It'll just happen.'

'How do you know that? We're *both* as green as grass. . . .'

She hugged him tight, her face pressed against his chest, so that he wouldn't discern her disappointment.

They had a good holiday, anyway, happy and comfortable with each other like the old friends they were. The sea breezes, the long walks, the history trails by bus to Battle, and to Lewes where they saw the ruins of the castle and became breathless as they tackled the steep gradient of many of the streets. They marvelled at the vast chalk outline on the downs of the Long Man of Wilmington. At Alfriston, they had lunch one day at The Star, the smugglers' inn, and another day they spent in Brighton, choosing bright pink rock to add to the collection they were taking home for the girls. The last two days they stayed put in Hastings. They bought delicious ice-cream from the little parlours on every street corner, and walked out to sea along the pier.

They packed their bags reluctantly on Friday evening. They had slept well all week, but on their last night in the hotel they were both restless. They talked for a while, then determined to get off to sleep.

Florence drifted into a delightful dream where she was floating in sun-warmed water under cloudless blue skies, calling out to Manny to join her. She was jerked awake by Manny shouting and thrashing about in the bed. He was all too obviously having a nightmare.

When she had calmed him down and wiped the sweat from

his face and chest, after helping him out of his wringing wet pyjama jacket, she turned the light low and cradled him in her arms. 'There, there, it's over, Manny. Do you feel like telling me about it?' She whispered soothingly, as she had when her girls were young.

It was a jumbled account, but she gathered that it related to the night of terror and mayhem he had endured, when his platoon were ambushed as they pushed forward to gain ground; when his best pal was killed at his side; when Manny turned and ran for his life; when he was brought down by a single shot by one of his comrades for his cowardice. He lay where he was until first light, when the ambulance picked up the survivors.

'Only one person knew that I was running away, deserting - though it wasn't planned, I swear - and that was the man who shot me. He kept quiet, because there were things I could have told about him . . . He disappeared himself while I was in hospital.'

'I said it's over, and it is. You were just a young lad, Manny. You have to forgive yourself.' *I know that* she said silently to herself.

'You don't think badly of me for it, then?'

'No. We've all done things on the spur of the moment which we are ashamed of.'

'Not *you*, Florence!' He kissed her then, in relief at having confessed to her, and his ardour was kindled by her passionate response.

It wasn't the bridal suite, but it was certainly a honeymoon night.

Early next morning, she still lay contentedly within the circle of his arms, waiting for him to wake. His eyelids flickered, he stroked her bare skin, reassuring himself that he wasn't dreaming.

'*Green as grass*,' she murmured fondly. 'Not any more, dear Manny. . . .'

126

PART TWO

Fourteen

THE tramcar picked up fewer passengers at the Paradise stop in the early, blustery days of March,1926. The employment situation was increasingly grim. The main news in January was that Allied troops were at last preparing to leave the Rhineland Territory, seven years after the end of the Great War. This event was not approved by some politicians, in and out of government, who expressed their reservations as to the outcome. Other headlines this month shocked the nation: the Shakespeare Memorial Theatre at Stratford-upon-Avon was destroyed by fire, although thankfully, ancient relics were saved. There were calls for a national fund to build a new theatre. All were urged to contribute, but many would be unable to do so.

Rose Marie had a travelling companion, Lilli, in the mornings. You didn't discuss your private lives on the tram, she thought, but she knew how much Lilli missed her daughter. Yvette was settled with her father, but there was no likelihood yet of her mother being allowed to visit. Lilli was being punished for leaving Sam and running away with their daughter.

Rose Marie received promotion in the new year., She joined the older women in their small workroom, dealing with alterations, and delicate beadwork for the wealthiest clients. She was encouraged to try her hand at designing, and her aptitude was praised by her mentors. Yet she missed the camaraderie of her contemporaries in the workshop. There was a worrying rumour going round that if workers left Belling's employ they would not be replaced.

Florence and Manny had spent the months since their marriage making the changes to the pie shop. She was very proud of her gleaming new kitchen and the splendid New World gas cooker with the double oven. The eating area at the front was crowded most days, but prices had to remain at their lowest. They had delayed taking on extra help, because of this.

She worried sometimes whether she had been too impulsive in spending her windfall, if it was the right time to expand the business. Then she looked at Manny's beaming face, and saw how he had grown in confidence and proved himself in the partnership.

Although Florence missed Josefina, she knew it was for the best when Stella took a lease out on a house in Bayswater and set herself up as a singing teacher in the large front room. Josefina had to change schools, but now her mother looked after her in their own home.

One Friday evening, when most of the clearing-up was done, Florence took off her rubber apron, wiped it clean and hung it on its peg.

'Can you finish up, Manny?' she requested. 'Then I can get our supper on. It's just the two of us, with Rose Marie spending the weekend at Russ's. What d'you fancy?'

'You look weary. Why don't I get us some fish and chips, after I'm done?' he asked.

'Your night for the pub, remember - yes, that's a good idea. Thank you!'

She was bending to place the plates in the warming oven in the kitchen upstairs, when he arrived with their instant meal. 'Give me the parcel; it might need hotting-up.' she said. Then she turned her attention to cutting and buttering two thick slices of bread.

He hugged her round the waist, from behind. 'You're filling out, but it suits you.'

'Contentment, I reckon,' she told him. She didn't turn round right away, waiting for the tell-tale blushing to fade. 'Right, you can dish up, Manny; make sure I get my share of the chips!' His comment decided her: she mustn't put off her visit to the doctor much longer.

Numbers had not decreased at the pub, but fewer pints were pulled. Manny made do with his single mug of bitter. A newcomer was seated at the piano tonight, thumping the keys, playing fragments of popular tunes. The stranger drained his glass, looked round hopefully, but there were no offers to replenish it. He banged down the piano lid and departed.

'I'll sit by you, Manny,' the old cleaner from the bakery said. She still wore her apron and the kerchief round her head.

He looked up, in surprise. 'Don't often see you in here, Nan.'

'Got the push tonight. Can't afford my services in these hard times, they said.'

'I'm sorry, Nan. What's your fancy? My treat.'

'Gin, dear, ta. Need something stronger'n stout.'

When he returned with her drink, she downed it in one gulp.

'Don't look so worried, dear, one's enough! Now, what's this I hear about your wife?'

'Florence? What d'you mean?'

'Being in the family way, like. Ain't she said?'

He couldn't admit to that, Florence would be humiliated.

'Not to all and sundry, no. Too early.' He rose. 'Well, better get on home.'

'Well done!' she called after him. 'Don't say I said anyfing!'

Manny walked back along the street in a daze. He felt a bit light-headed, but one beer wouldn't have that result, he thought. He recalled squeezing Florence's waist earlier and his teasing comment; she'd seemed a bit flustered after that. If Nan's assumption was true, why hadn't she told him?

There was a figure standing outside the shop. As he approached, he saw who it was.

'Knocked on your door; guessed where you'd gone. Thought I'd wait here,' Buck said, just as if they had parted company only yesterday.

'You didn't disturb Florence I hope?' Manny said sharply, not greeting him either. He looked up at the first-floor windows. There was no light showing.

'I haven't been here long; place was in darkness then. What's up?'

'What do you mean?'

'I dunno. Just a feeling I got.'

'Well, you might as well know. Florence and I were married a few months ago. We use my old place for storage.'

'I didn't expect that ... neither of you seemed the marrying kind.'

'Look,' Manny said, key-ring in hand, 'We can't talk out here. I suppose you're after a place to sleep tonight?' He dealt with the gate to the basement, they went down the steps, and he inserted the key in the lock. 'Wait 'til I light the lamp.'

There were still a few sticks of furniture, including Manny's old bed.

'Blankets and a pillow,' Manny told Buck. 'I'm not rousing Florence to fetch some linen. I don't deal with that side of things. Anyway, it's only for one night, eh?'

'Can't you be more helpful than that, old mate—'

'I'm not your old mate!'

'I been working ever since I last saw you, thanks to Florence helping me out. But the work's dried up, and I'm on the look-out again.' Buck sat down on the bed. He looked dejected; there was none of the old blustering.

Manny's innate kindness rose to the surface. 'Hungry?' he asked gruffly.

'I should say so. Me old trouble flares up, if I don't eat regular.'

'Well, I'll go now, but will come back a bit later with something for you to eat and drink.'

'Thanks,' Buck said, tussling with his boots. Then he stretched out under the blankets.

Manny made his way upstairs. The kettle was simmering on the hot-plate of the stove. He made a large tin mug of tea, stirring in plenty of sugar. He took the last two pies left over from the day's baking from the larder. Then he carried a tray down to the basement. He was reminded of that night in the police cell, where he had been shown kindness and given hope.

Some time later he eased himself into bed beside his slumbering wife. Cautiously, he slid an arm round her waist. Yes, now he could detect the slight swell of her body and the fullness of her breasts.

She stirred, murmured, 'I do love you, Manny. . . .'

He experienced a sudden rush of tears to his eyes. It was a minute or two before he could manage a reply, he felt so choked. It was the first time she'd said that. He realized that she was awake now, awaiting his reply.

'I love you, too, Florence. Goodnight, I'm sorry I disturbed you.'

'You don't want to talk, then?'

'Not tonight, eh?' Manny caressed the nape of her neck with his lips. 'Tomorrow will do.'

Rose Marie and Russ spent the evening in the little Soho restaurant where you could linger over your coffee. The staff were in no hurry to clear the table and were discreet.

'Better to arrive home after dark,' Russ decided. 'When the neighbours are not about.'

Rose Marie hadn't put up any resistance, when he told her his mother was staying with his aunt for a few days, and that they would have the house to themselves. It was their first chance to spend a night together since she'd decided against it on her birthday eve.

'After all, we're engaged,' he'd reminded her, earlier in the week. 'I'd get married tomorrow, if it was possible, you know that. . . .'

It was cold standing on the doorstep while Russ fumbled for his key.

'Hurry, I'm shivering!' Rose Marie hissed.

'I'll soon warm you up!' he said audaciously, as he ushered her indoors.

They crept about the house as if they thought it could tell tales, and turned the lights on and off in the kitchen and then the bathroom. It wasn't long before they drew the curtains in Russ's small bedroom, when Rose Marie noted the single bed.

'How can we both sleep on that?' she asked.

'Oh, I thought sleep was the last thing on our minds,' he teased.

'Well, you can close your eyes while I undress,' she ordered him.

'Why?'

'Because I say so, because—'

'You feel guilty,' he finished for her. 'Stop worrying about what Florence would say.'

'But I do!' She stood there irresolute.

'Come here,' he said softly. 'No more talking, leave any unbuttoning to me.'

Some time after midnight, a cab drew up outside the house.

Mrs Short paid the driver and then trod quietly up the front path. She noted that there wasn't a light showing in Russ's bedroom. Maybe he hadn't yet returned from his evening out with Rose Marie. He certainly wasn't in earlier, she thought, when she rang intending to say she'd decided to come back tonight, when Aunt Bea's daughter turned up unexpectedly for the weekend.

Mrs Short poured herself a glass of milk to take upstairs, she was too tired to make herself a sandwich, although she had missed out on her dinner. She went into the bathroom for a quick wash and then hesitated outside Russ's door, before retreating to her own room.

'Russ,' she called. 'Are you in bed?'

There came no reply. She turned the doorknob cautiously, feeling for the light switch.

'Mother, what on earth?' Russ exclaimed, jerking up in the bed.

Mrs Short's astonished gaze flickered to the face on the pillow beside him.

Rose Marie, in her confusion, sat up, too, clutching the sheet hopefully around her.

'You must forgive me intruding like this,' Mrs Short apologized stiffly. 'We will talk in the morning, Russell. Goodnight Rose Marie.'

When she left, switching off the light as she did so, Russ turned to Rose Marie.

'I didn't know she was coming home, honest! I'm so sorry, Rose Marie, you must feel mortified. I know I do.'

She surprised him, as she so often did. 'Well, as we've been rumbled, we might as well make the most of our illicit night of passion; it could be ages before we get another chance....'

Lilli had agreed to work late. She didn't mind, because the evenings seemed to drag now Yvette wasn't with her. Rose Marie hadn't returned to share the flat, and she could understand that, because she knew that she was hardly good company.

Her job had not proved as interesting as she'd hoped. The telephone callers said very little, merely stated a time when they wished Mr Solon to call. Only a few clients called at the office, and then her employer would send her out of the room to make tea, and to bring it to them 'in about half an hour, if you will, please, Mrs Bower.'

Mr Solon had been out most of today. When he returned, there were some clerical tasks he needed her to help with. She had been practicing on the typewriter at his suggestion for some weeks now, and there were urgent notes which he required typed-up. Names and places figured, which surprised her, but she told herself he must be convinced by now that she kept any curiosity to herself, and that anyway these facts meant nothing to her.

Lilli was still slow at locating the keys. Two foolscap pages took her over an hour.

'Thank you,' Philippe said. 'This is most kind of you. Now, Lilli, unless you wish to hurry home, I would like to show my appreciation, by asking you to dinner. The food provided to the apartment block where I live is excellent. What do you say?'

She experienced a brief flashback to the time she and Stella took the little girls to the Golden Domes, when he turned up unexpectedly; Stella's warning to be careful, not to agree to meet Philippe in his flat. She had been wary of him then.

'I should like that,' she said now, reaching for her hat and coat.

He picked up the telephone receiver. 'I will order our meal now, Lilli, then we won't have to wait too long the other end.'

Despite working for him for some months, Lilli still had no idea where he lived. They took a cab through unfamiliar residential areas, until they came to a tall building set well back from the road. They were admitted by a commissionaire, then took a lift up to the third floor.

He opened the door with a flourish. 'Welcome to my home, Lilli; I hope you approve?'

Wide-eyed, she took in the thick carpeting, fine furnishings, the cut-glass decanters and bottles of wine ranged on the bar shelf at one end of the room.

'No kitchen; I don't need it, but I can make tea, or percolate coffee. The bedroom is through there; the bathroom is off it. Hang your outdoor things in this cupboard, and use the facilities, if you wish, to freshen up before our meal,' he suggested.

'The maid has laid the table.' He sat down in a comfortable club armchair with his newspaper. 'Take your time.'

Lilli, washing her hands in a basin shaped like a shell, appreciated the hot water and delicately perfumed soap. She gazed solemnly at her reflection in the gilded mirror above the basin. She had little natural colour these days; she brushed on a touch of rouge and reddened her lips, then fluffed her hair with her comb. What am I letting myself in for, she wondered.

The food was wheeled into the living-room on a two-tier trolley. They sat on opposite sides of the table. The waiter served them with poached salmon, garnished with slices of cucumber and parsley, with hollandaise sauce; crusty rolls with curls of pale butter. Lilli was taken back to the days before the war when she was allowed to take dinner occasionally with her parents in the long dining-hall at the château. White wine sparkled in the fine glasses, and Lilli lost count of the times Philippe topped up their drinks. The dessert was one she had not enjoyed since she arrived in England - how Yvette would have relished it, she thought - peach melba, eaten with long-handled spoons.

Lilli felt a little muzzy, but happy, as she sat later in the other armchair, waiting for Philippe to serve the coffee. The table was cleared, as if by magic, and there was soft background music from the elegant gramophone with the curved horn.

She was almost asleep when the cup of dark coffee was placed on the table at her elbow.

'Lilli, can you hear me?' She nodded, smiling. 'Drink your coffee, now.'

She sat up obediently and lifted the cup to her lips, made a little face. 'What's in it?'

'Just a trace of cognac,' he said smoothly. 'It's getting late. Is it indelicate of me to suggest you are, well, a little drunk?'

She giggled, downed the coffee in a gulp. 'Am I?'

'Yes. I think it would be best if you stayed here tonight.'

'Where? In your bed? Where would you sleep?' She knew she was slurring her words.

'In my bed, yes. I can use the couch in here. Come on, let me assist you.'

Lilli lurched to her feet, felt his steadying arm around her, as they went into the bedroom.

'Would one of my pyjama jackets do?' he asked, going to the chest of drawers.

She nodded. 'Thank you, Philippe.'

'You will excuse me. I will go through to the bathroom, allow you to get in bed.'

Lilli flung her clothes off in gay abandon, donned the loose jacket and climbed between the fine Egyptian cotton sheets. 'This is nice. . . .' she said aloud, in approval.

Philippe stopped by the bed to wish her goodnight. He looked almost boyish with his hair dampened, and wearing a knee-length towelling robe.

'May I kiss you, to say thank you for your company tonight?' he asked. Without waiting for an answer, he leaned over and pressed his lips to hers.

'Don't go,' she heard herself saying, as if from a distance. 'Please don't go.'

Rose Marie sat at the breakfast table, listening to the raised voices in the kitchen. She wondered when it would be possible to escape, to go home.

Mrs Short came in first, and she actually smiled at Rose Marie. 'Well,' she said ruefully, 'I gather that the deed is done, and indeed that it is not the first time. I know what I told you when we met, Rose Marie, but I can see that you two are desperate to be together, now, rather than later. If you want to marry this wretched son of mine, well, you have my blessing. You'll be as poor as church mice, though.'

Rose Marie jumped up and rushed over to hug Russ's mother. 'No, we wouldn't! I didn't say anything before, but Florence came into some money when she married Manny, and she generously shared her inheritance with Stella and me. If, as my guardian, she will give me her permission, we could tie the knot this summer!'

'Sounds good to me,' Russ said, having heard it all from the doorway. 'Look, Mother wants you to stay, as we planned, so we don't have to rush back to your place today and upset any plans Florence and Manny have made for the weekend.'

*

Florence woke first, and gave Manny a kiss. 'Time to rise and shine, old boy.'

'Hang on a minute,' he said. 'I've got something to tell you—'

'And I've got something I'm bursting to tell you!'

'Let me speak first. It's *Buck*, he arrived last night, wanting to stay.'

'Oh, why didn't you wake me, and say?'

'I - I'm not really sure. But I couldn't send him away.'

'No, of course you couldn't. Is he downstairs?'

'Yes. Don't be in a rush to see him. We'll do the usual chores first. You've got something to say now, haven't you?'

'It will keep,' she said. 'If you get too excited, you'll ruin the pies!'

He smiled. He'd already guessed, after all. Then he paused, at the door, on his way to get washed. 'Another thing,' he said, 'I didn't hear Lilli come in last night. . . .'

Fifteen

IT was after nine on Saturday morning before Florence found a moment to call on Buck. There had been no sign that he was up and about.

She left Manny serving an early customer, and went down the steps to the basement. She hesitated, then opened the door with her key. If she knocked, she reasoned, Buck might appear in a state of undress, in view of any passers-by in the street.

She called out from the dingy hallway. 'Buck? It's me, Florence.' Then she became aware of a moaning sound from the bedroom. Without thinking, she opened the door and went in. The room was in darkness, so she crossed swiftly to the window and pulled the curtains back. 'Buck?' she said again.

The groans were repeated. She went over to the bed, in some apprehension. The unmistakable stench of vomit made her clap her hand over her mouth. She had been fortunate in scarcely suffering from morning sickness, which had helped keep her secret until she believed the early danger of miscarrying was past, but now she felt nauseous. She forced herself to turn back the blanket to reveal Buck's face. His eyes stared back at her. For a moment she thought the worst, then she saw his lips move, heard the hoarse whisper, 'Florence, I'm sorry I—'

'Don't try to talk,' she said gently. 'You obviously couldn't help it. What did Manny give you to eat last night - not those pies we had over?'

'Yes, don't blame him; he meant well.'

'You should have told him you were ill,' she stated. 'Look, I'll have to fetch him to help.'

She tapped on the shop window, beckoned to Manny. Fortunately he was on his own. Florence explained briefly what had occurred. 'I'm sorry, but you'll have to clean him up. Put on your rubber apron, and fill a bucket with hot water and carbolic. I'll take care of the shop, but turn the notice back to closed for ten minutes, while I go upstairs and ring the doctor. He should be at his surgery by now.'

When she came down again she carried a bundle of bed linen, towels and two of her late father's calico nightshirts. She left these on a table in the basement for Manny to collect.

'The doctor will be here soon, Manny,' she called out. 'I've brought a few things for you to make Buck more comfortable. I must open the shop now, there's someone waiting.'

Saturday mornings were always busy, as they closed at 1 p.m. Florence caught a glimpse of the doctor when he arrived, but she was serving a customer when he left. She thought, I'll have to go along to the surgery when Manny relieves me here.

When Manny emerged from the basement, he went round to the back area to empty the bucket, then dumped a heap of soiled blankets in the dustbin. He came in through the scullery at the rear of the shop to cleanse his hands at the sink.

'I'd better get changed before I take over,' he told Florence when she looked in.

'How is he?'

'Resting. Doc gave him a powder, like he did you that day, to settle him.'

'I'll go and see him, find out what's what, later,' she said.

'Well, I can tell you we're stuck with him for a few days.'

'Don't sound so doleful! I'm sure he's grateful for what you've done, Manny.'

'I did it for your sake, not his,' he admitted.

'That doesn't sound like you, my dear!' The shop bell clanged, and she was gone.

The doctor was tidying his desk. The surgery was over.

'I'm sorry to disturb you,' Florence began.

'I expected you. I couldn't say much in front of the patient. Sit down, Miss Flinders.'

'Mrs Manning,' she reminded him.

He smiled. '*You* should have been to see me before this. We might as well have a chat today, after I deliver the verdict on your friend. He has had this problem, I suspect, for years; it is a chronic condition. Likely a duodenal ulcer, caused by stress.'

'What can be done?'

'Rest, a bland diet. He mustn't worry so much. He is need of good friends like you.'

'Not friends who feed him pies,' Florence said ruefully. 'We'll take care of him, Doctor.'

'I am also concerned whether you are taking care of yourself. Hop on to the couch. Just remove your top clothes. I can feel the extent of your pregnancy through your petticoat.'

Florence relaxed as they had told her to in hospital, and the gentle probing of his fingers was not intrusive. She closed her eyes. Did he suspect, she wondered.

'Everything seems to be in good order,' he observed. 'You may dress.' He sat down at his desk, to make some notes. Once more, Florence took the chair facing him.

'Now, I estimate you to be around four months pregnant. Does that tie in with your own calculations?' he asked, looking up at her over his reading glasses.

'Yes. I was married almost five months ago,' she said defensively.

'I realize that you may be distressed by my next question. But I must know, for your own sake. This is not your first pregnancy, is it? You gave birth some years ago?'

'Yes,' Florence almost whispered.

'You, ah, were forced to part with that baby, I assume?'

'I was not allowed to acknowledge her.' Florence realized instantly she had made a slip. 'How old were you then?' he asked quietly.

'I was seventeen. My father was horrified at my predicament. I wasn't allowed out when I began to show; he said no one must know. It was a difficult birth, but my father employed a midwife - she wasn't local - but no doctor came. . . .' She paused, recalling the pain, then, 'I was told having another baby would be good for my health. Thirty-five isn't too old is it?'

'My dear Mrs Manning, not at all, despite the long gap between the pregnancies. Have you told your husband the good news?'

'Not yet, but I will today! Please doctor, can I ask you not to say—'

'You are my patient. Any discussion between us is confidential, I assure you.' He rose to see her out. 'However, I am sure your husband would not condemn you for what occurred long before he knew you. Think about it, eh?'

'Thank you, doctor,' Florence said gratefully.

She hurried back to the shop and to her relief found Manny on his own.

'What did the doctor say?' he asked.

'About Buck? A stomach ulcer, he thinks. Buck needs rest.'

'So do you,' he said, pulling out a chair for her behind the counter.

'You guessed?' She appreciated his obvious concern.

'Yes, and, before that doorbell goes, I want you to know I'm over the moon!'

'Oh, Manny, I'm so glad!'

'We won't say anything to Buck, eh, he'll be gone in a few days, I hope.'

'I promise. Well, I'm going to make him a bowl of arrowroot. That should help.'

They had both forgotten Lilli, with all that had been going on.

Around this time Lilli awoke at last, unaware of the time. She padded into the bathroom. There were signs that Philippe had already made his ablutions; a shaving brush on the basin, with a stick of lathering soap. She turned to bolt the door. She couldn't resist the opportunity of taking a long, hot bath. She turned on the taps and let the water run to a luxurious depth, adding bath crystals from a jar on the shelf. There was a towel on a chair, with a note, written by Philippe, saying simply, FOR YOU LILLI. With this was a new flannel and toothbrush. Had he been out to the shops already? She glanced at her watch before removing it. 2 *p.m.*! How on earth had she slept so long? She stepped into the water.

Later, as she dried herself, she realized she hadn't brought her clothes. She wound the towel round her, went through into the bedroom. The door there was still closed. 'Where on earth are my things?' she exclaimed. No answer came from the next room.

The only thing she could do was to retrieve the pyjama jacket from the bathroom basket.

She ventured fearfully into the living-room. On the table was a glass of orange juice, two rather limp croissants on a plate and a dish of jam. How long had that been there? She suddenly realized that she needed something to eat. Well, this was obviously her breakfast.

Then Philippe came in. He looked preoccupied. 'I had to go out. I am sorry, but I couldn't wake you earlier to tell you. I'll make you some coffee, shall I?'

'Where are my clothes?' she demanded, aware of her scanty attire, her bare legs.

'Ah. The maid calls early for the laundry. By the way, she is in my personal employ. I thought you would be glad to have your garments cleaned.'

'What d'you expect me to wear in the meantime?'

'You look very chic as you are.' He removed his coat and hat, then his jacket, rolled up his shirt sleeves. 'It's warm in here. Shall I turn down the heat?'

She didn't deign to answer that. 'I want to go home, Philippe. As soon as I get my things back. Last night, well, that was wrong, *very* wrong; I am still a married woman—'

'What do you think happened last night?' He was actually smiling. 'Can you remember?'

'Thanks to whatever you gave me to drink, no!'

'Then I will enlighten you. I kissed you goodnight and despite your pleas, I left you.'

Lilli felt a wave of relief sweep over her. 'You're sure?' she insisted.

'I would not say so, if I was not.'

'I'm sorry,' she managed. He handed her a cup of coffee.

'Black, I think, don't you? Look, Lilli, I have this to tell you. You must remain here for a while. I have received disturbing news regarding your situation.'

'What do you mean?'

'I have learned that further efforts will be employed to obtain from you that which you insist you have no knowledge of. You will be safe here, it is a secure address.'

'I want to go home,' she insisted. 'What will my landlady think?'

'You must write her a letter saying that you have had to go away unexpectedly, on special assignment. Ask her to ensure your flat is locked and that nothing is touched. You will enclose a month's rent, which I shall give you. I will have this letter delivered by hand.'

'What about my clothes? I can't manage with what I have.'

'I will send Annie out for whatever you need. She has good taste; she was not always a servant, but she is very diligent. She will keep you company in the mornings when she cleans the flat. Just remember her loyalty is to me. Here, I am known as John Brown.'

I must humour him, Lilli thought, fool him into thinking I will do whatever he wants. Thank goodness, my Yvette is with her father. *He* won't let anyone get at her.

Josefina opened the door at her mother's request. Stella was teaching at the moment. Just as her friend Yvette had done the day she was taken away, she shrieked, '*Daddy!*'

Jose stepped inside, then put his baggage down. 'You've grown,' he observed.

'Of course I have! I was only five last time you saw me, and now I'm eight! You didn't send me a card on my birthday last month,' she said reproachfully.

'I see you bear grudges, like your mother. Where is she?'

'She is teaching; she mustn't be disturbed,' Josefina said firmly.

'She didn't get my letter? I wrote that I was coming.'

The door of what they called the music room opened. Stella came out, followed by a plump girl holding a sheaf of music.

'Take our visitor through to the other room please Josefina, while I see Miss Hobbs out.'

Jose and Josefina were left by themselves for some time. When Stella joined them, it was obvious that she had changed her dress, literally let her hair down, in a thick single black plait down her back, and hastily applied make-up.

'Josefina,' Stella told her daughter. 'Why don't you do your piano practice? Your father and I need to talk.'

'I don't want—' the child began mutinously.

'*Go*. I'll call you in a little while.'

When Josefina had reluctantly departed, Stella faced Jose. 'What are *you* doing here?'

He looked at her appreciatively, at the rapid rise and fall of her bosom, the lustrous hair.

'I missed my beautiful wife, my singing partner . . . When you wrote with your new address, I took stock of my life. Oh, the girl was gone by then. I was crazy for her, but it didn't last.'

'You want me to sympathize with you, I suppose?' She stood there, her anger palpable.

He rose in one swift movement, and before she could stop him, he had hold of her and was kissing her passionately. Stella went weak at the knees. Her resistance evaporated.

'Stella,' he murmured. 'You'll take me back, won't you?' He added, rather unfortunately, 'If only for Josefina's sake, eh?'

She pulled away then. 'You've always regarded our child as an encumbrance!'

'I promise to do better. She's got your spirit, I like that.'

'She *looks* like you. . . .'

'I'm happy you think that.' He pulled her to him again. 'Now you have a proper home, a new career, can you find room again for me in your life?'

A small voice spoke from the doorway. 'Can I come in now? Is everything all right?'

Stella whispered in his ear. 'You can stay tonight, but you'll have to convince me. . . .'

'One night will be enough for me to do that,' he assured her. He let her go. 'Come in Josefina, and tell me all about yourself, since I last saw you.'

'It'll take a long time to do that,' Josefina began uncertainly.

'And I've got plenty of time to listen. Let's do that, while your mother makes the tea.'

Buck accepted the bowl of arrowroot blancmange, laced with a dash of sherry, gratefully. He was sitting up in the nice clean bed now, and even with the stubble on his face and the dark circles under his eyes, he looked better than he had earlier.

'Don't rush off Florence,' he said. 'It's good to see you again.'

She found a chair, sat at a distance from the bed. 'Need to take the weight off my feet.'

'You've got more flesh on you, it must suit you, marriage.'

'It does. Eat up, there's a good chap. It'll line your stomach.'

He did as she said. When she took the dish from him, he suddenly seized her arm.

145

'Don't do that!' She sounded alarmed.

'Oh, don't worry, I ain't got the strength for what you're thinking . . . But I can recall when you didn't mind, can't you?'

'Whatever d'you want to bring that up for? I'd better go.'

'I never told no one you know. Only your father suspected, and then he kicked me out.'

'We were both so young and giddy; I think that's the expression.'

'It was the first time for both of us. I loved you, Florence.'

'No, you didn't! You just couldn't help yourself, that's all.'

'I never forgot you, or what happened,' Buck said. He slumped back on his pillow.

'Well, I certainly managed to.' she sounded fierce. 'My father made sure of that.'

'I never meant to blight your life—'

'You didn't! One mistake, but I rose above it, and now I've married my Mr Right.'

'I'm glad you think that. Well, you had better go, and don't worry, my lips are sealed.'

As she climbed the stairs to her flat, Florence thought, 'Please God, let it be so. . . .'

'What's up?' Manny said, when he saw her face. 'Buck not spoken out of turn?'

'I'm just tired that's all,' Florence sighed. 'I guess I need an early night.'

Manny sat her down and eased her shoes off. 'I'm going to take real care of you from now on,' he promised. 'And as we have the place to ourselves, an early night sounds good.'

Just then, they heard the knock on the front door below. Manny went down and came back with a letter in his hand.

'It's addressed to you, Florence. Came by hand.'

Florence opened it cautiously. When she unfolded the single sheet of notepaper, she discovered two guineas wrapped in tissue. She read the letter, looking puzzled. At last she looked up, said slowly, 'It's from Lilli. You'd better read it. I don't know what to make of it.'

Lilli went to bed that night in a peach-coloured silk nightgown, so sheer that she quickly covered herself with the bedclothes.

146

She didn't want Philippe to get any ideas. She feigned sleep when he went through to the bathroom, as he had the previous night, but this time she had made sure she remained sober. She needed her wits about her. If this was all a dream, she thought, it was a very disturbing one.

When he had gone, she let the tears wet her pillow. She cried silently because she had made a mess of her life, and suddenly she thought of Sam, her husband. In the early days, before they came to England, they had been so in love. He hadn't been impatient with her then, as he was when she rowed with his mother. If only they could have set up home on their own! Supposing she never saw Yvette again . . . I couldn't bear it, she said to herself. I've got to get away from this place, and go to Sam and throw myself on his mercy. Surely he would forgive me?

Josefina cuddled Yvette's doll in her arms, whispering to her. It was a comfort, even though naturally the aristocratic Clarice did not answer. Her long-lashed eyes closed automatically when Josefina put her down on the pillow.

'I know Yvette said you were for show, and not to be played with, Clarice, but I know you like to be cosy in my bed with me. You may have a hard head, and arms and legs, but you've got a nice, soft body.' She squeezed Clarice round her middle. 'You're losing a bit of your filling; I must get Mummy to sew you up.' She lifted the dolls dress and petticoat and examined the tiny hole she had poked with her little finger, curious to see what Clarice was made of. The answer was fine wood pulp. Mummy would want to know what the dust was on the sheets.

She wondered if her father really was as pleased to see them as he said he was. He had never taken much notice of her before. Nor had her mother, really, until recently. Aunty Florence was the one she missed most. Then Rose Marie, but they both had other people in their lives to love now. A tear trickled down Josefina's cheek. Stella had forgotten to come in to say goodnight, just told her to take herself off to bed. She couldn't go to sleep without a goodnight kiss. She made her mind up, climbed out of bed, and tiptoed along the landing to her mother's room. She turned the door handle, but the door wouldn't open.

'Mummy!' she called out. 'The door's locked!'

After a moment, came her mother's muffled voice. 'Go back to bed, Josefina!'

As she turned sadly away, there was another voice. Deep, masculine. She couldn't make out words, but then she heard a brief snatch of laughter. Then there was silence.

Sixteen

Rose Mane waited until after tea to talk to Florence on Sunday afternoon. Florence and Manny seemed a trifle preoccupied. Before they sat down to eat, Manny took a tray, covered with a clean tea-towel, downstairs. Rose Mane deduced there was someone staying in the basement. Who? she speculated. She looked at Russ, sensing his apprehension now the initial euphoria had lessened. There was still an important hurdle to cross, she thought.

Her chance came when she and Florence were by themselves for a few minutes in the sitting-room while the men went down to the yard bunker to fetch more coal for the fire.

'Florence, I have something important to ask you,' Rose Marie said. 'Russ and I want to get married this summer. Oh, I know I said we were in no hurry – and please don't think this is because we *have* to, because we *don't* - but, well, we've *decided*, only, of course, I need your permission, and—'

'You're worried I'll refuse, eh?' Florence smiled at Rose Marie's worried expression. 'Well, I do feel you are both rather young, but you've made your minds up, and it's obvious you are very much in love. Who am I to keep you apart? You have my blessing.'

Rose Mane jumped up, hugged her tight in her relief. 'Thank you, Florence!'

'Go easy, my dear. I'm not up to bear-hugs just now!'

'What d'you mean? Oh, Florence, you're not ill again?'

'Far from it. Can you bear to wait until September for the wedding? You see, I'm expecting a baby in August, and I'd like to look my best for your big day.'

'What wonderful news! Hope it's a boy this time after all us girls! You're going to be just like the mother-of-the-bride and I'll make sure you have a lovely outfit trom Belling's!'

'It may still have to be a larger size,' Florence remarked ruefully.

'What does Manny think about all this?'

'Ask him; here come the coal carriers!'

By the middle of the week Buck was up, but not exactly raring to go, despite heavy hints from Manny. He had a proposition to put to Florence, when he could catch her on her own. In the meantime he decided to impress her with tidying up the basement rooms.

She came across him, broom in hand, disposing of cobwebs in the corners.

'Thank you, Buck! We meant to spring clean in here, but we're so busy in the shop—'

'I realized that, and I thought I could help.' He paused, then, 'I was wondering, Florence, if you could do with an extra pair of hands in that respect?'

'Could I! But the truth is, we can't afford it, Buck. We're just breaking even now!'

'Look, let me do my bit. I'm not asking you to pay me; bed and board would be enough. Doc said I shouldn't go tramping about looking for work, sleeping rough and that. Well?'

'I'd have to discuss it with Manny; we're partners in the business since we wed.'

Buck thought to himself, crafty old devil! Didn't know he had it in him.

It was her turn to hesitate then, but he was going to find out soon, if he stayed.

'I don't know if you realized, but I'm expecting a baby, Buck.'

There was a mere flicker of his eyelids. 'You can't afford *not* to have me, then.'

'Well, It does seem . . . I'll speak to Manny later. I came to say, it being early-closing day why don't you join us for lunch?'

'I'd be glad to. I mean no offence, but I look forward to a square meal after all that pap!'

'*No!*' Manny said explosively, when she told him of Buck's idea.

'You don't like him, do you? In a month or two, Manny, I'll be carrying all before me, and I won't be able to manage what I do now.'

He showed instant concern. 'I guess I'm jealous. He knew you long before I did.'

'I could never have married him! Manny, I always thought of you as a kind person.'

'I try to be. All right, Florence. Let's give him a month's trial.'

They were in the shop, clearing up. Florence pulled the blind down on the door. She gave him a quick kiss. Then she gasped. She took his hand, placed it firmly on her stomach.

'The baby, Manny, I just felt it move for the first time. . . .'

'So did I,' he said, in awe.

'There you are, then, that's the bond we have between us, and *no one* can spoil that.'

There had been months of strikes and hardship for the country's workforce. In May, negotiations finally collapsed between the coal miners and the mine owners. All the other unions came out in support and a general strike was inevitable. For nine seemingly interminable days industry was at a standstill.

Clerical workers in the Capital were not involved in the national strike, but the transport service was badly affected. The tramcar no longer ran along the route to Paradise corner and Rose Marie found herself without the means to get to work.

Many others took to the bicycle again, having not ridden one for years; some determined to walk from the suburbs. Those who normally reserved their motoring for weekends, decided to drive to work, offering lifts to colleagues. Empty lorries returning to base were flagged down and young women in stylish clothes climbed nimbly on to the tailboard of these vehicles for a twopenny ride, to cheers and waves from the army of walkers.

'Don't do anything I wouldn't do!' soon became a familiar call.

'*You're* not getting a ride on the back of a lorry!' Florence said firmly to Rose Marie.

She didn't have to: that first morning, there being no trains or buses, Elmo Turbot-Watts came to the rescue and collected Russ from his home. *En route* they stopped for Rose Marie. They also picked up some stragglers along the way and there was relieved laughter as they squeezed into the back of the van.

'Who's for a game of sardines?' asked a cheeky office boy.

'There were only three girls in the workroom,' Rose Marie reported that night to her sister. 'Mrs Belling asked me if I would mind helping out. I enjoyed myself, though there was more chat about the wedding than treadling. Anyway, orders are right down.'

'Pie sales were actually up, all those hungry hikers on their way to the city! We had to do another baking. Although the butcher warned me he doesn't know when he'll get the next delivery ot mutton.'

'The strange thing is,' Rose Marie said, 'folk are so cheerful. Whistling as their feet turn the pedals, talking to strangers, helping where they can. Mr Turbot-Watts says people rise to a challenge, like they did in the war.'

'I don't imagine the miners are whistling any tunes, poor devils,' Florence mused.

'You're with the workers then? Not management?'

'Of course I am. Mr Baldwin says the government are determined not to yield, they are urging volunteers to keep vital services going. I miss the newspapers, there's only the news printed by the political parties, and all that pontificating by them on the wireless, eh?'

After nine days the TUC capitulated and there was a general return to work by their members; however, the miners stood firm tor several more months, despite the suffering and hardship their communities were forced to endure.

Some firms had inevitably gone to the wall. Others cut down on staff. The 'whistling', as Florence predicted, abruptly ceased. The Depression was fast becoming a fact.

Lilli had been away for four months by July. Florence and Manny were partially reassured by the monthly rent which came with a brief covering note from their friend. Josefina was still in regular correspondence with Yvette, so they knew she was all right. Florence took it upon herself to write to Lilli's husband Sam to advise him of his wife's absence. He thanked her for her concern but wasn't sure what he could do, except:

If this continues much longer, I will come up to London when I can, and try to find this man Solon, who must know where she is.

'You really must stop worrying about it,' Manny told her, when he read the letter. 'I can't help thinking she's with this bloke because she wants to be. But why is she hanging on to the flat?'

'Perhaps she isn't sure that this is a permanent arrangement. Her husband actually sounds like a decent man, though he was wrong to snatch Yvette as he did. Maybe he hoped that would force Lilli to return to him, despite him insisting he didn't want to see her.'

It was a Friday evening, but Manny hadn't made his weekly visit to the pub since Buck took up residence in the basement. He wanted to be around in case Buck seized the opportunity to keep Florence company. Familiarity was certainly not to be encouraged.

Florence was nearing the end of her pregnancy. On doctor's advice she was only working in the mornings now. Manny was actually glad of Buck's help in the shop. He couldn't fault his work. Buck tackled all he was asked to do, and the customers liked him. After a month, they managed to pay him, a basic wage. Manny remained wary of his erstwhile comrade. However, Buck had Sunday lunch with them, at Florence's insistence.

'I can't seem to settle this evening,' Florence remarked presently, shifting on the sofa.

'Let me rub your back,' Manny offered. He'd noted her pale face, the occasional grimace; her evident discomfort. He loosened the ties of the kimono, which she'd changed into after supper; insinuated his hands under the straps of her nightgown to begin the gentle massage.

'Thank you, that helps,' she breathed gratefully after a while.

'I'm glad,' he said softly. 'I like our Friday evenings on our own, don't you?'

'You know I do. Though I wonder what Rose Mane is up to with Russ every weekend.'

'You can guess as well as I can . . . His mother must know, eh?'

'They'll be married soon, of course, but—'

'You sound more like her mother than her sister!' Manny teased.

Florence took a deep breath. Was this the time to tell him? 'Manny,' she began.

He looked solemn, sensing the importance of what she wanted to say.

'Manny, there is something I should have told you, before we got married.'

'Yes?' he prompted.

'There's no easy way to say it. You see, Rose Marie *is* my daughter. . . .'

'I don't understand why you couldn't trust me.'

'It's not that. I suppose I've had to live with the lie since before she was born; my father forced that on me! I was sixteen when it happened. I was ignorant of the facts of life, Manny. Rose Marie doesn't know. How can I tell her now, when she's so happy and in love?'

'Who was it?' he demanded harshly.

'It doesn't matter. I never told him. He was only a boy. We were both—'

'As green as grass? What you said to me?' He sounded more sad than reproachful.

'Yes! Yes!' She was sobbing now, clutching her swollen belly. 'Can you forgive me?'

'Can I forgive you?' he repeated. 'Dear Florence, I *love* you! How you must have suffered over this all these years . . . But I don't know how or when you can break the news to Rose Marie, that's a fact.'

Florence let him wipe her tears away with his handkerchief. Then he held her close, and rocked her in his arms.

'It was the best thing I ever did,' she whispered. 'Marrying you. Soon, I'll be able to tell the world I'm the mother of your child!'

'And I'll be so proud to hear you say that,' he said.

Lilli was already in bed when Philippe arrived back at the apartment that night. She thought, I must go through with it, I can't go on like this. If I can fool him into thinking I'm happy living with him, he may relax the rules and then, when I get the opportunity to run, I'll take it.

She hadn't been out of the flat since she arrived. The only company she had during the day from Monday to Friday was Annie, the maid. She thought wryly, *my jailor*. She was not even permitted to open the window. As if she could escape that way - it was a sheer drop.

Lilli found the relationship between Annie and Philippe intriguing. Annie may have worn a neat black dress and white apron, but she also wore sheer silk stockings and her hair was startlingly blonde and expensively Marcel-waved. Annie had purchased Lilli's new clothes; they were stylish and the lingerie was exquisite - *seductive*, she thought, wondering if this was Annie's choice, or her employer's. Annie, Lilli thought, does not like me. Maybe she's jealous. She obviously feels passionately about the man she calls Mr Brown. . . .

In the beginning, Lilli had thought of writing to Sam, explaining her dilemma and appealing for his help. Then she realized she didn't even know the address of this place, and, anyway, how could she trust Annie to post a letter? She would likely pass it to Philippe. She tried not to think about Yvette. Surely her little girl must feel she had rejected her?

She always left her bedside lamp on low so that Philippe could pass quietly through to the bathroom before retiring. She feigned sleep, but was vibrantly aware of his presence when he paused by the bed and looked down at her, before wishing her a good night. That was all.

This evening they had dined together, but, as usual, he had excused himself after the meal. What was this mysterious business he had to attend to, she wondered?

Now, as he entered the room, she consciously forced herself to relax, to stretch her arms as if suddenly awakening, then opened her eyes as he stopped by the bed.

He said merely, 'I apologize if I disturbed you, Lilli. Go back to sleep. It is late.'

Instead, she sat up, pushing back the covers. She was clad in the most sensuous of her nightgowns, a Parisian affair in bias-cut oyster satin which left nothing to the imagination. Surely he must note the agitated rise and fall of her bosom, she thought.

'I'm not tired any more; I just sleep a lot because I'm bored,' she stated. 'I eat too much for the same reason, I must have put on weight.' She was well aware it suited her.

'It is my fault, I admit it, that you feel like that. But, what can I do?'

'Talk to me. You owe me that, Philippe. How much longer must I be here?'

'I cannot say. Have you thought, Lilli, very hard about the reason for this? There must be an answer, if not an obvious one. You possess something which, if you give it up, will ensure you can return to a normal life.'

'I've told you all along, I have absolutely no idea what these people want from me,' she asserted defiantly.

His hands were warm as they steadied her own gesturing hands. Very gently, he began to stroke her arms with an upward motion until he reached her shaking shoulders.

'Lie down,' he said soothingly. 'You are trembling.'

'I'm frightened. You see, I thought,' she whispered, as he eased her down in the bed, 'I would try to. . . .'

'Seduce me?' he sounded amused. 'Would you prefer the alternative?' He reached out, clicked off the light. 'I won't be long. There is no need for pretence in the dark.'

When he touched me, Lilli thought, I knew he desired me, as I do him. . . .

Seventeen

FLORENCE and Rose Marie were having a heart-to-heart discussion late on Sunday evening. Manny wisely left them to it, and went to bed.

'Had a good weekend at the Short's?' Florence asked casually.

'His mother keeps on about the wedding . . .' Rose Marie sounded rather disgruntled.

'Well, it's only natural. She's excited; we all are.'

'I thought it was the *bride's* mother who fussed about clothes and wedding cake.'

'The cake is sitting snugly in the tin; I'll ice it after the baby arrives when I'm more myself.'

'I'm very pleased for you, you know I am, because you'll be a *real* mother at last, and you've certainly had plenty of experience in that role with Stella, me and Josefina, but I'm not at all sure I want a baby myself,' said Rose Marie thoughtfully.

'You may change your mind. Meanwhile, make the most of being just the two of you.'

'Oh, we are! Dear Florence, you won't have the embarrassment of telling me what's what before the wedding, will you?'

'You know it all, do you?' Florence said wryly.

'I don't suppose *you* did! Was it rather a shock? Sorry! I shouldn't have asked that.'

Florence looked ruefully at her baby bulge. 'As you can see, I found out. Actually . . .' She hesitated, gathering courage. 'I was impulsive myself at your age. . . .'

Rose Marie exclaimed, 'Whatever do you mean?'

'It's time I told you. It's been on my mind, with the wedding coming up, and arrangements to make: you'll need your birth certificate—'

'I'm aware of that! You're not trying to tell me I'm adopted, are you? Why, everyone says how much I look like you!'

Florence took a deep breath. There was that niggling, fleeting pain again, she thought.

'That's always been a comfort to me. You see, I was only allowed to keep you, on promising my father not to tell anyone I had given birth to you.'

There was a long silence. Florence could see the disbelief on Rose Marie's face.

'How *could* you!' she said at last.

'It was the only thing I could do. I was just seventeen, younger than you are now, still an innocent child really, my father had seen to that.'

'The man concerned took advantage of you?' Rose Marie demanded.

Florence shook her head, putting out a tentative hand, only to be rebuffed.

'Tell me!'

'He was a few months older than me. I suppose I was looking to fall in love, and so was he. My father and stepmother had gone to a temperance meeting at the Tabernacle. Stella was in bed. He was keeping me company. We sneaked into my parent's room, and one thing led to another. We couldn't stop ourselves. My father caught us together and the lad was lucky to escape with just a thrashing. My stepmother was kind; she stuck up for me, despite him railing at her. I was never able to tell my . . . friend, about the baby, about *you*, Rose Marie.'

'Were you in love with him?'

'I thought I was. It was nothing like I feel for dear Manny now. Can you forgive me?'

'I wish you had told me years ago, so I could get used to the idea!'

'I wish that, too. . . .'

'Well, I'm going to bed, it's all too much to take in tonight.'

Even as Rose Marie rose and made to leave Florence without the usual affectionate kiss on her cheek, Florence cried out. There was a spreading damp patch on her nightgown.

'Quick! Call Manny, I think my waters have gone! The baby's on its way.'

Rose Marie ran out of the room, shouting for Manny. He appeared in his pyjamas. 'Whatever is it?'

'Florence!' She was sobbing bitterly now. 'She told me I was her daughter, then I was mad at her and she suddenly screamed. She's in labour Manny, and it's all my fault!'

He gripped her arm, turned her round. 'Stop it! You'll have to help me. She loves you Rose Marie,' he added reproachfully.

'I know, of course I do! I'm so sorry. . . .'

Florence had prepared herself for a long drawn-out labour, which had been her lot last time. However, the new baby was obviously in a great hurry. The pains intensified rapidly and Manny tried not to panic. Rose Marie pulled herself together, rang for the doctor. He would have to cycle from his home, further out than the surgery.

The doctor's calm voice told her what to do. 'Protect the bed with newspapers or brown paper, if you have it. Boil plenty of water. Plait a length of torn sheeting, tie to the bedpost and allow your sister to pull hard on it when the time comes.'

'How will I know when that is?' Rose Marie cried.

'Mrs Manning will tell you. Reassure her, rub her back, sponge her face. I will be as quick as I can. Ask her husband to unlock the front door, turn on the light in the hall.'

Manny heard the knock on the door as he shot back the bolts. Surely it couldn't be the doctor already? Buck stood there.

'What's up? All the lights blazing! Is it Florence? Can I help?'

'Doc's on his way. Go back to bed. You'll have to look after the shop tomorrow.'

'What about the pies?'

'Who cares about the bloody pies?' Manny yelled uncharacteristically.

'Good luck then.' Buck took the hint, retreated down the basement steps.

The little white cat nipped indoors ahead of him. Blanche had declined to move upstairs with Manny and despite Buck's indifference to her, she'd attached herself to him.

He was about to turn her out into the yard when she began weaving in and out of his legs, purring. Buck actually bent over and stroked her.

159

'All right, I give in. Reckon you're the only real pal I've got, despite your silly name.'

Rose Marie fashioned a rough plait, having ripped up a good sheet in her desperation. She fastened it above Florence's head and positioned her hands firmly round the rope end.

'Pull when you want to, Florence!'

'Doc's here!' Manny rushed to the kitchen door to let him in.

He stood there, divesting himself of his jacket, rolling up his shirt sleeves, requesting a clean apron. He opened the black bag and put it ready on the bedside table. He motioned to Rose Marie to move aside, so that he could examine Florence.

'I need a bowl of hot water and soap, to wash my hands. Can you fetch that for me?'

Rose Marie went out thankfully, but Manny hovered uncertainly by the open door. The next moment, the doctor was bending over his patient, encouraging her to pull on the rope, and the baby literally shot into the world, into the doctor's hands.

Rose Marie had to step over Manny who had keeled over from the shock and was slumped in the doorway. She stood there, slopping the bowl of water, staring incredulously as the tiny infant was slapped, bawling indignantly, into life, then given to Florence to hold.

'It's a boy, Rose Marie, what we hoped for. . . .' she said faintly.

The doctor hauled Manny to his feet, led him to the bed.

'It's a boy,' Florence repeated.

'What are we going to call him?' Manny was still swaying slightly.

'We did mention Flinders, or is that too solemn?'

'Flinders,' he considered for a moment. 'How about Flynn, my mother's maiden name?'

'Flynn, yes, that sounds right. What d'you think Rose Marie?' Florence asked.

However, Rose Marie had set down the bowl and gone away.

'Better make the tea,' the doctor advised Manny. 'It's time to eliminate the placenta, and as you appear to be squeamish . . . please tell your sister-in-law I can do with her help.'

Manny hadn't the faintest idea what the placenta might be, but he went off obediently.

The baby was washed by the time Manny returned, having taken his time, and Rose Marie was carefully dressing him in one of the loose flannel gowns Florence had sewed so painstakingly. Florence too had been made comfortable, she was reclining against plumped-up pillows in the bed.

'I must leave you,' the doctor said, drinking his tea in one long draught. 'But I will return to make sure all is well, before morning surgery. On my way home I will put a note through the nurse's door to ask her to come at seven. You had booked her, as I suggested, for the laying-in?'

'Yes doctor.' Florence's voice sounded husky. She held out her arms for the baby. 'I made the crib up today. I must have tempted fate! He's rather small, are you sure—?'

'He's slightly premature, but nothing to worry about. Well done, my dear!'

'Thank you, doctor, for everything,' she told him.

'I'll see you out,' Rose Marie said quickly. 'Then I must get to bed. Work tomorrow! Sleep well, Florence.'

'I believe I will! Thank you for your support, Rose Marie, it means a lot to me.'

After they left, Manny placed the baby carefully in the crib alongside the bed.

'He's asleep,' he whispered.

'He won't wake up properly for a day or two, as I recall.' She smiled ruefully. 'But then we'll really know he's here! Manny, come to bed, you must be exhausted.'

'Not as much as you are!' He left the light low, settled himself thankfully beside her. 'You can kiss me, you know. . . . You'll have to be up and about before the nurse comes.'

'I realized that. Also that I must put a sign up on the shop door - CLOSED DUE TO UNFORESEEN CIRCUMSTANCES.'

'Only for one day, Manny, then you'll have to get Buck to help with the pie-making!'

Florence thought, *Buck*. He must never know that he fathered Rose Marie, nor must Manny. I mustn't tell her either. She'll need time to get over knowing I'm her mother. . . .

The nurse, plump and comfortable, was already in charge of mother and baby, when Rose Marie emerged from her bedroom, carrying a suitcase. She'd waited until she heard Manny go into the bathroom, and she wanted to leave without creating a scene. She placed a letter addressed to Florence on the table. She'd written in pencil, at dawn:

Dearest Florence,
You will feel I am deserting you just when you need me, but I can't help it. I feel so mixed up inside. I must get away.
    I will stay with Stella. I will telephone her first, after work.
    Don't say anything if you speak to her earlier, will you?
    You must believe me when I say I love you still, and that I am glad your baby has arrived safely.
    Please don't upset yourself about all this; it will not be good for you.
    You and Manny are a family now, and I need to go my own way. Grow up quickly, I suppose!
    Take care, dear Florence, and thank you for keeping me as you did, that means a lot to me.
    Your affectionate Rose Marie.

Manny didn't hear the door close behind her. He crossed to the kitchen window and looked out. She was standing with two others, waiting for the tram. He saw the case at her side, on the pavement. It must be too heavy to hold for long, and he could surmise why.

He turned, saw the letter. Despite seeing that it was addressed to Florence and not to both of them, he opened it with shaking hands. This was completely out of character. He read it through several times as if mesmerized, unsure what to do with it.

The nurse came through into the kitchen. 'Oh, Mr Manning,' she enquired. 'Is there any chance of a light breakfast and a large cup of tea for your wife?'

Manny pushed the letter behind the clock on the mantlepiece, with a couple of bills.

'I'll make something shortly,' he said. 'Is everything as it should be?'

The nurse smiled. 'Your wife is already worrying about how you will manage without her! I told her very firmly to stay

162

where she was; she has to rest while she establishes the breast feeding. Premature babies need a bit of coaxing, of course.'

'We had thought of asking old Nan to come in daily to help with the chores, but we hadn't got around to it,' said Manny, looking embarrassed at the mention of breast feeding.

'That is an excellent idea. I shall, of course, deal with the baby's laundry myself.'

Fifteen minutes later, Manny carried the breakfast tray to Florence. She sat up in bed with a bemused expression on her face. She looked young and rather vulnerable this morning.

'I'll get the baby bathed while you eat in peace, and talk to your husband.' Nurse scooped the baby up in her capable arms and departed with a crackling of starched apron.

Manny placed the tray carefully on Florence's knees. 'Soft-boiled egg, I tapped the top, and fingers of bread and butter, like you used to do for Josefina - remember?'

'Of course I do! I still miss her, but now we've got our little boy, we're a family again!'

'Florence, I've got something to tell you; you're not to upset yourself,' he began.

Instantly, she showed alarm. 'What is it?'

'Rose Marie - she's decided it's best if she stays with Stella for a bit.'

'Why?' Florence put down her apostle spoon beside the eggcup.

'Well,' he invented. 'She can't do much to help, having to go out to work all day, and she seems to think it will be nice for us to be on our own, with the baby.'

'Hardly that,' she pointed out. 'Nurse'll be here for a fortnight. Not at nights, I know, but . . . there must be more to it than that. She's still upset, I reckon.'

Manny felt guilty as he thought of the letter behind the clock. 'She'll get over it.'

'You're right. Perhaps it's for the best,' she said unconvincingly. 'I suppose I'd better eat up. I need my nourishment. The baby will need feeding after his bath. It means a lot to me, Manny, you know, to be able to nurse him myself. The first time, well, I had to get back to work, making pies and that. My milk dried up.'

163

'You'll have all the time you need to look after Flynn, I'm going to make sure of that. It's only natural and right. I can see to the pies and the shop; Buck can work full-time. And I'm asking old Nan to come in daily, to do the chores - under your supervision, of course!'

'You're in charge, that's obvious,' she said, and her smile showed she didn't mind at all.

Manny pinned the notice to the shop front. He'd already told Buck he'd got the day off, and about the baby's unexpected arrival. He wondered if Buck had seen Rose Marie depart with her case, but he didn't say.

He didn't know why he hadn't realized it before: the only young man Florence would have known at the time Rose Marie was conceived was Buck, her father's assistant in the pie shop. All the facts pointed to that. Maybe it was just as well Rose Marie had left here, before any probing began. Like Florence said, it was time to forgive and forget what happened in the past. He must never reproach her, and he was determined he would never enlighten Buck.

Eighteen

'ARE you feeling unwell, Rose Marie?' Mrs Belling asked. She'd just popped into the small work room with a ball gown which the owner had decided needed to be re-fashioned. 'No hurry for this,' she added. 'Normally, I would have suggested the client look at our new range, but we're all penny-pinching these days, it seems.'

Rose Marie looked washed-out. She'd missed out on breakfast, but she didn't feel like eating. Her mind was still in a turmoil after yesterday's events.

'My sister had her baby last night. I was wondering,' she began hesitantly.

Mrs Belling had her informant in the showroom. She already knew that Rose Marie had arrived this morning carrying a suitcase. Her protegée had been unsettled ever since she decided to get married this Autumn. She sighed. Rose Marie had seemed to have a good career ahead of her, but ... she hoped the girl wasn't pregnant.

'Take the day off, my dear. Tomorrow, too, if you need to. Your sister will be glad of your help, I'm sure.'

'I'm going to stay with my other sister for a while,' Rose Marie floundered. Did that sound heartless, leaving Florence in the lurch?

'Ah, too much going on at home?' Mrs Belling suggested tactfully. 'You obviously need a rest from the domestic scene, and work is slow, so off you go.'

Twenty minutes later, Rose Marie was on a bus to Bayswater, to the roomy terraced house in a pleasant area near one of the many public gardens.

When Stella opened the door to her, still in her housecoat although it was gone half past nine, her eyes widened in surprise.

'Rose Marie! What on earth—?'

'You haven't heard from Manny then?'

'Come in! I'm afraid I haven't tidied up yet. Did you know that Jose is back with us? He took Josefina to school this morning, then he had shopping to do for me; I'm determined he pulls his weight here until he finds a job! Manny - why on earth would he telephone me?'

'Florence had her baby last night. It's a boy,' Rose Marie said.

'Oh, that's good news, isn't it? I didn't know it was expected yet.'

'It - he wasn't.' Her face crumpled. 'Oh, Stella, I feel it's my fault. I upset Florence, you see, but it was such a shock when she told me. . . .'

'Told you what? Sit down do. I'll put the kettle on. It appears you've come to stay?'

'If you'll have me!' Rose Marie was crying now in relief.

'Of course I will. Tea first, then let's get the explanations over, before Jose returns.'

'Now,' Stella said, lighting her first cigarette of the day. Jose had encouraged her to take up the habit again, although she knew it was bad for her voice. 'I'm listening, Rose Marie.'

'Can I ask *you* a few questions first? It's important.' At Stella's nod, she continued. 'Do you remember your mother?'

'*Our* mother, surely! Yes, of course I do. I was about Josefina's age, when she died.'

'Do you remember me being born?'

Stella hesitated. 'Well, Father was very Victorian - children weren't told about such things, they just had to accept them after they'd happened. I imagine I was kept out of the way until after the event. In fact, I believe I was sent to stay with an old aunt for a couple of weeks. When I came home, Mother showed me this little baby in a crib, and said it was my new sister. I was very put out! Florence sat me down and talked me round.'

'Did she have much to do with the baby?'

'Not then, she had Mother's shop chores to do as well as her own. But after Mother died unexpectedly, well, Florence had to look after you and me, as well as make the pies, though Father employed a woman to help in the house and in the shop. After we lost Father, Florence was struggling to cope with it all, until Manny came.'

'Stella, this is going to come as a shock to you, too. Florence is my *real* mother. Father, as you refer to him, although he was your step-father, was actually my *grandfather*.' Rose Marie was surprisingly calm as she stated this; it was Stella who dissolved into tears.

'How *could* they think they were doing the right thing? What a mess!'

'We'll never know now. A lot to do with Father's pride, I suppose.' They both heard the key turning in the front door lock. 'Jose's back! Please, Stella, keep this to yourself, won't you? It's really just between Florence and me, after all, but maybe Manny knows. . . .'

'I must ring them. Congratulate them on the birth of the baby. Has he a name?'

'Flynn, Manny's choice, I think.'

'I like it, don't you? Just one more thing: what about Russ? Won't you have to tell him?'

'I'm going to call the wedding off,' Rose Marie said flatly.

'Hello, anyone at home?' Jose called out from the hall.

'In here,' Stella answered. 'A nice surprise - Rose Marie's got a few days off; she's come to stay with us. Unload the shopping, then you can take her case upstairs to Josefina's room.'

Jose was obviously delighted to have his pretty young sister-in-law around. Rose Marie, aware of Stella's reaction to his flirting, realized that she couldn't stay there too long. She excused herself after lunch saying she needed a nap, after a wakeful night.

'I'll make sure you're not disturbed,' Stella said, tight-lipped. 'Take the spare bed by the window, Josefina sleeps on the one near the door. She'll be back from school soon after four.'

Rose Marie took off her shoes and lay down on the single bed. Although she was so tired, her mind was in too much of a turmoil for her to immediately succumb to sleep.

How can I tell Russ? she thought. Do I have to? Can't I just say I've changed my mind? He'll be terribly hurt of course, but it's all so complicated. Another difficult letter to write. . . . She fell into an uneasy sleep.

She woke with a start, wondering where she was. Josefina looked down at her, smiling, displaying new gaps in her teeth. She was holding Yvette's French doll.

'Oh, Rose Marie, we're together again! I've missed you so much!'

'Come here,' Rose Marie held out her arms. 'Not half as much as I missed you!'

Later she said, 'Did Mummy tell you about Florence and Manny's little baby?'

'Yes! It's very exciting. We're going over to see them on Saturday. I can hardly wait! Does that mean he's my cousin? I get all mixed up with our family, sometimes!'

'So do I . . . Look, you go downstairs and have your tea. I've a letter to write. You can show me where the postbox is, can't you?'

' 'Course I can! See you in a while, then, Rose Marie.'

Rose Marie unlocked her case, located her writing pad, envelopes and a stamp.

Dear Russ,

I don't know how to tell you this, but I must. Please believe me when I say it is not in any way your fault, but I cannot marry you in September. Forgive me for not giving you the explanation you deserve. It is too painful for me to do so. I am staying with Stella for a while, but it will not be a permanent arrangement.

I am devastated to let you down. There is no one else involved – *I love you*, that hasn't changed – but I pray you will meet the right girl in the future.

Please tell your mother and Sadie that I will miss them, too. I will, of course, return your ring. Please, I know I should do it myself but I can't! Will you let the vicar know the wedding will not now take place.

My darling, don't think too badly of me.

Your broken-hearted Rose Marie.

'Russell, there's a customer waiting,' Mr Turbot-Watts

reminded him. 'What on earth is wrong with you today? That's the second time I've had to tell you. You know I'm busy.' He was sorting out his shelves of classic books.

Russ had a dazed look on his face. He went obediently to enquire what it was the customer required. 'Yes sir, I believe I can locate a copy for you. Why not have a browse round the shop meanwhile. . . .' The words came automatically.

His employer had overheard. With a sigh, he abandoned his task and came over to whisper discreetly in Russ's ear, 'I know where to put my hands on it. Get busy with dusting the books on that chair, for me, will you?'

Rose Marie's letter, which had arrived by the early post back home, was in Russ's inside jacket pocket. He didn't need to take it out and read it again to know what it said. Like Rose Marie so recently, he was in a state of shock and disbelief.

'Now,' Elmo, as Russ had recently been invited to call him, said, as they closed the shop for their half-hour lunch break. 'Feel like confiding in me, old boy? I don't know much about affairs of the heart, that's true, but I'm told I'm a good listener. I promise not to give advice unless you ask for it.'

'Rose Marie has called the wedding off. I received a letter this morning. I couldn't bring myself to tell my mother.'

'That's understandable. But, naturally, you must, as soon as possible.' He cleared his throat, took a swig of tea, but left his favourite sandwich, sliced liver sausage on rye bread, untouched on the plate. 'Is that unwanted advice? If so, I apologize.'

'No, you're right. I'll tell her tonight. Rose Marie asks me to contact the vicar at St Mary's, too. We have an appointment with him this Thursday evening, you see.'

'Feel like telling me why this has come about? Lover's quarrel?'

Russ shook his head vehemently. 'No! We spent the weekend together at my home. She did tell me privately that she was rather fed-up with all the wedding talk - my mother does keep on about it, I'm afraid. My sympathies were with Rose Marie. I told her so.'

'Where is your fiancée? At the dress shop today?'

'She is staying with her sister Stella in Bayswater. She is obviously not at work.'

'Take the afternoon off, if you wish to visit, talk to her.' Elmo's bald pate glistened with his concern. 'Don't do it on an empty stomach. Eat your lunch, my boy.'

After Russ had gone, Elmo decided, on impulse, to shut the shop for the afternoon. His other assistant, if he could be termed that nowadays, had not turned up for work this week. He thought he would call at Jacob's room nearby and enquire after his health. He said to himself, 'I suppose I worry more about my staff than most employers, because I have no immediate family. I care about my young assistant as if he was a favourite nephew, and I'm touched he looks up to me. But then, he has no father to talk to. . . .'

The news was not good regarding Jacob. His landlady had sent for the doctor.

'Poor old chap, he set off for work yesterday as usual, then come back and said he'd lost his way. Now he don't seem to know at all where he is. I suppose this means the infirmary. I can't see him at the shop no more.'

Elmo took out his round leather purse, handed her a gold coin. 'Look after him, won't you? Let me know if you need more.'

'Thank you, sir. I'll keep you informed,' she said.

Walking back, idly looking at the competition from the other book shops, Elmo mused, Jacob's not the only one who's lost his way. Russ will be devastated if Rose Marie has really changed her mind.

'I'm so sorry, Russ,' Stella said helplessly, keeping him standing on the doorstep. 'She won't see you. She's shut herself away upstairs.'

'Can't Florence do something, find out what's wrong?' he appealed.

'Oh, I see you don't know! Florence had her baby on Sunday night. She mustn't be upset, at the moment. In a week or two, well, maybe she can help. What about your mother?'

'I haven't had a chance to tell her yet.'

'Look, why don't you go home now and do just that? I'm afraid I'll have to go, I have a pupil waiting for my attention.' As

170

he turned to leave, Stella repeated, 'I'm so sorry Russ, so very sorry.' She hesitated, then added, 'Don't do anything *silly*.'

'Don't do anything silly,' was said by the nurse to Florence, as she went off duty before lunch. 'However, I can tell you intend to get out of bed the minute I close the door. Nan, I expect you to see she sits in her chair; does nothing except look after the baby. I'll be back later on.'

'I'll do me best,' Nan agreed. Manny was in the shop, and Nan had chicken soup bubbling gently on the stove. Nurse had insisted on a light but nourishing diet for her nursing mother. Just as well, Nan thought, tucking a stray wisp of hair beneath her mob cap, I brought my lot up on soup, lots of it, made from cheap odds and ends.

Nurse was right. Florence appeared, still a trifle unsteady on her feet so she sank gratefully into the chair Nan hastily pulled forward.

'You've done a good job in here Nan, thank you,' she observed. 'Soup smells good. I hope I get time to enjoy it before the boy wakes up.' She hadn't got quite used to calling him Flynn yet. It seemed a bit old for a baby, she thought.

Nan handed a little sheaf of papers. 'Found these behind the clock when I dusted. Guess Manny stuffed 'em there and forgot 'em, eh? I didn't read 'em,' she added ingenuously. ' 'Cause I can't read, you see.'

'Bills!' Florence sighed. 'Manny can deal with those. What's this, I wonder?'

She read Rose Marie's letter in silence. Why hadn't Manny given it to her? She knew the answer, of course. He didn't want to upset me, not now, she thought. She tucked the letter in her pocket.

There was a wail from the bedroom.

'His lordship,' Nan said, eager to lift him out of the crib for a quick cuddle before she passed him on to his mother.

Calm down, Florence told herself sternly. She's had time to think about the situation. Russ and Stella between them, they'll talk her round.

Nineteen

'NICE day,' Annie observed, sounding quite friendly for once. Lilli, toying with her breakfast at the table, looked up in surprise. Annie had just arrived.

'How would I know? I haven't been outside for so long,' she returned.

Annie replenished Lilli's coffee, poured a cup for herself, and to Lilli's surprise, sat down.

'Didn't you realize Mr Brown's not here? He's gone on one of his assignments, as he calls 'em.' Annie actually smiled at Lilli.

'No, he's often not here when I get up.' Lilli was wary of this friendly approach.

'Don't you ever wonder why you sleep so sound? About that nightcap he makes you?'

What a fool I've been, Lilli thought; *of course*. She said faintly, 'No, surely not?'

'You're not a woman of the world, that's obvious. Been playing you along, has he?'

'What d'you mean?'

'I mean, letting you think he *will*, when he *won't*. Teasing you, like.'

'*Pardon*?' Lilli pronounced with a gallic intonation.

'Look, he's like a cat with a mouse. He keeps you between his paws and when you let him know you're ready to give in, he get's bored with the game, and goes off. That's what he's done today. Left me a note with the doorman. 'Carry on as normal,' it said.'

Lilli set down her cup in the saucer, making it rattle. 'You've got the key - let me out!'

'I'm sorry, I really am, 'cause I know you must miss your little girl - he told me that much - but I daren't. Well, must get on. Finished? I'll clear the table.'

Lilli retreated to the bathroom. She was shaking. A quick wash. I must get dressed, she thought. I have to find a way of getting Annie on my side. This is my chance. . . .

She riffled through the expensive garments in the wardrobe. How could he think they would compensate for what she'd lost: her child; yes, her husband, too; her freedom; her friends in Paradise buildings; even her job at the Golden Domes - sheer hard graft maybe, but she'd earned every penny, and her efforts had been appreciated. Philippe had led her on all right, trapped her and finally humiliated her, as he had the other night.

She'd actually been prepared to allow him to make love to her, but he'd walked away from her with a mocking, 'Goodnight, Lilli.' She'd felt so ashamed, yet relieved.

Thank goodness he did reject me, she thought now, as she found what she'd been looking for, her plain office dress. It smelled faintly of dry-cleaning fluid, but it was her own.

When she emerged from the bedroom, she was aware that Annie approved.

'That's the first step,' she said. 'But you mustn't think I'll unlock the door. I'm a prisoner, you see, in my own way. He's got a hold on me, too.'

There was a lull in the pie shop. Manny decided to pop upstairs to the flat to see how his wife and son were doing. He left Buck in charge. The usual diners had been and gone, but there was the likelihood of customers when the next tramcar stopped outside.

Buck put a fresh tray of mutton pies in the oven just in case and checked the mushy peas. The doorbell clanged, and a woman stepped inside. A new face, Buck thought, as she chose a seat. She called over, 'Menu, please!'

He came out from behind the counter and pointed out the blackboard on the wall.

'Pie, peas and mash 6d; mug of tea 2d. Bread and butter 1d. All right?'

'All right,' she agreed with a smile. 'Though I prefer my tea in a cup.'

'Right you are,' he said. 'Won't be long.'

She moved the condiments aside when he returned with a loaded tray. He noted the bright golden hair, the saucy little hat tilted to one side. When she looked up to thank him, he saw that her eyes were wide and china blue; her mouth a startling scarlet. He thought, she'll leave her mark on the cup. She ain't so young close up, neither.

'Won't you join me?' she asked.

He was taken completely by surprise. 'Oh, I don't think—'

'Why not? Trade's slack ain't it? My treat. Or have you had your meal already?'

Bold as brass, like her hair, he thought, impressed. 'Er, no,' he admitted.

He fetched a mug of tea, a plate of bread and butter. He still had to watch his diet. Mash would have done, but he'd served her with the last of that.

'Turn the sign to closed for ten minutes,' she encouraged him, scooping up the peas on the back of her fork. He sat down, watching the door nervously.

After they'd eaten, the woman lit a cigarette. He declined when she offered him one.

'Better not. My boss wouldn't approve.'

'Expect you guessed there's more to it, than an invitation to lunch?'

'We-ell. . . .'

'I have news of your friend Lilli. Interested?'

'You ought to be talking to my employers. But it ain't a good time. Missus has just had a baby. They know her more'n I do.'

'You can pass it on, eh?'

'I've seen you before,' he remembered suddenly. 'You came here with a note from her.'

'That's so. She's in a spot of trouble . . . I'm sorry, I don't know your name.'

'Buck. That'll do. And you are?'

'Annie. That'll do, too. Here's her boss's address. That's where she is. She ain't allowed letters or visitors, so don't send the Law. She'll swear she's there voluntary, 'cause otherwise, it'll lead to trouble for her family, understand?' She handed him a piece of folded paper.

Buck nodded. 'Then what use is this bit of paper to anyone?'

174

A rapping on the door. He saw Manny's frowning face looking at him through the window.

'Must open up!' he told her. Customers were alighting from the tram outside.

'Well, I'm off. I can't leave Lilli on her own too long. You do what you think is best.' She placed a shilling on the table. 'Keep the change!' she grinned, there being none.

Then she ran past Manny, to catch the tram.

Manny didn't get a chance to remonstrate with Buck until after the shop had emptied.

'What was that all about, Buck? I trust you to look after the shop, and—'

'Here!' Buck said shortly. 'The woman had something to impart, like, in private.'

Manny looked at the scribbled address on the scrap of paper. 'What's this?'

'It's where Lilli is being kept against her will. Didn't you recognize the woman?'

Manny shook his head, obviously disbelieving.

'She's the one what brought the letters and the rent for Lilli's flat.'

'I never saw her; Florence dealt with that. Against Lilli's will, you say?'

'Yes. You'd better get back to your wife with that. Do nothing until I can tell you what I know, later. Don't worry, I'll keep the shop open!' Buck experienced a sudden pain in his gut. Even bread, he thought, is no good to me when something happens to tax me.

Florence was resting on her bed, nursing the baby. Nan had finished her work for the day but Nurse would be back to carry out her evening duties.

'What's up?' she greeted him. She was glad that Manny was no longer bashful, when he came upon her like this. He was proving a caring father as well as a good husband. A little smile curled her lips. He just needed that bit of encouragement, she thought.

He sat down beside her, gently stroked the baby's downy head against her breast.

175

'He looks as if he's asleep, Florence,' he observed fondly.

'Concentrating on the job in hand, my dear. Well, tell me, eh?'

He placed the paper Buck had given him, on the bedside table.

'You can look at this, when the baby's finished. It's where Lilli is staying. A woman came in the shop and spoke of her, gave Buck that. He says he'll explain later. She's been kept against her wishes, I do know that.'

Florence jerked and young Flynn gave a protesting yell. She positioned him against her shoulder and began rubbing his back. 'Get that old wind up, my boy ... that's better! I *knew* something was wrong, despite the letters. They were too formal; it was her writing, but it didn't *sound* like her. I said that to you, didn't I? What are we going to do about it?'

'You're going to do nothing personally, but you can tell *me* what to do. Hear Buck out first, Florence. Shall I lay the baby down? Then I must get back to the shop.'

After he had tucked the baby in the crib, he bent over Florence to kiss her.

'What's that for, in the middle of the day?' she joked.

'To say I'm real happy, having you - and him. . . .'

'Manny, I feel exactly the same. But—'

'What?' he prompted.

'You shouldn't have kept Rose Marie's letter from me you know. Nan found it yesterday.'

'I didn't want you to be upset. I was waiting for you to get your strength back.'

'She's my daughter - yes, I can say it now! - and she needs me, that's obvious. Poor girl's all mixed up. I hope Stella can deal with it. I'll write to Rose Marie that's all I can manage at the moment. D'you think that will help?' she appealed to Manny.

He kissed her again. 'Yes, I'm sure it would. Have your nap first,' he advised.

It was the first time Buck had seen the baby. He stood there awkwardly in the kitchen, all scrubbed up after work, while Florence rested in her chair by the stove and rocked the baby's cradle from time to time. Nurse was folding the damp clean nappies and hanging them on the airer. She was obviously not going anywhere.

'What d'you think of him?' Florence asked.

Buck couldn't see much of Flynn, being a few feet away. 'Nice,' he said dutifully.

Florence glanced at Nurse. 'Could you keep an eye on the baby for a few minutes, please? A business matter, best if we discuss it in the other room I think.'

Nurse looked meaningfully at Florence's attire: flowing night-dress, gown and slippers.

Florence took the hint. 'When Mr Manning comes in, you can tell him to join us.' Buck followed her into the sitting-room.

'She's kind, but likes a gossip, I'm afraid. Now, Buck, I gather you had a visitor, who gave you Lilli's address. Manny believes she's being held there without her consent. That Mr Solon, I presume.' She swayed almost imperceptibly, sank down on the sofa. 'Take a seat, Buck.'

'Annie, that's her name, said he was Lilli's boss. You all right, Florence? You've gone very white,' he said.

'Don't worry about me, early days yet, as Nurse keeps saying. Tell me the rest.'

When he'd finished, she assured him, 'We won't do anything in a hurry.'

Manny heard her say this as he entered the room. 'Best if we send the information on to Lilli's husband,' he suggested. 'He's still responsible for her, after all.'

Another difficult letter to write, Florence thought. 'You leave it with us, Buck,' she said.

When Annie arrived back, to her consternation, she found that Philippe had returned.

'Where have you been?' he demanded.

She thought quickly. 'Ain't I allowed time off to visit me poor old Gran? She's nearly ninety and she can't get out, so I do her shopping for her, when I can.'

Lilli must be in the bedroom, she surmised. Had anything been said? Lucky she hadn't let on where she was going. He had a subtle way of extracting information. Never violent, that was something.

'I had a job for you to do. Too late now, you can carry it out tomorrow morning. Go and find out why Lilli won't speak to me. She's crying her eyes out in there.'

'I shouldn't have gone out like I did. She don't like being on her own, and you'd told me you were going away.'

'So you thought, because I allow you to come and go, you'd neglect your duties?'

She bit back a retort. It wouldn't be wise to alienate him now, she thought.

Annie closed the bedroom door behind her. Lilli was lying on the bed, coverlet askew, red-eyed but no longer weeping.

Annie said softly, 'What's up?'

'He hadn't gone away at all. It was a trick, to see what I might try, I think. I said I didn't know where you'd gone.' Lilli whispered.

'I went to me Gran's,' Annie said, just in case he was eavesdropping. 'That's all.'

'Philippe made me write another letter to my friend, to say I want my things. To pack them up for you to collect. Not clothes, my personal possessions. I've very few of those.'

'That's good, you'll be glad to have your bits and pieces,' Annie said in her normal voice. 'I'll expect I'll fetch 'em for you tomorrow. Come on out now, and I'll make us all a nice cup of tea, and there's some of that coffee cake from yesterday. You like that, eh?'

'I want a word with you, Mr Manning,' Nurse said firmly. She'd persuaded a weary Florence back to bed, pointed out the commode in the corner, and told her she was not even to walk to the bathroom. 'Your wife's exhausted. She wanted to write some letters, but I said no. Sleep and plenty of it is what she needs, or her milk will go. You've got a hungry baby there. Will you make sure she stays where she is for a couple of days?'

'Of course I will.' Manny was worried. 'You ought to get home now, Nurse, to your family. I'll take Florence her supper on a tray.'

He made up his mind there and then: he'd tell Florence that he would deal with it all. He'd phone Stella later and insist that Rose Marie speak to him. Then he'd write to Lilli's Sam.

Florence has been so independent all these years, he said to himself, but she's got to learn to share all these responsibilities now.

Stella had a great deal to say. Manny had a job to take it all in. Despite his bewilderment, he realized she was trying to tell him that Rose Marie had left. She hadn't given any indication that she was going, until after Josefina had gone to school. Then she came downstairs with her case packed and asked if she could ring for a taxi.

'I said,' Stella gabbled. 'Where are you going? What about your job?And have you enough money?' She told me she was giving notice at Belling's, that money was no problem because she had been saving the money Florence shared with us for her wedding, only now there wasn't going to be one. . . . She was going to stay with Sadie, Russ's sister. She'd spoken to her on the phone last night but Rose Marie didn't tell me then what they talked about. Apparently, she's going to take charge of Sadie's wardrobe, help with changes of costume, and will look after her backstage while she's on tour. "I'll still be sewing, I expect," she said. I asked her if Russ knew and she said yes, Sadie had told him.'

'Have you an address for her?' Manny enquired anxiously. He wasn't sure what Stella meant, about no wedding. He'd have to tackle Rose Marie herself about that.

'Yes, I'll bring it with me when we come to see you all on Saturday. I must go, Josefina's really upset, poor child, because Rose Marie went without a word to her. . . .'

'Just one more thing,' Manny said quickly. 'Leave it to me to tell Florence. She could do without all this trouble right now.'

Twenty

MANNY was behind the counter in the shop when Annie called back on Friday morning.

'Spoke to Buck yesterday. He said your wife has just been confined, so I thought I'd give this letter to you, then wait in the shop until you come back with what's requested, like.' She handed him the envelope with Florence's name on the front.

'Oh, you're Annie, I presume,' he said.

Buck came through from the back room carrying a bowl of peeled potatoes.

'Just delivering this to Florence,' Manny told him, brandishing the envelope. 'Annie can do with a mug of tea perhaps. Will you take care of it?'

Buck nodded. 'Got some brewing. A cup, not a mug, eh? Sit down then, Annie.'

While Annie sipped the hot tea, Buck transferred the potatoes to a saucepan.

'Why have you come back again so soon?' he enquired presently.

'Nosey, ain't you? If you want to know, I'm collecting Lilli's possessions.'

'Does that mean she's decided not to come back, I wonder?'

'Look, Buck, I told you a few things yesterday I shouldn't have. Can't think why.'

'You took a shine to me,' he said boldly.

She smiled. 'Perhaps ... I guess we're two of a kind. Both taken some knocks in life. Both done things we shouldn't have. You'd like to put things right, like me.'

'You got it,' he told her. 'Another cup of tea?'

Upstairs, Manny waited while Florence read the note.

'You're not getting out of bed,' he said firmly. 'Where's the key to Lilli's flat? I'll do it.'

'Not clothes, or toys, she says, just her *treasures*. Funny way to put it . . . Key's in the table drawer. Come and show me what you've got, before you hand it over, eh?'

The task was soon accomplished. Manny spotted Josefina's Spanish doll on the dressing table. He tucked that under his arm. He recollected the little girls exchanging their favourite dolls. She'll be over on Saturday, he thought, I'll return it to her then.

'Poor Lilli,' Florence sighed. 'Nothing of much value here. Unless the empty scent bottles are crystal glass. Yet she obviously came from a posh family in France. She must have left it all behind her. Something more to report to her husband, though.'

'I said I'd do that, tonight.'

'All right. I'm holding on before I write to Rose Marie, though. I'm hoping she'll decide to come with Stella and Josefina when they visit.'

'You never know,' Manny said, as he clicked the attaché case shut. But he *did* know, he thought. Rose Marie was probably on her way to the Midlands right now. . . .

Birmingham. Rose Marie arrived late Friday afternoon. Sadie was there to meet the train and hurried her away from the station. They jumped into a waiting cab and were driven at speed through the roar of the traffic to a modest hotel on the outskirts of the great industrial city.

'You're sharing my room, I hope you don't mind?' Sadie asked. 'Not much space, but it's comfortable. Bathroom just along the corridor. It's plain cooking here but plenty of it. They don't object to serving dinner when you get back from the theatre. There's some big names on the bill, but I miss the London scene. I'm told this theatre really comes into its own in the pantomime season; maybe I'll still be here then!'

She took in Rose Marie's doleful expression. 'You must be hungry!' Sadie exclaimed contritely. 'I'll ring for a sandwich and pot of tea for you to be brought up here. I never eat, as you know, before a performance. You've time for a quick bath first. We need to leave for the theatre in about an hour. Unless you would rather relax here, after your journey?'

'I'm tired,' Rose Marie confessed, 'but I don't want to be on my own. I'll come.'

'Oh, good! Look, I don't want to know the ins-and-outs of what's gone wrong between you and Russ. I don't think *he* understands why, either! I just thought, Rose Marie must want to get away from it all, have a complete change of scene.'

'You were right, Sadie. I'm very grateful for your concern.'

'Off to the bathroom now before someone else bags it, and your refreshment will await you on your return!'

'What shall I change into?'

'Whatever you like, as long as its comfortable. Shoes, in particular!'

After a soak in hot, scented water, Rose Marie felt much better. The hotel towels were huge and soft. She wrapped one round her while she washed her hair in the basin. Now she had removed all the grime and smoke from the journey, she thought, despite her fluffy, damp hair. No time to set it. The food completed the revival process.

It was still light, a pleasant summer evening, when they emerged from the hotel to find another waiting cab. The rush-hour was over, the traffic less; this time Rose Marie enjoyed the ride through the city.

Backstage, Rose Marie was introduced to passing artistes, but most were too preoccupied to talk; the stalls were already filling with smartly dressed people, but the real buzz of excitement emanated from the gallery above.

'There's still a lot of wealthy folk in Birmingham, despite the slump in business. Then there's the other side, where people work long hours for low wages to turn out all the stuff with the label, *Made In Birmingham*. They like a night out too and the gallery is their choice. Cheap and cheerful! Sheer escapism. I'm glad to do my bit in that respect.' Sadie told Rose Marie.

The orchestra tuned up, while Sadie led Rose Marie to her dressing room.

'Just a cubby-hole really, but then we're not the stars of the show! Better than the communal dressing room, though. You never know who might have used your powder puff!'

Sadie selected a frock from the rail, hung it on a hook on the

182

back of the door.

'What can I do?' Rose Marie ventured.

'Well, you can learn about stage make-up, while I apply the greasepaint! I don't expect you to work on your first evening, you know! We haven't discussed all that yet.'

'I only posted off my resignation to Mrs Belling, this morning . . . she won't get it until tomorrow. So officially I still work for Belling's.'

'You'll lose your wages in lieu of notice, I suppose. Are you all right for money? Don't worry about the hotel, I've done a deal with the manager on that.'

'I've got some savings.' Rose Marie realized that neither Russ or his mother had told Sadie about her windfall. She added quickly, 'How long before you're on stage?'

'We're the final act before the interval. It's a good spot.' A rap on the door made Sadie look up. 'I expect that's Stan. He's staying in our hotel too, with his friend. They would have come here earlier. Open the door, there's a dear.'

Stan wasn't talkative. Rose Marie was already aware of that. Dedicated to his dancing, she thought wryly, when he greeted her with a brief nod.

'You're late,' Stan reproved Sadie. He was already immaculate in his dress-suit.

'I've never let you down yet have I?' she returned. 'Well, you've got time for a quick one in the bar, while I get changed. I'll see you backstage.'

'Dashing about, when you should be resting before the performance,' he complained.

'Family come first with me, you know that. Off you go!'

'Family,' Rose Marie said a little later, as she held the dance frock clear of the make-up on Sadie's face and neck. 'Is that really how you think of me?' She regarded Sadie's reflection solemnly in the mirror.

'You know it is. I took to you the minute we met! Mind you, I worried a bit about my young brother sweeping you off your feet like that. I did wish you hadn't decided to marry so young, before you'd had a chance to further your career. Your sister, now, seems to have given up her's for teaching, when she has a lovely voice. Wasn't she married at your age?'

183

'Yes, but Jose wasn't the best choice she could have made. Although their daughter is very special to Florence. I think the world of her, too.' She changed the subject. 'Shall I tidy your hair for you? It's rather ruffled at the back.'

'Please! I can see you're going to make yourself indispensable to me!'

Later, Rose Marie sat on a chair in the wings, with a sideways view of the stage. Not quite the same as sitting in the stalls she thought, recalling with a pang the day she had met Russ. She'd clutched the dress box from Belling's on her lap. He'd flirted with her, and she supposed that was when they fell in love. So much had happened since then.

The Charleston was still a favourite here. Sadie's energetic steps, the billowing of her flame-coloured short skirts, the swinging of her long, knotted rope of glittering beads, the bandeau round her head, all added to the charisma of the dance. Stan was a perfect foil, with his smouldering good looks; the audience must surely believe, as Rose Marie had in her youthful *naïveté*, that these two were lovers. She mused, it's an illusion, but it was real enough between Russ and me.

A voice in her ear startled her. 'Can you see well enough?'

'Yes, thank you,' she murmured shyly. She made out a tall man in the shadows, then as the spotlight followed the dancers across to that side of the stage, she glimpsed his face with high cheekbones and dark eyes, above the roll-neck collar of a black jersey. He smiled.

'I should introduce myself, in a stage-whisper, naturally! I am Jack Dawes, the theatre manager. You must be Rose Marie, Sadie's sister-in-law?'

'Not exactly, but Sadie's a good friend,' Rose Marie replied.

The dancers were taking a bow, to enthusiastic applause. With a wave, they came off-stage. When Rose Marie turned round, after congratulating them, Jack Dawes had gone.

The curtain came down. 'Time for another cup of tea, and a change of costume,' said Sadie, leading the way to the dressing room. 'Stan prefers his tot of whisky.'

'I met Mr Dawes,' Rose Marie told Sadie. 'He seemed to think I was your sister-in-law.'

'I suppose that's how I think of you! I imagine you put him

184

right? He's a grand chap.'

Rose Marie nodded. 'I haven't stopped loving Russ, you know. We were so close, but I believe it would have hurt him more if I had stayed.'

'I said I wouldn't pry, and I'll endeavour to keep to that. I have a dilemma of my own, Rose Marie. Jack Dawes, well, he's asked me to marry him.'

'He seems very nice. He's certainly handsome!'

'Not so young, though, did you notice? He was married to an actress, but she left him a few years back. He's bringing up a young son, who's at boarding school. He's quite frank about it: he'd like to get married again; have his boy home with him all the time, not just for the holidays as he is now.'

'You don't want to take on his son?'

'It's not that, Rose Marie. I'm selfish. I don't want to give up my dancing. Besides, I have to help support my mother.'

'That's hardly selfish! Still, I'm not the one to give you advice, Sadie, am I?'

'Well, I have to agree! But in case you're wondering, I'm not in love with Jack, and he isn't in love with me! We're, well, *comfortable* together, but that's hardly *romantic*, is it?'

Lilli's meagre possessions were lined-up on the table. Philippe lifted the stoppers from the perfume bottles, sniffed them. He turned the bottles in his hands thoughtfully.

'These are old?' he queried.

'They were my grandmother's. She lived with us after my grandfather died and my father inherited the château. When she passed away, my mother said I could have them. The perfume still lingers. I kept them in my lingerie drawer,' Lilli wished she hadn't said that.

'Then you must do the same, here,' he said smoothly. Then he sighed. 'It is obvious that there is nothing here which anyone would want.'

Lilli bridled at that. 'I brought my treasures, as I call them, from my own country. They are precious to me. I hope you will tell the people you work for that I obviously do not have what they are looking for. Surely, now, you can allow me to go?'

He shook his head. 'Supposing you have concealed something

from me or, rather, that your friends have?'

'Don't be ridiculous! If only you would tell me what you believe I have?'

'A secret gift from your father, before he went off to war.'

'I have no recollection of that!' she insisted. 'Why won't you believe me?'

'Look, pack these things back in your case. Cast your mind back. You must remember! As soon as you tell me, you will be free.'

'Then I shall be here for ever,' she cried, with a flash of her old spirit. 'Because I am telling you the truth!'

The Saturday matinée, and this time Rose Marie had a younger companion in the wings. Ronnie Dawes was eight years old, very like his father to look at.

'Don't be a nuisance,' his father cautioned.

'I'm waiting for the ventriloquist to come on. I like his dog; it's really funny!'

'You relish the bit, I suppose, where the stage-hand comes on with a mop and bucket. Well old Larry doesn't think that's so hilarious.'

'Well, the ventriloquist shouldn't make the dog say, 'I gotta go' then, should he?'

'Ronnie always has to have the last word,' Jack said, ruffling his son's hair. 'I reckon *he'll* be a ventriloquist one day.'

'Which turn do you like best?' Ronnie asked Rose Marie when his father had gone.

'The dancing, of course!' she replied promptly. 'All those sequins were sewn on by me!'

After the show, Jack invited Sadie and Rose Marie to spend the time before the evening performance at his home nearby. 'Ronnie enjoys your company and so do I,' he said gallantly.

It was a town house, but with a small, secluded garden. They sat on a stone seat on a perfect square of Cumberland turf, and were served with chilled lemonade with a slice of real lemon and shortbread biscuits by the housekeeper.

Ronnie bounced a ball on a paved area, until his father mildly requested he desist.

'We'll have a day out in the country tomorrow shall we? Find somewhere you can kick a ball as much as you like.'

'Can we take a picnic?' Ronnie's face brightened up.

'You know I'm not much good at packing picnic baskets! We'll find a nice pub, where we can sit outside, and have whatever we fancy to eat. How about that?'

'Can Sadie and Rose Marie come too?'

'Why don't you ask them? They may have other arrangements.'

'Have you? Go on, say yes,' Ronnie pleaded.

'We haven't, and we'd be pleased to come,' Sadie said promptly. 'Rose Marie will be surprised, I think, to see the beautiful countryside around the city. Will you call for us, Jack?'

'We certainly will,' he said. 'Is eleven o'clock too early in the morning?'

'We'll be ready and waiting, won't we Rose Marie?' Sadie asked.

Rose Marie nodded, smiling. She thought, Sadie may consider Jack is not serious about her in *that* way, but *I* can tell he is!

Later, when they were back in the dressing room at the theatre, and Rose Marie was pressing a chiffon scarf carefully with a cool iron, she said, 'It should be fun, tomorrow.'

'Mmm.' Sadie was laying out the sticks of greasepaint on the make-up shelf. 'I suspect that you've already guessed that the life of an artiste is not always a giddy whirl! Not as it was when my mother was wooed and won by a minor member of the aristocracy! More sober times, I suppose. Maybe I'll end up like your sister Stella, teaching rather than performing.'

'Maybe you'll get married.' Rose Marie folded the scarf carefully.

'You think I should take my chance with Jack?'

'You'd have a ready-made family, and a comfortable home. A permanent place in this theatre! You're wrong about him not being in love with you: it's obvious to me he is.'

'Just as it's obvious to me,' Sadie retorted, 'you and Russ are made for each other!'

Rose Marie made her mind up. 'I *will* tell you the reason why I fled, Sadie. It's rather shocking I'm afraid. It concerns my family.'

'My dear, what could be more shocking than what happened to

187

my father? We've had to live with that, especially my mother. But we've never kept it a secret. Things are always easier to deal with, Mother says, if they are out in the open. I'm ready to listen. . . .'

'Oh, I didn't expect to find you still in bed!' Stella exclaimed, looking round for somewhere to lay down the flowers she had brought.

Josefina said in her forthright way, 'Now, Mummy, you have to remember that Aunty Florence is no spring chicken! See, I know what that means now!'

'Come here,' Florence invited. 'Give your ancient aunt a kiss! I've missed you, dearie. You may lift the baby up for a cuddle, Stella. I know the little blighter's awake.'

'What a way to describe your baby,' Stella reproved her with a smile, but she was soon rocking little Flynn in her arms.

'Rose Marie decided not to come, then?' Florence asked after a while.

Josefina opened her mouth, then closed it, after a look from her mother.

'Not today, but you'll see her soon, I hope,' Stella said quickly.

Manny came in with Carmen, the Spanish doll. 'Thought Josefina might like this back.'

'Oh, good!' Josefina squealed. 'I wondered where she was. I've got Clarice, of course, Yvette's doll. She says I can keep her 'til she sees me again, but Carmen's my favourite.'

They heard a knock on the door. Buck's voice. 'Someone to see you.'

Manny opened the door. A tall man stood beside Buck.

'I'm sorry to disturb you,' the man said, as Buck clattered back down the stairs.

'Who are you?' Manny queried.

'My name is Sam Bower. I am Lilli's husband, Yvette's father. I was waiting for news from your wife, but became impatient. I decided to come and find out what the situation is.'

'It's not the most convenient time to call, but you've come a long way, so you'd better come in,' Manny said.

More complications, he thought. How could he shield Florence from further worry?

Twenty-one

'C AN you entertain him for a bit?' Florence asked Manny. 'Tell him I've got visitors, and the baby to feed shortly too. Make him a cup of tea, eh? We'd appreciate one, too! Where's he staying tonight, oh dear!' She was becoming agitated, her face flushed.

'Calm down,' Manny said soothingly. 'I'll see to it all. Will you keep her out of the kitchen, Stella?'

'I certainly will.' Stella was still cooing over the baby. 'You realize this will probably give me ideas?' she sighed to Florence, when Manny had returned to their unexpected guest.

'That might not be a bad thing.' Florence's response surprised Stella.

Stella glanced at Josefina. Her hair hung down her back in a single braid like her mother's. She's grown up a lot since she left here, she thought. Cottons on more than we give her credit for. But her expression gave nothing away.

'It would make me stay put, you mean?' Stella asked. 'What about Jose?'

'Time he grew up and faced his responsibilities. Or did the other thing. . . .'

'What's that?' Josefina was listening in after all.

'You don't want to know,' Florence said. 'Would you like to hold your cousin for a while? I'll put my dressing-gown on and then we'll beat the retreat to the sitting room. I'm all hot and bothered propped up here in bed.' She threw back the bed covers.

'But, Manny told me the nurse said—' Stella began.

'I mean to stop acting like an invalid, get back to normal. Come on!'

Manny poured two mugs of tea for himself and Sam. He

refilled the teapot and set up the cups and saucers, the jug of milk, the bowl of sugar lumps, on the tray. He'd overheard the exodus from the bedroom into the sitting-room. It probably wasn't Stella's fault, he thought, resigned. Who could stop Florence when she was in a determined mood?

'Excuse me a moment, I'll just take this tray through. . . .'

'I appreciate that your wife has a new baby, but I was hoping to speak to her, later.'

'Later, as you say. You are welcome to stay here tonight, in Lilli's flat.'

'I'm grateful,' Sam said. 'I admit I was hoping you'd suggest that.'

On his return, Manny realized something. 'I posted a letter to you yesterday. Didn't you get it?'

'I left before the first post. Why, has something happened?'

'We know where Lilli is. She's being kept against her wishes. She was told what to write to us. I'm sure she would have written to Yvette, if she could. They were very close.'

The big man flinched. 'Lilli deprived me of my daughter, it's hard to forgive her that.'

'She must have had her reasons. You should have sat down together and talked about your problems. Things fester if you don't.' Manny surprised himself. I know that, he thought. All those years I wasted, thinking about what Buck did to me in the war. He got his just desserts many times over; I struck lucky, with Florence.

'An address you say? Is it far from here?' Sam demanded.

'A few miles. You can't go there tonight. We'll work out the best way to go about it.'

'Who gave you this information?'

'A woman called Annie. The chap who brought you up here spoke to her first. She's seen Lilli, it seems she's not been harmed,' he emphasized, guessing Sam's fears.

Stella came through with the tray, followed by Josefina. She said to Manny, 'Look, I think we've stayed long enough for a first visit. Florence is back in her room, seeing to the baby. Leave her undisturbed for a while, eh?'

'We'll come again soon. I'll make sure of that,' Josefina added firmly. ' 'Bye, Manny.'

'Pick your bag up,' Manny said to Sam Bower. 'I'll take you upstairs and show you the flat. The bed needs making up. There's a basin in the WC; cold water, but have a wash and brush up. Take your time. When you return, I'll see if Florence feels like talking.'

'I was wondering,' Sam said tentatively, 'if Lilli's friend, Rose Marie could tell me anything. Yvette talks a lot about her. She may know something that you don't.'

'Rose Marie left home recently. I'd rather you didn't mention that to Florence.'

'I gather you've family problems, too. I'm sorry to involve you with mine,' Sam said.

The baby, replete, dropped off to sleep. Florence kissed him, then lay him in the crib. She looked at herself in the long mirror. Still those hectic spots of colour in her cheeks. She took a few deep breaths, then sat down at the dressing table to tidy her hair. She wanted to dress, but felt too weary to make the effort, despite the bravado she had shown Stella earlier.

Manny's anxious face greeted her when she emerged from the bedroom.

'What have you got lined up for supper?' she asked. 'We must ask Sam to join us. We can talk over the meal.'

'I was going out for fish and chips, but—'

'Well go now, before he returns. Three cod and chips, remember. I'll lay the table.'

'Florence . . .' He gave up. 'I'll be as quick as I can. Just that then, I'll do the rest.'

Manny met Buck outside the shop. They fell into step.

'Not going to the pub are you?' Buck asked. He was all dressed up.

'No. Chip shop. Our visitor's staying over. He tell you who he was?'

'I heard him tell you. Let's hope he deals with the problem. You shouldn't have that on your plate right now. Florence doing well, and the baby?'

'Thank you, yes. Well, cheerio, have one for me, as they say.'

'Doc's told me to stick to soda water, but I like the company.'

Buck sat nursing his glass of fizzy drink. The hoped-for company had not yet materialized. He'd come out rather early he supposed. A newspaper had been left on his table. He opened it up for something to do. The touch on his shoulder startled him.

'May I join you?' Annie stood there, looking solemn.

'Yes . . . How'd you know I was here?'

'The shop was closed, you weren't at home. Saturday night, so I worked it out.'

'Can I get you a drink?'

She shook her head. 'I can't stay long. I might have been followed.'

'I can deal with that, if necessary,' Buck asserted forcefully. 'What's up?'

'Quite a lot. Mr Brown, as I call him, didn't find what he was hoping for in Lilli's stuff.'

'Well, perhaps he'll give up then. Let her go.'

'He said not. But I have a feeling he's lying. He brought back a lot of papers, files, from his office and locked 'em in a trunk the other day; I don't think he's been back there since. The doorman at the apartments – he's my uncle by marriage, he got me the maid's job and a room in the staff quarters - told me privately that Mr Brown's given notice; he's leaving.'

'Things been happening our end, too. Not that they tell me much. Lilli's husband arrived this afternoon. He's staying over the pie shop tonight. Working out what to do I reckon.' He added, 'Who is this Mr Brown really, d'you know?'

She shook her head. 'He's a bleeding mystery man. Wish I'd never met him!'

'How did you?'

'Not the way you're guessing! I had a nose round his apartment when he first come there, and, well, I fancied an item or two, and when he found out it was me as did the nicking, he said he wouldn't report me if I did a special job for him. . . .'

'Why are you telling me all this?'

'Felt I could trust you.' She stretched a hand across the table. He took it.

'First time anyone ever said that to me,' he said gruffly.

The pub was filling up. He released her hand. 'You'd best get back.'

'You're right. I'll call a cab. Quicker. I'll be in touch when I can.' Then she was gone.

192

Lilli was asleep in her chair. Philippe sighed as he moved stealthily around, packing his clothes into a large suitcase, personal items in a smaller one. He piled these on top of the trunk by the door. It was a pity, he thought, that he could not explain to Lilli why the time had come for him to leave; to apologize for drugging her glass of wine at dinner this evening. He would catch the boat-train tonight. Tomorrow, he'd travel across France and further still. A new identity, a fresh assignment with, hopefully, a more positive outcome. If he failed again, he knew what he could expect.

The telephone call made to the cab-station, he paused for a moment beside Lilli, looked down at her. It was fortunate his masters in the secret world of espionage were not aware that he had actually fallen in love with her. This was not the time for regrets.

'*Au revoir*,' he said softly to Lilli, as he opened the door to a discreet knock.

The doorman had come to help with the luggage. A note passed hands. The man would keep his mouth firmly shut, likewise Annie. Who would believe Lilli?

As one cab drew away, another arrived. Annie encountered her uncle in the foyer of the apartment block. He gave a brief nod. She instantly comprehended.

'She still here?' she asked breathlessly.

He nodded again. Glanced around to make sure they were alone. 'Glad he's gone, eh?'

'I'll say!'

'Take the lift,' he told her.

Upstairs, Lilli stirred, looked around her, uncomprehending at first. Then she struggled up, staggered toward the door. It was ajar. Philippe had left without locking it! She pulled at the handle, went outside, then stopped, swaying, gazing at the staircase opposite.

The lift doors opened and Annie took in the situation immediately. She ran across the thick carpeting along the corridor and pushed Lilli back inside the room. She closed the door behind her. As Lilli opened her mouth to feebly protest, Annie panted, 'I've got the key!'

Lilli sat down abruptly, tears spilling down her face. 'I had a chance. . . .'

'You still have! More than that. You're *free* Lilli! Mr Brown has gone, for good. Look, I'm going to make you some strong, black coffee, 'cause I reckon he gave you something to dope you, before he went. He didn't want you raising no alarm, like.'

'You'll help me, Annie, won't you?' Lilli's voice was slurred. 'You see, I don't know where I am even, and I don't want to stay here—'

'You won't have to. I'll take you home. But not in this state, eh? I'll pack your things while you drink as much of this as you can.' Annie poured the first cup of coffee.

She took the shabby suitcase which contained the items from Lilli's flat, rolled the glass scent bottles in a silk nightdress apiece, tipped the contents of the lingerie drawer on top, but left the expensive clothes in the wardrobe. She thought, I can get rid of those later; she won't want 'em. She made an exception of Lilli's coat, hat and shoes, which she had been wearing the night she came here.

Lilli was on her third cup of coffee. She looked less limp, Annie was pleased to see.

'All right, that'll do. Put your shoes on, and your coat and hat. It's past nine, so it'll have to be another cab, but I'm flat broke now.' She made a face. 'Unless you can help?'

'My bag in the bedside cabinet, I've still got my wages in my purse. . . .'

'Right, ready? Hang on to me!' Annie guided Lilli out. 'Not the stairs, the lift.'

The cab driver was the same one who'd brought Annie back nearly an hour before.

'Where to?' he asked. Her companion looked the worse for wear, he noted.

'Where you got me from, Paradise Street. To the pie shop on the corner.'

'Too late for an 'ot pie, I s'pose?' he joked.

' 'Fraid so, but you'll get a tip for your trouble,' Annie replied.

Buck was about to go up to the first-floor flat to tell them what had been said in the pub. He'd waited until he judged they would have finished their meal. Then he spotted the two women alighting from the cab. He hurried over to take the case from Annie. He could tell the younger woman needed the support of the other.

'Oh,' Annie said in a matter-of-fact way as she encouraged Lilli up the stairs. 'I should've said before, Buck told me earlier, your husband's here. He won't have to break down Mr Brown's door tomorrow, now.'

Manny opened the door, gazed incredulously at Lilli, flanked by the other two.

He turned, yelled, 'Florence, Sam, she's back. *Lilli's back!*'

Then Florence was hugging Lilli and Lilli was crying, 'You've had the baby, oh Florence!' while Sam just stood there awkwardly, dumbstruck, it seemed.

'We'll go,' Buck got in at last. 'I reckon any explanations can wait until the morning.'

'Thanks,' Manny told him. 'He's right,' he said to Florence. 'Anyway, Sam's got the right to know it all first.'

'I just want to get back in my own bed. . . .' Lilli said faintly.

Sam found his voice. 'I'll take you up to your flat. Is it all right for me to stay with you tonight? I can sleep in Yvette's bed,' he floundered.

'I suppose so. . . . Goodnight, it's good to be home,' Lilli told the others.

A protesting wail came from the bedroom. 'Here we go again,' said weary Florence.

'We'll leave you now, too,' Buck put in.

He and Annie went down the stairs, as the other two made their slower progress up.

They shivered a bit out in the night air in the street.

'How are you going to get back?' Buck asked Annie.

'Well, I've done enough rushing about for today. You've got a bed I can use, haven't you?' she said daringly. ' 'Sides, they might want to hear my part of it, in the morning.'

'I've only got one bed,' Buck said. 'I can manage in the chair.'

'We'll see about that. Ooh, you've got a cat, all ghostly and white at night!'

'You don't like cats?'

'But I do. Will she let me pick her up, I wonder?'

'She don't allow that as a rule,' he began. But Annie already had the cat in her arms.

Took old Manny seven years before he got together with Florence, he thought, and I've only known Annie seven days!

Lilli undressed quickly in the bedroom. She put on the expensive nightdress which Philippe had bought her. It was too late to find out where her own clothes were. She suddenly felt wide awake, although she had a dull headache. Someone had made the bed up; despite the flock mattress, she felt comfortable, as she never had in Philippe's luxury bedroom.

She could hear the narrow bed next door creaking as Sam got in. He was a big man, she thought, he's not going to sleep well on that. It might even collapse!

Sam was obviously having difficulty in getting settled. Finally, she called his name.

He stood there in the doorway, peering at her in the dark. 'You want me?'

'Get in the far side of this bed, Sam. I shan't get to sleep with you groaning in there.'

'Are you sure?'

'Look, we slept in the same bed for nearly seven years—'

'And the last five of those you kept to your side, and I kept to mine,' he stated.

'You know why that was. Your mother—'

'You can't blame her for everything. It was her house.'

'That was the problem.'

'You refused to make up after we'd had words—'

'She was listening in.' Lilli said, as he pulled some of the covers off her side.

'How could she help it? Thin walls, and you screaming in a foreign language.'

'All you had to do, to shut me up, was to say sorry, put your arms around me and—'

'Like this?' he whispered, moving closer. He got a firm grip on her slippery silk-clad waist. Her resistance melted away. No more fighting, she thought. I've been such a fool. We both have. She raised her face for his kiss. Time to make up. . . .

'Like *that*,' she agreed, much later.

Twenty-two

ELMO was doing his best to keep his young assistant busy. The fact that he himself had to take off time for two funerals meant that Russ was in charge of the bookshop on both occasions.

Old Jacob had succumbed soon after his collapse, which Elmo regarded as a blessing, for Jacob's sake. There was a handful of mourners, including Jacob's landlady. They had a good wake, provided by Elmo, and it was, as he said in a heartfelt address to those present, the final page in a life dedicated to literature.

A few days later, he was summoned to Norfolk on the passing of his uncle. Most of the village turned out to celebrate a real character, one known to them all and respected for his endearing eccentricity as well as his great knowledge and love of books. Elmo was very touched when he learned there was to be a collection to raise money for a commemorative headstone in the churchyard. So much good port flowed after the ceremony, back at the pub, Elmo deemed it wise to ring Russ and say he had decided to stay that night and return the following day. He'd had the foresight to bring an overnight bag.

The landlady of the White Hart showed him his room, with the remark, 'This is the one your friends used when they came up here to see your uncle. Well, naturally, they paid for *two* rooms, but I guessed they had other ideas ... Maybe they've married since?' she speculated.

'Not yet,' Elmo added firmly. 'Well, I must bid you goodnight. It's been a long day.'

She had the last word. 'Lovely young couple, made for each other. . . .'

Elmo thought, I really can't stand by any longer and do nothing. Russ may not appreciate advice from one who is, after all, unqualified to give it, but I'll do it, all the same.

Russ had been well occupied during Elmo's absence. Piles of books on chairs had been sorted and slotted into the appropriate place. He needed to blot out the thoughts that it was now September, that it was over six weeks since Rose Marie had joined his sister at the theatre, but most of all that this coming Saturday was to have been their wedding day.

He had heard nothing from Rose Marie since she had written to him from Stella's. Sadie made her usual weekly telephone calls to their mother who had assured him that his sister was looking after Rose Marie, but that Russ must continue to be patient meanwhile.

Elmo arrived at the bookshop not long before closing time. He gave an approving look at the tidy display shelves and then went into the back room to put the kettle on.

'Come and join me, boy: we need to talk. Leave the door open in case we have a last-minute browser.' The tea was soon made and the biscuit tin opened. 'Thank you, you've done well. *You* deserve a break now.' Elmo dipped his ginger biscuit in his tea.

'I'd rather keep busy, it takes my mind off things,' Russ replied. 'Did the funeral go off well? It was a fine day here.'

'Yes, the sun shone, though the east wind blew, but the mood was light-hearted. We celebrated his life in the traditional manner. He was a good age, Russ, eighty-four. Retirement finished him, but then he didn't call his books work anymore than I do.' He paused, drank deeply of his tea. Then, 'The White Hart landlady remembered you and Rose Marie. Dropped a heavy hint that, ah, you'd had a bit of a, um, honeymoon night there. . . .'

'I'm sorry. That was taking advantage of your generosity.'

'My dear boy, I am not criticizing you in any way. The landlady said you were made for each other. I heartily agree. Now, what do you propose to do about it?'

'What can I do?' Russ sounded defeated.

'Now, I'm aware of the significance of tomorrow's date. I wouldn't have mentioned it, but it's your Saturday off and I don't like to think of you being utterly miserable at home. If she won't come to you, you must go to her. If you haven't resolved your differences by Monday, take the following week off. Don't forget that was supposed to be your honeymoon.'

'I don't know what to say to you,' Russ began.

'Then don't. Just make sure you return with Rose Marie.'

The journey to the Midlands seemed never-ending to Russ. After spending a wakeful night going over and over what to say to Rose Marie, he was impatient to arrive at his destination.

It was stuffy and malodorous in the carriage. Two of his fellow travellers were pipe smokers, who added to the fug. Wanting a breath of fresh air, despite the grunts of disapproval, he forced the window down and poked his head out. A blast of steam from the engine alerted him to his foolhardiness just as he received a painful smut in his right eye.

He staggered back from the window, feeling desperately for his handkerchief in his coat pocket. One of the pipe smokers leapt to his feet, not to administer first aid, but to pointedly slam the window shut. A middle-aged woman in a corner seat next to the corridor was kinder.

'Give me your handkerchief; I have a bottle of water in my bag. I'll dampen it for you.' She did so. 'There, hold it to your eye. The cold and wet will help.' She leaned over him solicitously suggesting he rest his head back against his seat. 'I had to do this for my eldest son once. He suffered in silence like you. Being a stoic helped him get through the war, I believe, although he lost his life just before the Armistice. . . .'

Russ closed his other eye. He was in agony; not capable of conversation.

Later, when he left the station and was wondering what to do, he was directed to a chemist, where his eye was examined by the proprietor, soothing drops applied and a pink celluloid eye-patch provided. The advice was to keep this on at least overnight.

He caught a bus to the theatre, hoping to arrive there before the matinée began.

'Miss Short's dressing room?' the stage-hand repeated. He spotted Jack Dawes and his son Ronnie backstage. 'Mr Dawes,' he called. 'This gentleman is asking for Miss Short.'

Jack came over immediately, held out his hand. 'I'm Jack Dawes, the theatre manager, and you must be Russell, Sadie's brother. She advised me you were coming. I'll take you to her. Ronnie, put the seats out in the wings, please.'

When Jack tapped on her door, Sadie opened it immediately. 'I might as well come with you now, Jack.' She put a finger to her lips, whispered to Russ, 'She doesn't know. Go in. She's tidying up behind the screen. I'll see you later.' Then she was gone.

Russ closed the door quietly behind her. He waited, irresolute, for a few seconds, then cleared his throat. It had the desired effect: the screen folded back and Rose Marie was revealed, in a pair of Sadie's old practice tights and an oversize jumper with holes at the elbows. Her hair was ruffled, her face pink, and she clutched a brush and dustpan.

'More glitter than dust,' she said in a matter-of-fact sort of way. 'Sequins and discarded dancing pumps. . . . What took you so long, Russ? I've been waiting for you to come and find me! Why on earth are you wearing an eye-patch? You look like a pirate!'

'You might show some sympathy. I got a smut in my eye from the train!'

Rose Marie dropped the brush and pan with a clatter, held out her arms.

'D'you want me to kiss it better?'

'That might help.' He moved slowly towards her. 'You're still wearing your ring!' He sounded almost accusing.

'Well, I was going to send it back, as I said, but I forgot.'

His arms went round her compulsively and he almost squeezed the breath out of her.

'You *didn't* forget, did you?'

'No,' she whispered. 'How could I?'

'What was so terrible that you couldn't tell me? Why did you run away like that?'

'Sit on the couch and I'll tell you. Sadie got it out of me and she made me realize that you wouldn't love me any the less because of it, Russ.'

They sank down on the couch still holding on to each other. 'I do love you. I forgive you. Did you realize that today should have been our wedding day?' he asked her.

'I've been crying on and off all morning about that; look at my puffy eyes! I could do with an eye-patch, too.' Her voice trembled. 'I need kissing better, like you. . . .'

'Is anyone likely to disturb us?'

'Not for some time. Oh, Russ, can we ever get back to the way we were?'

'I know we can,' he said simply.

Later, they sat together in the wings and watched Sadie dance. She came breathlessly off stage to embrace them both.

'Let's go back to the dressing room, we can't talk here!' Sadie urged.

When they were ensconced, Russ told her, 'I'm taking Rose Marie home tomorrow.'

'I'm sorry to let you down. I'm so grateful for all you've done for me,' said Rose Marie.

'It meant I could keep an eye on you, make sure you were all right, for Russ's sake as well, and for Florence. She's been through a lot, too.'

'I know. I do know. . . .'

'When I said about going home,' Russ said, 'I meant you must go straight to Florence.'

'I don't know how I can make it up to her; what to call her now—'

'*Florence*. Just as you always have.'

'I shall miss you, you kow,' Sadie said after breakfast next day. 'I'll be back for you wedding of course. I have to make sure Mother doesn't buy an unsuitable hat! But I hadn't realized until you joined me how lonely my life can be. Perhaps I should settle down too. . . .'

'Well, you've had a firm offer,' Rose Marie said in her old mischievous way.

'Ah, Jack. D'you really think I should accept?'

'You'd be daft if you didn't! He doesn't expect you to give up your dancing, though you'd have to give Stan the boot, and you could be a fairy in the Christmas pantomime!'

'You'd all come to cheer me on, would you?'

'Of course! Don't hang about, Sadie. I know it's not what you dreamed of when you first went on the stage, but, now you've caught the right person, don't let him escape!'

'Not quite the way I would have put it,' Sadie said drily. 'Oh, Rose Marie,it means so much to me to see you happy again, and everything sorted out.'

'Well, I still have to face Florence, and try to put things right between us.'

They were waiting in the hotel foyer for Russ to alert them that the taxi had arrived.

He came hurrying up. 'The baggage is aboard!'

'Not yet, I'm not,' said Rose Marie. 'I want to say goodbye and thank you for everything to Sadie first.' As she hugged his sister, she whispered, 'You're going out with Jack and Ronnie later on, aren't you? Say *yes* today! Don't forget.'

'I won't. I might race you to the altar!' Sadie added, 'Not a great romance for me, eh?'

'You could be pleasantly surprised! I know Florence was. Must go!'

'Someone coming up the stairs,' Manny warned Florence, as she nursed the baby by the fire.

'Go and find out who it is then, while I make myself respectable!'

He opened the door, could hardly believe his eyes, then called out, 'Florence, it's Rose Marie and Russ! Come quick!'

Florence emerged from the sitting room in a fluster, babe in arms.

'Rose Marie, oh, my dear, you're back!'

'Pass Flynn to me, then you can give her a proper welcome!' said Manny. 'Russ and I will have a chat in the kitchen. Why don't you two go in the other room?'

'Let me have a good look at you,' Florence said, when the embracing was over and they were sat down. 'You seem more . . .' she hesitated.

'Grown-up?' Rose Marie suggested. '*You* look younger, being a mother suits you!' Then she realized what she'd said. 'I suppose, well, I might have believed you were my sister, but you were always a mother, really, to me.'

'I'm glad. I don't expect you to call me that, you know.'

'I wasn't intending to. Can we just go back to where we were? Talk things over like sisters do? *We'll* know the truth, of course. That's what matters.' She bit her lip to hold back sudden tears. 'Can you ever forgive me, Florence, for leaving you in the lurch?'

'If you can forgive me for deceiving you,' Florence wiped her own eyes. 'I thought I'd ruined everything for you, that you'd cancelled the wedding because of my confession.'

'I thought I'd spoiled your big moment - having your baby - by going off as I did.'

'I was distraught, I must admit. . . .'

'So was I, Florence. All this could have gone on longer, if Russ hadn't come to me and told me he wanted me back, and he was sure you did, too.'

'You'll be married after all?' Florence had to know.

'Of course we will! As soon as it can be arranged. Manny must give me away, you'll be the mother of the bride and Josefina will get her wish to be our bridesmaid! Any chance of your famous Bombay toast for supper, I wonder?'

'Manny'll make it, if I ask him nicely,' Florence said. 'First, let's call the others in and discuss the arrangements!'

At eight o'clock, Russ rose reluctantly to leave.

'You don't have to go, you know,' Florence said unexpectedly. 'You can stay here.'

'I think I should,' he looked at Rose Marie.

She nodded. 'Yes, you have to tell your mother what we've decided about the wedding. You've to go work tomorrow, and I want to catch the early tram to Belling's, to ask very humbly if I may have my job back! I'll see you out.'

At the foot of the stairs, they kissed. 'No night of passion,' he whispered regretfully.

'We've many more of those to look forward to,' Rose Marie said.

'I'd got used to not getting up at the crack of dawn,' Rose Marie yawned over her porridge. 'But it's not so frantic in the kitchen nowadays, is it?'

'Not since Manny and Buck make all the pies at the back of the shop. They've got a new assistant now, Annie. She comes in later, keeps the place tidy. You could say I'm a lady of leisure nowadays, well, almost. Flynn sees to that,' Florence said ruefully.

'He's a beautiful baby, Florence! Does he – look anything like I did?'

'Something, I think. Just as imperious as you were, with his yells to see to his needs immediately!' Florence looked at Rose Marie. 'Father would remind me where my duty lay.'

'Oh, Florence!' Rose Marie glanced at the clock on the mantle-piece. 'Well, time to go. I may be back sooner than I intended if Mrs Belling turns me down. But, anyway, Russ is coming after work, if that's all right, because we're going along to try to explain to the vicar. . . .'

She dropped a quick kiss on Florence's head, and then on Flynn's, in his mother's arms.

It was raining, a dampening drizzle, but Rose Marie hurried across the pavement to the waiting tramcar, with her mackintosh collar turned up. Her stockings were splashed with the muddy water lurking in the gutter and her rubber overshoes squelched as she hopped aboard.

'Nice to see you're back again,' the conductor observed, clip-ping her ticket. 'Last time you travelled on the tram you had a suitcase with you. Had a good holiday?'

'A change of scene, but it's good to be back,' she said.

Mrs Belling gave her an unexpectedly warm welcome. She didn't ask 'Why?' She actually hugged Rose Marie and told her, 'Plenty of work awaiting your attention, upstairs!'

'No,' she said later. 'I didn't engage anyone in your place. I had a feeling you'd return!'

Twenty-three

'Now Lloyd George is leading the Liberals, things are bound to improve,' Florence observed. She turned the pages of the *Daily Mirror*, spread out on the kitchen table. 'They said we were sliding into a deeper Depression after the General Strike but unemployment's dropping. Now, I reckon our young couple can start their married life this Saturday with hope for the future.'

'What about us?' queried Manny. 'We're celebrating our first wedding anniversary. We've got something to show for it too,' he added proudly, as he dandled his son on his knee.

Florence looked up, smiled. 'All that good sea air helped! I'd love to visit Hastings again, wouldn't you? But we can't take another holiday with the wedding to pay for. We're lucky we've got our outfits from last year, eh?'

'Rose Marie said you should have something new. I presume she's given in?'

'I told her, what a waste! I only wore the costume once, after all. Getting pregnant soon after we were married put a stop to that. Thank goodness I've got my figure back!'

'I can see that,' Manny said boldly.

'And I intend to keep it that way, so don't get any ideas about adding to the family!'

'*Yet*,' he murmured under his breath. He'd get round her, in a year or so, he thought.

'Rose Marie, you know, is going to carry on at Belling's. They're not making so much *haute couture*, as they call it, but more clothes the working girl can afford. She's modelling that line for them, next month. Right now, she's putting the last touches to her wedding dres.'

'She won't be showing off any clothes if a baby comes along, as it did for us . . . I suppose you'll want to get back to the old routine before too long, won't you?'

'You all seem to manage the pie shop very well without my help,' she said ruefully. 'But as for a baby, I think that's far from Rose Marie's mind, right now. Well,you'd better join the workers downstairs, no slacking, and pass the boy to me!'

Annie was serving the lunchtime customers and Buck was at the counter, when Manny returned. They made a good team, and her presence eased the wariness between the men.

She looked smart in her new patterned overall with the matching cap restraining her blonde locks. Manny suspected she sometimes stayed overnight here, but he didn't pry.

'Wedding plans all in order?' Annie asked, as she came into the back for more pies.

'Seems so,' Manny told her. He had some other news for her. 'Lilli and her family are coming for the wedding. They'll be staying with Stella, Florence's sister, for the weekend. Josefina wanted Yvette to be a bridesmaid, too. You and Buck, well, you'll hold the fort here for us, of course, but you're welcome to join us in the evening about seven after the meal. We'll save you some cake! You'll see Lilli then. We fixed the wedding for the afternoon, as Florence thought the baby was too young to take out to a restaurant.'

'Thanks, that'll be nice. Everything all right with Lilli?'

'Seems so. She wrote Florence they've got a place of their own now.'

'That's good. I was wondering, Manny, what you're going to do with Lilli's flat?'

'Let it again, I suppose. Why, are you interested?'

'We might be. Me and Buck. Ain't said nothing to him yet, though—'

'Annie!' Buck's voice startled them. 'Where's them pies?'

Manny said quickly, 'It'd have to be a *proper* arrangement, Florence would insist on that.'

'So would I, whatever ideas you've had about me!'

Manny thought, as he peeled another lot of potatoes and hoiked out the eyes, I reckon she'll be the making of old Buck. It's rather dismal down in the basement, I reckon I can persuade

Florence to let them have the top flat. Why shouldn't he have his chance to move up in life as well, like me? I could forget about him and Florence that time, then.

'I've decided to accompany Sadie back to Birmingham on Sunday. I want to meet this Jack Dawes she's suddenly announced she's going to marry at Christmas. She's not doing so without my approval!' Mrs Short told her son firmly.

'Oh, mother, he's eminently suitable - a really nice chap! A few years older than Sadie, but he has a good home, a secure job, and they're both in the same business, of course.'

'What about the child?'

'He and Sadie get on well. She says Ronnie reminds her of me at that age!'

'I'm not sure whether that's a compliment or not! You've been mysterious about your honeymoon, Russ. Can't you give me a hint?'

He tapped his nose. 'I promised Rose Marie I wouldn't tell.'

'Well, where are you going to live when you come back?'

'I haven't the faintest idea. We've been concentrating on the wedding, on being together. I suppose we'll have to decide between staying in Paradise and here!'

'I plan to stay with Sadie for a while. You can come back here after the honeymoon, eh?'

'Thanks, Mother, I'm sure Rose Marie will agree that's a good idea.' Russ said.

'Another thing, you haven't said who your best man will be.'

'Elmo, of course, he's the one who helped get us back together! I never kept up with the chaps from school.'

Mrs Short suddenly wiped her eyes. 'I've always said you're too impulsive, but on this occasion you needed a push in the right direction. Rose Marie explained to me why she left like that, but I assured her we're more enlightened nowadays. Florence is a splendid person.'

'Then we can all look forward to the wedding without a care in the world,' he said.

'I'm not sure,' Rose Marie sighed. 'It was such a good idea having the wedding in the afternoon. All this hanging about, and having to dodge out of sight if someone calls.'

'Keep still, do,' Florence reproved her, as she hooked up the back of the wedding dress. 'It must have taken you ages to sew these on, Rose Marie, but you can be proud of all your hard work, it's a charming frock . . . unusual.'

'Well, it was bound to be, as I designed it myself!'

The dress was the fashionable shorter length, in sumptuous palest pink satin, with swirls of tiny sparkling stones on the bodice, modest at the front, but low-cut at the back. With it, Rose Marie wore matching satin shoes with rhinestone buckles. The short veil would be positioned carefully on her head at the last minute, secured with pinned-on artificial rosebuds.

They were in Florence's bedroom, with the door firmly closed. Flynn was being entertained in the kitchen by his father. Manny would be glad when the bridesmaids arrived!

Florence draped a protective cloth round Rose Marie. 'Now for your hair. . . .'

'Those waves cost me a fortune at the hairdressers, be careful.'

'D'you want a tap with the hairbrush?' Florence joked. As she brushed, she gently pressed the waves back with her fingers.

When she took the cloth away, she told her, 'Now look in the long mirror.'

For a long moment, Rose Marie stared solemnly at her reflection.

'I don't look like me,' she said at last in a small voice.

'You're looking at a beautiful bride, my dear. No tears, don't you dare!'

'I hope you'll be proud of me one day. . . .'

'I couldn't be prouder of you than I am now, Rose Marie.'

A tap on the door. 'Are you ready?' Stella's voice. 'The girls are waiting, and so is the wedding car to take us all together, hope you don't mind, and I'll hold the baby, shall I? Your flowers are on the table. Jose has gone straight to the church, with Lilli and Sam.'

'We're ready,' Rose Marie replied. There were gasps from those waiting when they saw her in all her splendour. She picked up her bouquet of pink and cream roses and Florence draped a shawl round her shoulders.

'You mustn't catch cold!'

'There's a crowd waiting outside the shop to give you a cheer,' Josefina said, excited.

'Oh dear, I hadn't expected that! Let's go and face the music then!'

The bells were ringing; inside the church choirboys were singing; there were polished pews and extravagant hats on shingled heads. The lamp standards were wound round with pink ribbon and there were flowers on every windowsill. These decorations had been earlier arranged by Mrs Short and Sadie to surprise the bride.

As she walked down the aisle on Manny's arm, followed by the bridesmaids, also in pink with Juliet caps, Rose Marie sensed he was more nervous than she was. She gave a cheery little wave with her bouquet as she passed each pew and visibly quickened her pace, out of step with the music, as she approached Russ, waiting with Elmo at the front. She passed her bouquet to Josefina, then she slipped her hand in Russ's with a squeeze to show all was well.

'Here we go,' she whispered, making him smile.

The solemn promises were made, prayers were said and hymns were sung. The vicar, who had looked anxious until the bride arrived, visibly relaxed. Then formal photographs were taken plus informal snaps with box cameras by the assembled guests.

Florence was beginning to wonder if she had been rash in inviting so many back to the rooms over the pie shop. But there was plenty of food put out ready in the larder, she reassured herself; the ham and chickens already carved; the bowls of salad and dishes of relish; just the tea to make when they got back and the bread to cut; the splendid wedding cake to stand centre-table.

Thank goodness, she thought, Flynn slept in Stella's arms throughout the service! Stella looked really maternal, as she never did when Josefina was a baby. Maybe, she mused, Stella has taken my advice and there's a happy event in the offing. Jose's attitude to family life certainly has improved. He's even teaching pupils himself - the Spanish guitar!

She turned her attention to Lilli and Sam, who were taking a lift in Elmo's van, together with the little girls, who refused to be parted. Sam had his arm firmly round his wife's shoulders, and it was obvious to Florence that they were well on the way to a happy ending.

'How are you getting back?' Florence asked Russ's mother and sister.

'We're expecting a taxi cab to come for us shortly,' Mrs Short replied. 'Look, your sister is signalling you to take the baby, I believe. She and her husband can come with us. We'll be with you soon!'

The bride and groom sat in the front of the big wedding car; Florence and Manny in the back, with Flynn. She jigged the hungry baby in her arms to prevent him crying.

'You see to him first, when we get home. I'll get the guests settled, with a glass of something to keep 'em happy,' Manny whispered in her ear. 'We'll be the first back!'

The wedding breakfast went off smoothly, thanks to all their hard work beforehand. Elmo made a splendid speech, Manny a more hesitant but equally heartfelt one.

At six o'clock Mrs Short, Sadie and Elmo said goodbye, and the congestion eased a little in the sitting-room.

'Elmo has tickets for the Fred and Adele Astaire musical,' Mrs Short told them.

'I should be able to give old Stan a few tips afterwards,' Sadie laughed. 'George Gershwin's wonderful music, how I'd love to be in a show like *Lady Be Good*.'

'Enjoy yourselves!' was the chorus.

Florence rushed out to the kitchen to cut two more pieces of wedding cake. 'Take these back for your fiancé, Sadie, and his son. We must wish you all the best for your own wedding in December.' She paused, 'I want to thank you for all you did for Rose Marie. . . .'

'I'm glad it had this happy outcome,' Sadie said sincerely.

When Buck and Annie arrived there was more cake-cutting and glasses of wine.

Buck looked sheepish in a jacket which Lilli recognized. Philippe must have missed that one, she thought. Annie had obviously emptied the wardrobe in his flat after his departure.

'It's funny how things turn out,' Annie said to Lilli. 'I suppose you can say I met Buck through you, in a roundabout sort of way. And you got back together with your Sam when it seemed you never would. Did you ever discover what Philippe was looking for?'

Lilli shook her head. 'No. But strangely enough, after all these years, my mother got in touch with me . . . I can't help wondering if *he* had something to do with that.'

'You'll see her again will you?'

'Not yet. A lot to sort out first. I need to know if she was involved in my abduction.'

Rose Marie joined them. 'We'll be off shortly. I have to get changed first - I don't want to advertise the fact we're just married. . . .'

'I don't know why not,' Lilli said, giving her a hug. 'Anyone can see that.'

'Oh, well! Excuse me, anyway.' She beckoned Florence to follow her into the bedroom.

'We said we wouldn't tell anyone, but, in case you're worrying where we're off to so late in the evening,' Rose Marie confided to Florence, as she helped her out of her wedding gown, 'we're spending tonight in Park Lane, W1: Elmo's wedding present to us! D'you know, I think he rather fancies Russ's mother – taking them to a show no less!'

'Not a very ladylike expression,' Florence mildly reproved her.

'Well, I think she thought I was an abandoned hussy when she caught Russ and me in an embrace the first time I visited her house!'

'Hmm . . . just tell me, are you going further afield tomorrow, I wonder?'

'I'm afraid you'll have to wonder until our return. Not out of the country, though!'

Florence hung the wedding clothes in the wardrobe. She turned, then held out her arms. 'One last hug in private! Is everything all right between us now?'

'Darling Florence, it is! I can leave knowing you won't be lonely with Manny and Flynn to fill your life, and you can be sure I'm ready to be a good wife, if not a conventional one!'

'Two baths in one day, but I couldn't slip between these fine sheets without, could I?' Rose Marie asked Russ, padding into the hotel bedroom wrapped round with a towel.

'Don't interrupt me when I'm shaving. That's twice in one day, too!'

'Is that so I can relish the smoothness of your face?' She allowed the towel to drop.

He turned from the basin, still lathered up, shaving brush in hand. 'Not at all, I don't want to snag that impressive linen with my beard. Oi! Don't mess my side of the bed up.'

'I'm testing the mattress. At least the bed doesn't creak, like the one at your mother's.'

'That bed was only intended for one,' he reminded her. 'Do put something on, Rose Marie. I'm going to ring room service and ask for an omelette to eat in bed, only I won't say the last bit, of course. Despite all we ate in Paradise, I have a distinct hollow feeling.'

'So have I. I fancy an omelette too, with a jug of percolated coffee and cream.'

'Well, perhaps we ought to eat at the table, after all. You haven't got a pinny.'

'All right,' she climbed out of bed, smoothed the eiderdown. 'Where's my dressing-gown?'

Some time later, they switched off the lights and turned back the covers again.

'Are you looking forward to returning to the inn in Norfolk tomorrow?' she asked. 'No one could possibly guess that's where we're going.'

'Except for Elmo, as we're borrowing the van. I said we'd collect it at ten.'

She wriggled her way into the centre of the big bed. He rolled towards her.

'I had the same thought,' he murmured, enfolding her in his arms.

'I'm so glad I married you,' she whispered.

'Can't you stop talking for a while?'

'You know the answer to that,' said Rose Marie demurely.

And, of course, he did.

Twenty-four

'I can whistle through the gap in my teeth!' Yvette demonstrated. It was a shrill sound.

'Shush!' Josefina winced. 'The grown-ups will be cross if we wake them up. Sunday morning, remember. Mummy said we were to stay put in my bedroom until we heard the call to breakfast. I mentioned we were hoping for eggs and bacon but *she* said she wouldn't be frying *that*, after all we ate yesterday. Well, I suppose they called that a breakfast, didn't they?'

'Can I come in the other end of your bed? We can see each other better then, and we can play with our dolls, can't we, like we used to.'

'All right. I shall miss Clarice you know, when you take her away. Oh, mind where you're putting your feet - they're cold!' Josefina complained as Yvette wriggled down in the bed.

Yvette, like Josefina, had shot up in height since they were last together. Her fuzzy curls had disappeared; her grandmother apparently disapproved of curling rags. She, too, now had plaits, though hers stuck out in a comical fashion because her hair was so fine.

'Do you like being with both your parents?' Yvette asked, as she checked that Clarice was still in good shape.

'Do you?' Josefina countered, hoping that Yvette wouldn't spot what she had dubbed Clarice's appendix scar, cobbled together by herself, because Stella had been 'too busy'.

'We-ell . . . I'm glad to get back to French cooking - my gran uses so much suet! And our new house is actually very old, and poky, 'cause we can't afford much rent, and Maman hasn't got a job, 'cause Daddy says "wait and see". I don't know what for.'

'I wish sometimes I could go back and live with Florence—'

213

'So do I! Well, in Florence's top flat. We had each other then, didn't we?' Yvette said.

'Even though we fell out sometimes! I'll tell you a secret. My mummy's going to have a baby! I'll have a brother or sister she says, though that's not much use to me, now I'm getting older, is it? I heard Mummy telling Daddy he's got to knuckle down - whatever that is.'

'I think you're very lucky! It's not fair, why can't Maman have another baby?'

'Maybe she isn't trying what mine did to get one.'

'What's that?' Yvette was intrigued.

'I'm not sure. I might ask Aunty Florence. She'll know, as she's just had Flynn, eh?'

'Oh,' exclaimed Yvette accusingly. '*What's this*?' She held Clarice up, her soft body uncovered, revealing the clumsy stitching.

'She needed an emergency operation.' Josefina tried to sound convincing.

'Got any scissors?' Yvette demanded crossly. 'I can sew properly; French girls always can. Spanish girls obviously can't—'

'*Half*-Spanish,' Josefina reminded her. 'I've got a pair in my girls' sewing box.'

'Give them to me! Then find me a fine needle and a reel of cotton!'

Josefina sat on her end of the bed, not daring to interrupt her friend's concentration.

Snip, snip, went the tiny scissors. Yvette's face was like a thunder-clap.

'Look at this,' she cried wrathfully. 'A great big hole!'

'It *was* only a tiny one—'

'Yes, until you poked your fingers inside!' Yvette demonstrated. Her expression changed to one of puzzlement. 'What's this?' She dug deeper, and the filling trickled out.

Josefina watched in amazement as Yvette pulled something free, a small suede bag with a drawstring top. Yvette opened it up, and then gasped. 'It's full of beads!'

'Put it back!' Josefina urged.

'No, I'm going to call Mummy. It could be hidden treasure!'

'It looks like what you said it was, beads - old, *black* beads!'

'Why are you making all this noise, so early?' Stella said crossly from the doorway.

'Yvette's found something inside Clarice's tummy she wants to show Lilli!'

'I'm here,' Lilli yawned, having come from the bedroom next door. 'Show me what?'

'There's something else,' Yvette squealed. 'A piece of paper, folded very small.'

'Careful,' her mother advised. 'Give it to me. Run and fetch your father.'

When Sam arrived, and the paper was smoothed out, Lilli perused it carefully.

'What is it?' Stella asked.

'It's written in French. I'll translate . . . it appears to be a copy of my father's will! The address is our family château in France. It is dated August, 1914.

My dearest Lilli,

I have been called to defend our country in the certain knowledge we shall soon be at war again. I must ensure that my affairs are in order, but I hope you will not read this until you are a grown woman, many years from now, and the secret is out. Because I do not have a son, the château will pass to my brother, or if he pre-deceases me, to his son. He must honour his promise to care for your mother and you, if I die in this conflict. Your mother will inherit some money and artefacts which do not belong to the property.

To you, my only child, I bequeath my grandmother's necklace of rare black pearls. You may never wear them but you will have them as your security if you encounter hard times. I have pondered how to keep the necklace safe, if the enemy should come to our gates. The doll is always with you, I pray no one will suspect.

My love always, Lilli. Your father.

'It is signed by him.' Lilli looked up with tears in her eyes.

The children were quiet now, very solemn. It was Sam who spoke first.

'Did your father sew the doll up himself, do you think?'

215

'As he always mended my toys, I imagine that he did. My mother must have wondered where the pearls had disappeared to, after he left us. She couldn't be sure, of course, but she must have suspected I had them,' Lilli said.

Sam put his arm round her. 'Come back to our room now, we need to talk.'

Stella said quickly, 'I'll keep the girls occupied. Get dressed, you two, then come downstairs and I'll cook you that breakfast you asked for, even if it does turn my stomach.'

In their bedroom, Lilli handed the pearls to Sam. 'Look after these while I get dressed.'

'We can't go home this afternoon as we planned. Tomorrow, we must find a solicitor and ask his opinion. Then we ought to have the necklace valued at a reputable jeweller's.'

She discarded her nightdress, thinking his words over, not conscious of her nakedness.

On an impulse Sam came up behind her. He said softly, 'You must wear the necklace once. Let me fasten it for you. . . .'

She spun round. 'I know what you're thinking,' she whispered.

'Do you?' He seemed mesmerized by the necklace gleaming against her pale skin.

'Yes. It's just as if we're falling in love all over again.'

'It's raining, like the last time we were here,' Rose Marie observed, as they drew up outside the White Hart Inn.

Russ opened the van door on her side with a flourish. 'Well, it's Autumn now, what d'you expect? Anyway, we didn't let the weather bother us then, did we? And this time we don't need to creep about between rooms upstairs.'

'I suppose we could have plundered the nest-egg and gone abroad,' she mused. 'Then the waves would have been nice warm ones under blue skies, not,' she patted her hair ruefully, 'the kind of waves which flatten out when it's wet.'

'I don't mind where I am, as long as I'm with you,' he said.

The landlady recognized them. 'Mr and Mrs Short, congratulations and welcome! Would you like to order your evening meal now, before you go upstairs to unpack? I expect you could do with a pot of tea. I'll bring one up in a while, shall I?'

'Please,' Rose Marie smiled.

They changed into more casual clothes in the bedroom. Rose Marie put on a woollen frock in cherry red with long sleeves, thicker stockings and flat shoes. As she combed her hair, which retained a slight curl, Russ pulled a thick jersey over his head.

'That looks like a cricket pullover,' she said.

'That's because it is. A relic of my school days. The back knitted by my dear sister in stocking stitch, the front by my mother, because of the cable pattern. It's a favourite of mine.'

'Florence does all the knitting in our family, but at least I can sew!'

'You're a marvel at that!' he said fondly.

Later, they enjoyed their meal by a blazing log fire. Plates of tender beef stew, with Norfolk spoon dumplings, whole small carrots and onions, covered in rich, glutinous gravy. The second course was just as filling, apple pie with clotted cream.

Rose Marie leaned back in her chair, after the table was cleared.

'We should sleep well tonight, if we don't suffer from indigestion,' she said.

'We need a spot of exercise,' he thought. 'Let's go for a stroll.'

'It's almost dark,' she reminded him.

'Round the green then, and back. The fresh air should revive us. Come on!'

They came upon the old chapel. Curious, they tiptoed up to the arched side window and peered in. A figure moved in the gloom, made more eerie by a single dangling lightbulb.

'D'you think it's a ghost?' Rose Marie clutched at her husband's arm.

'Old Mr Turbot-Watts? Stop being so fanciful!' He didn't sound too certain himself.

They'd been spotted. A face appeared the other side of the window, staring at them. A man, with a broom in his hand.

'Yes?' he called. 'Do you want me? Come round to the front, if you do.'

'We can't admit to just being nosey,' Rose Marie shivered. It was chillier here in the evening than in London. 'We'd better apologize. . . .'

'Come in, I can do with some company,' the man said

cordially. 'It's a trifle spooky in here, but I had an hour or two to spare, so I drove over to get on with the sweeping. I bought the old place at an auction: I hope to live here when it's habitable once more, and make a studio up in the gallery. I'm an artist, or rather, I want to be. My profession was as a bookkeeper, not a bookseller, and suddenly realizing I was dull and almost middle-aged, I made up my mind to be reckless, as I wasn't permitted to be in my youth. . . .

'You knew the previous occupant, you say? How about giving me a hand in here for an hour, and telling me about him. I've heard he was very eccentric. By the way, my name is Graeme, and you are?'

'Rose Marie.' She almost added Flinders. 'And Russ. We're staying at the White Hart.'

'Rather late in the season for a holiday,' their new friend said cheerfully.

Rose Marie was glad it was dim in there, so he couldn't see her blush.

They told the story of the old bookseller, and smiled as they recalled their meeting.

'Wait a moment,' he said, as they were about to leave. 'I've got something of his you might like to have as a memento. I found it up on the gallery, luckily in a dry corner.'

It was a book, entitled *Exploring the Australian Outback*, with colour plates interleaved with tissue. Inside, was inscribed, 'Elmo T-W, 1876.'

'It was published in Sydney. I wonder if the uncle went there when he was younger? I think we should give it to our Elmo,' Russ said, as they walked back to the inn. He added 'It makes me wonder if we should do something like that, before we settle down.'

'Well, why not? But I'm ready for bed now, after all that brush-work,' Rose Marie told him.

'So am I. I hope you're not too tired. . . .'

'I didn't say that, did I?'

They exchanged a lingering kiss under the porch of the White Hart. The door swung open and they were caught in a beam of light.

'Just about to send out a search party,' their jolly landlady remarked. 'We called last orders half an hour ago. Thought you must be lost. Newly-weds! You're all the same, lose all sense of time. Going straight up?'

'We are,' Russ sounded sheepish. He brushed a cobweb from his jacket.

'Have a good night then, my dears.'

'We will, I'm sure, in that comfortable bed,' Rose Marie said.

'No hurry for you to get up in the morning.' The landlady had the last word.

Flynn had deigned to fall asleep at last. Florence and Manny settled thankfully into bed.

'It seems so quiet here, doesn't it,' said Florence, with a catch of her breath, 'without Rose Marie. No one up top, either. Just the three of us. It'll take a bit of getting used to.'

Manny patted her arm. 'You'll miss her; we both will. About the flat upstairs: Annie mentioned she might be interested in renting that. What d'you think?' He didn't quite have the nerve to mention Buck, too.

'She's a real good sort. She works well with Buck. Yes, why not.'

'He likes her, I can tell. You never know. . . .'

'What are you trying to say Manny? Out with it!'

'You'd better talk to Annie. Seems she and Buck, well—'

'They're a couple, is that it? That doesn't surprise me. Did you think it would?'

He nodded. 'That's all right then. Florence. . . .'

'Yes, my dear?' She encouraged him with a kiss, snuggled up to him.

'Now we can, well, *relax* a little, do you think we can, you know. . . .'

'Get back to normal married life, is that what you mean? I thought you'd never ask!'

Twenty-five

Spring, 1927

THERE were daffodils with golden-frilled trumpets in the Municipal flower-beds along the front at Hastings. Clear blue skies above with a watery sun giving the illusion that it was much warmer than it was. The sea was more honest in its grey swell, and the beach was visited only by the swooping, querulous gulls.

Florence and Manny didn't mind the buffeting wind at their backs, and Flynn, bouncing about in his new pushchair, peeped over the mackintosh cover which shielded him, and pointed at the things which caught his attention, like the pony and trap bowling by along the road; the noisy motor with blaring horn, an open-top charabanc, where the folk sat huddled under blankets and grimly held on to their hats.

Flynn was eight months old, forward for his age, his proud parents believed. He was already trying to pull himself up by the furniture at home, and attempting to balance on his chubby legs. Today, he wore a wool coat and leggings, with tiny lozenge shaped buttons, not an easy garment to remove in an emergency, as Manny and Florence knew to their cost. Despite the fact that he couldn't yet toddle, his feet were encased in smart kid boots, and on his head he had a woollen cap with earflaps and ties under the chin, knitted by Florence, which he was intent on taking off, so that he could throw it overboard.

'Foolish child,' his mother chided. 'I'm aware I don't look my best in a cloche hat, but I've got the sense to keep it on.'

Manny, propelling the chair, grinned. 'Nothing like a blast of fresh sea air, Florence.'

'I know. I'm not grumbling; it was my idea to come here for the weekend.'

'Let's sit on that bench for ten minutes. It's difficult to discuss the situation with the couple in the house hovering around. I realize they're anxious to sell to us, but—'

'We've got a lot to consider before we make our minds up,' she finished.

Florence prudently tucked a square of muslin in Flynn's collar. She fished in her bag and brought out a rusk. 'That should keep him happy, until it gets all soggy and disintegrates. Now, you'll agree it was a good plan to stay in the boarding house to see how it is run?'

'Well, yes. But it's still hard for me to take in that you want to leave the pie shop.'

'I've been there all my life, until now! Our honeymoon was the first time I spent a night away from there. It's not really the place to bring up a family, as I know from when the girls were young.

'When Lilli sold that necklace for all those thousands of pounds, she was really generous, not only giving half the money to her mother, so she could be independent of her brother-in-law, who appears to have been the one behind all Lilli's troubles, but seeing Annie all right too. Annie confiding in us that she was thinking of buying an established business, and running it with Buck, well, I suppose I shouldn't have suggested right away how about Paradise pies? You'd have to promise to keep the name, I said to Annie.'

'You didn't give *me* a chance to think about it, either.'

'I'm sorry, Manny! Did you feel I would be depriving you of your livelihood?'

He shook his head. 'It wasn't that. Since we married, well, you've shared everything with me. I've been determined not to let you down.'

'You haven't! My dear chap, now Flynn's weaned, I need to return to work. Not the slog of making pies day after day, but another business where we can work and thrive together. This seems ideal. Guests all summer, we can share the cooking, and out of season, we'll be able to live on the proceeds! Enjoy taking Flynn out and about. Having the family to stay. Think how Josefina would love it here.'

'You've won me over, Florence,' Manny told her. 'As you always do!'

It was a brisk walk, some of it uphill, to the smart white-painted villa with green shutters and a small front garden enclosed by black railings embellished with gilt paint. *The Hollies Guest House – Vacancies,* a swinging sign announced.

'Six bedrooms,' Florence marvelled, 'and not a whiff of a pie!'

'Fully furnished,' Manny said. 'That's a good selling point.'

'Well, we can leave all our furniture behind, too!'

Florence lifted Flynn from the pushchair. 'There, your daddy can fold that up! This is going to be your new home in a short while, Flynn. We'll have to make it May, after Stella's baby comes, because I must be there for that. Well, are you pleased?'

She hadn't noticed the baby had rusk smeared all over his glove. With a toothless beam, he proceeded to transfer the gooey mess to her cheek, as she bent to give him a kiss.

Mrs Short worked more flexible hours than her son had. She usually arrived at the bookshop around ten in the morning. Elmo was grateful for her help, so he had the kettle boiling and the biscuits out on a plate before she made her entry.

It was already three months since Russ and Rose Marie had announced that they were off on their great adventure to Australia.

'I won't be leaving you in the lurch,' Russ assured Elmo. 'Mother will hold the fort until we get back!'

'Oh, and how long is that likely to be?' They couldn't say, they admitted.

Rose Marie had been with him, having already advised Mrs Belling that as usual, she was acting on impulse, but that Russ would look after her, and she hoped to come back to Bellings with lots of fresh designs.

Elmo told them they had his blessing. 'Better go now. I suspect the country is still heading for a financial crash. If times get really hard, you'll have a good time to remember.'

Now, he said to Alma, as he was permitted to call her, 'I think you deserve a few days off. I'm sure you'd like to visit your daughter . . .' he cleared his throat. 'I could drive you there this Sunday, if you like.'

'That would be nice. Why don't you shut the shop and have a break as well?' she asked. 'Sadie and Jack would make you very welcome, I know.'

What am I letting myself in for? Elmo thought. Then he smiled. 'I'd like that,' he said.

Others were house-hunting, too. Lilli's new baby was due in four months. Sam came up with a surprising suggestion.

'The Regal Cinema, they're on the look-out for a new manager. I'd like to apply for the post. It's rather run-down, but you've got the know-how haven't you from your Golden Domes days. It would give us a good excuse to move further from my mother, without hurting her feelings. There's a new estate of family houses not far from the Regal. What d'you think?'

'Well, if you think being a cleaner at the cinema qualifies me to advise you, I say yes!'

Lilli was so happy nowadays, she would have agreed if he'd wanted to go to the moon!

She rather hoped the baby would be a girl, because then they could please Yvette and call her *Pearl*.

Rose Marie and Russ were sitting under a gum tree, poring over a map. The weather was still hot, and the flies bothersome. She took a swig of luke-warm water from a billy-can.

'Haven't you located that spring yet?' she asked. She moved her sun helmet, wiped the sweat from her neck. She thought, oh to be in England now that April - or rather March – is here. I wouldn't care how much it rained - I'd dance about in it and get soaked.

As if he could read her thoughts, Russ said, 'I fancy being back in London and I could just do with one of Florence's pies. Do you want to go home?' He signalled the driver of the truck that they were ready to move on.

'I don't want to sleep in a tent tonight,' Rose Marie sounded petulant. 'No gazing up at the stars, back to the homestead tonight. By home, do you mean England? We haven't finished adventuring yet.'

'What does that matter?' He pulled her to her feet. 'I'm home-sick too. Shall we do it?'

'Why not?' she said. 'We've still got plenty of tales to tell. It'll be so good to see the family again; I've missed them. I'm still one of Florence's girls, after all. Everything will be just as it was . . . won't it?'